DRAGON FAE BOND

THE ELUSTRIA CHRONICLES: DRAGON FAE
BOOK THREE

CAETHES FARON

BECOME AN INSIDER

Get sneak peeks and stay up to date on new releases by signing up for the author's Insider Newsletter at

CaethesFaron.com.

1

When did my life become so unreal? Was it ever really normal?

Was my time at Moonlark Academy normal? I didn't have friends, not even then. Letting people in led to getting hurt. When had I learned that lesson the first time? It seemed as if I'd been born knowing it. My mother had birthed me then gone off on another Circle mission with my father.

Never trust anyone to stick around.

Alistair had been different. He'd been the first person to fight past my defenses. He wore me down through sheer determination. I never trusted anyone else at the Circle. Just him.

Partners were replaceable. No sense getting close. I trusted them in a professional capacity, but I never trusted any of them with who I was, with my identity.

Until Deacon. Where Alistair had forced his way into my heart, Deacon had charmed his way in.

Then a ghost from my past walked through the door at Bubbles and Brews, tumbling my fragile mind into unconsciousness. Julien. He was the only one to ever get close enough for romance. He made me feel things I never had before. He made me feel...normal.

As a young woman without parents who spent her teenage years training as an assassin, all I'd wanted was to be normal. He gave me that, and then I threw it away. I destroyed the perfect façade we'd created. He saw the real me.

Julien couldn't be here. He was in Elustria leading a normal life. This chaos, this insanity was no place for him. It had to be a vision, a hallucination brought on by my nether addiction. It was the only thing that made sense.

Among the madness of the nether addiction, Deacon was real. His strong arms had lifted me, cradled me against his chest. It was Deacon who brought me wherever I was, who had put me in this bed.

The inside of my eyelids glowed orange with light. It wasn't nighttime anymore. A sound filtered through my thoughts. A rumbling. I opened my eyes against the harsh light and looked down to find Pint curled up on the bed next to me, snoring like an old man, little puffs of smoke escaping his nostrils every now and then.

Sunlight poured in through a window across from the bed. It was the harsh light of the afternoon sun. I'd been out longer than I thought. The room was a good size and well appointed. The door to an ensuite bathroom stood ajar. A comfy reading chair complete with lamp and footstool sat in one corner. In the opposite corner past the foot of the bed sat a small desk and chair.

A woman sat in the desk chair. She had it turned facing the bed, watching me. When I looked at her, she jumped up. She wore the simple garb of the priestesses at the temple.

"Your Highness, you're awake."

I tried to correct her, to tell her I'm not a highness, but my mouth wouldn't open before she continued.

"I'll go get the Dragon Prince." The woman bobbed a curtsy and left the room in a hurry.

I had to be at the Syndicate compound if Drake was here. I remembered now. This was the room Drake had given me.

Pint stirred at the sound of the priestess's voice, and the door shutting roused him completely. He looked up at me, and his tail wagged. My little dragon reminded me of a puppy, but I'd never dare tell him that.

My mouth felt glued together. I needed something to drink, but shards of pain stabbed my head when I moved.

"Whoa, take it easy," Pint said as he stood and came closer to lick my arm.

Tired of lying flat on my back, I ignored him and pushed through the pain. It was bad enough I'd been out all night and at least half the day. I wouldn't spend one second more on my back.

On the nightstand sat a pitcher of water and a glass. I couldn't pour fast enough. My tongue sat thick and hairy in my mouth, and it soaked up the water as quickly as I could pour it down my throat. Water had never tasted so sweet.

As I drank, the reality of the situation descended on me. I groaned. "I'm so embarrassed."

"Don't," Pint said. "You've no reason to be."

"No reason? I passed out in a bar because I was so strung out on the nether that I hallucinated my ex-fiancé walking through the door. Not exactly the behavior of a prophesied hero, as you'd say."

Pint looked embarrassed on my behalf and curled up in my lap in a comforting gesture. I petted him absentmindedly as I drank my second glass of water.

"Trust me, no one looks at it that way," Pint said. "Everyone's just concerned about you."

As if that made it better. "Yeah, people love a hero they have to worry about."

I closed my eyes and luxuriated in the feel of the water going down my throat, but images intruded on my thoughts. Tendrils of the nether clinging onto my brain, keeping parts of my mind for itself. Dreams and nightmares that had tormented me while I'd slept burst to the forefront. Twisted images of Dorran, Alistair, Deacon.

And Julien, the image that had set this whole thing off. It was strange that after all this time I would see him. I hadn't even checked on him since this whole Dragon Fae business started. Maybe the hallucination was telling me that something was wrong. Maybe he wasn't safe.

I was torn between wanting to see everyone and hiding in shame. I was a spy and assassin. Self-control and discipline were supposed to be my hallmarks. "Pint, where's my void blade?"

"It's in the drawer of the nightstand," Pint said.

I rolled over and opened the drawer to check. My void blade sat there peacefully, as if it hadn't killed hundreds. I rolled back onto the bed. I wanted to know where Deacon was. I wanted to see him, but I didn't know if I could face him. He had his shit together, and I was just one fuck-up after another.

"I bet everyone's wanting to exchange me for a better model right about now. I mean, it's only been a week since I was anointed. Still well within the return window."

Pint looked uncomfortable and shifted his weight.

"What is it?" I asked.

He looked at the door, as if waiting for someone and then sighed and turned to me. "You've been out of it for two weeks."

2

"**W**ait, what?" That couldn't be. Two weeks? No.

Pint looked nervously at the door again. "You fainted two weeks ago. The priestesses have been tending to you. Apparently it has something to do with the nether. They've been performing spells and giving you potions to sustain you. They started to wean you off everything recently. They thought that maybe the potions kept you from waking up."

"But it can't be two weeks. Where is everyone?" I swung my legs over the side of the bed and tried to stand but quickly had to sit back down. My legs had a hard time handling my weight. It was the first physical proof that what Pint said was true. I braced myself and tried again, pushing through to walk to the window.

I placed a hand on the window frame for balance. My room faced the back of the compound, and I saw several small houses. There didn't seem to be much activity. The only movement was a little gray bird that flew up to the window, looked right at me, then flew off.

The door to the room opened, and Drake walked in. His eyebrows lifted in surprise at the sight of me at the window. "You're up."

"Yes, isn't that why you're here? The priestess said she was going to get you. Or are you surprised that I'm walking around after being bedridden for two weeks?"

Drake looked at Pint on the bed. "You told her?"

"Only that it's been two weeks." Pint fidgeted and looked away from Drake's glare.

Drake nodded and looked back at me. "The priestess said only that you were awake, not that you were up and about."

They were hiding something from me, both Drake and Pint. It wasn't natural that Deacon and Sybil weren't here. And what about Alistair? Surely at least one of them would've been here. "Where is everyone? Where's Deacon?"

I took a step toward Drake, ready to push past him and out the door to find Deacon, but Drake caught my shoulders. "He's not here."

I looked into Drake's dark red eyes. "Then where is he?"

"He's on a mission in Elustria."

A mission? Deacon didn't do missions solo. "What does that mean? And where are Alistair and Sybil?"

"Alistair's in Elustria with Deacon. Sybil is at the temple holding a summit meeting. The priestess went to get her after she found me."

I looked away to gather my thoughts. It felt like I'd passed out and woken up in an entirely different world. Was this a dream? It felt like it. "I don't understand. Why are Deacon and Alistair in Elustria? What's happened?"

Drake and Pint shared a knowing look. What weren't they telling me?

"I have some food on the way," Drake said. "Everyone will be back soon. Why don't you eat and freshen up?"

"No. The last thing I remember is being at Bubbles and Brews. Deacon was trying to help me home, but I was too unsteady. Then I hallucinated my ex-fiancé and passed out. Now I wake up, and Pint tells me it's been two weeks, and Deacon's nowhere to be found. Alistair and Sybil are both away. Tell me what's going on."

Drake got that same uneasy look he had right before he swore fealty to me and Deacon. This was the look of a man who didn't want to do what he was about to. Drake took a deep breath and said, "It wasn't a hallucination."

"What?" I remembered hallucinating Julien. That hallucination had bled into my dreams. It was what tipped me over the edge and made me pass out.

"The asshole's here," Pint said from behind me. He flew over and hovered next to my shoulder. Normally he'd land, but he probably thought I couldn't handle his weight right now.

"And you didn't tell me?" It wasn't like Pint to keep secrets from me.

"They made me swear I wouldn't tell."

I looked at Drake. "So you all thought you'd keep it a secret from me?"

"No, not at all. Deacon just wanted to make sure he could talk to you first. He thought if Pint told you, you would rush off to find Julien. Deacon knew Pint wouldn't be able to stop you on his own."

The reality sank in. "He's really here?"

"Yes, he's here."

To be honest, I didn't know if I wanted to see him or not. The man had rejected me, but I hadn't stopped loving him. And why had he shown up at all? Why after all this time? Was it a coincidence that he walked into Bubbles and Brews? My heart said it wasn't.

Pint landed on the bed. "I wanted to roast his ass as soon as he got here, but Deacon wouldn't let me."

"Good," I said. Pint had always placed the blame squarely on Julien's shoulders. He didn't understand that I had betrayed him. Julien didn't deserve whatever Pint wanted to do to him.

I wanted to know why Julien was here. I didn't want him to see me this way. Ever since he rejected me, I'd fully embraced my identity as a spy and assassin. The whole world knew that I killed people. I didn't even try to pretend like I could have a normal life.

I could barely contain my shame at becoming nether addicted. It was bad enough that Deacon had to see me that way. I'd tried to hide it from Alistair, but he saw me pass out at Bubbles and Brews. Julien saw that too. It seemed like he always saw me at my lowest points, and I resented him for it, which wasn't fair to him.

When Julien rejected me, he made it clear that he never wanted to see me again. Something must've happened for him to show up, unless it really was coincidence. I didn't believe that though. My followers in the enclave would've kept any outsiders away that night. But what had he been doing here for two weeks?

"Are you treating him well?" I asked Drake.

"Yes, he's being tended to. Deacon took control of his care."

That didn't comfort me. Deacon had made no secret of his feelings toward Julien.

What was I thinking? Deacon wasn't petty. That wasn't in his character. More than anything, Deacon was a protector. Duty defined his life, and he didn't have it in him to mistreat someone. He'd at least protected Julien from Pint.

One of Drake's shifters entered with a tray of food. It held a simple bowl of broth, some bread, fruit, and cheese. He set it on the desk and left.

"I'll leave you to eat and freshen up. The others will be back soon, and we can all talk," Drake said. "But before I go, I need you to promise me that you won't go looking for Julien. Deacon wanted to be the one to tell you he's here. It's bad enough we already broke our word to him. Please let me at least honor his wish that he speak to you before you see Julien."

"Of course." I sat at the desk. "I want to talk to Deacon first anyway."

"Thank you." Drake left me alone with Pint.

I quickly ate and showered. I pushed down the urge to make myself look nice for Julien. He wasn't mine to look nice for anymore. Besides, I didn't want to take the time. I needed to be ready as soon as everyone got back. I'd lost too much time already.

Once I was dressed with my hair up in a ponytail, I relaxed for the first time since waking up. That was when I felt it, the familiar hum of Deacon's magic. We were still connected from the anointing. In my confusion earlier, I hadn't noticed. Feeling his magic soothed me.

"So what's been happening, Pint?" I asked as I reclined on the bed with him next to me, my hand scratching the top of his head.

"I'm not quite sure. I've spent all my time here with you. Who cares about Elustria and Malev and all the others? That spineless blob of an ex-fiancé of yours told them something that's got everyone in a tizzy. I'm just ignoring it. I wanted to be here with you, be here when you woke up."

That was Pint, always loyal. We were two damaged creatures who understood each other. To be honest, I thought he wouldn't mind if the world burned around us as long as there was something for him to hunt. We were too cynical to believe the world held anything for us.

"You have to know something. How's Alistair? How's his hand doing? And what about Sybil and Deacon?"

"They're all fine. Alistair's hand isn't back to normal, but he says it's good enough. Sybil has been annoyingly perky." It was strange to hear him criticize Sybil at all. She'd had Pint in thrall with her endless supply of steaks. He'd had a little bit of a crush on her since she showed up in our lives. "I may have had a few harsh words with her. I just couldn't stand her constantly fluttering about telling me not to worry, that of course you'd wake up. I don't need that kind of positivity in my life."

It didn't surprise me that he left me hanging with Deacon. Pint had a bit of a jealous streak, and Deacon was the current target of it. I supposed it didn't matter. I could feel that Deacon was safe through our link. That was all that mattered.

"You don't have to stay here. You must be bored being cooped up in this room," I told Pint.

"No, I don't want to be alone." Even though he would never admit it, there was a hint of worry in his voice. Seeing me down for so long must've really troubled him. "Besides, I want to go burn off Julien's eyebrows, and Deacon's made it clear that I can't. Stupid bully dragon shifter."

I wanted to tell him to be nice to Julien, but magic washed over me, like a warm mountain breeze, rippling over my skin, filling my lungs. Deacon knew I was awake.

He was back.

3

Footsteps pounded down the hall moments before the door burst open, and there was Deacon. His broad shoulders and tall frame filled the doorway. The green eyes that were as familiar to me as my own had a shadow of worry and disbelief, like he didn't dare trust good news.

I stood, and his face transformed from worry to relief. He ran to me, pulling me into his arms and sinking his face in my hair. He breathed me in. I buried my face in his neck and ran my hand through his dark hair, holding him to me, assuring him that I was real. He still had the scent of Elustria on him.

His magic latched onto mine, making me gasp with surprise. He pulled back just enough to kiss me, his lips landing on mine with a desperate urgency, as if he needed to prove to himself that I was real. I melted into it, welcoming his tongue into my mouth. A zing of excitement went through me down to my core. How strange that his kiss could both give me strength and make me weak in the knees at the same time.

His lips pulled back, but he kept his forehead touching mine. "I'm sorry. I shouldn't have done that. I just couldn't help myself. It's really you. You're awake."

"Don't apologize." He trembled slightly beneath my touch. I recognized it as the release of stress. It was the same reaction as after a hard mission, when the mind knows it's over and the danger is gone but the body hasn't quite caught up yet. I'd really scared him.

It hadn't been worth it visiting the nether. Had I known this would be the result, I would've never gone. Deacon didn't scare easily, but my illness had shaken him. I didn't have the right to do that to him.

"I'm fine, really," I said. "Apparently a two-week nap is exactly what I needed."

Deacon let out a bark of laughter. "So they told you."

I pulled back to look in his face. "Oh, so you expect me to think this is the reaction you'd have if I'd only been out for a day?"

"I guess not." He pushed my hair behind my ear. The way he looked at me, it made me feel precious, special. "I was so worried."

The look in his eyes, it was as if he'd aged far more than two weeks. It dawned on me. "You thought this was it. You thought this was the end of the prophecy."

"I didn't know what to think."

I didn't like this, the worry on his face, the shadows in his eyes. "I'm fine. I promise. I woke up thinking it was the next morning."

Before he could say anything, a light knock sounded on the door a split second before it opened to reveal Sybil and Alistair. Deacon quickly stepped back, as if we'd been caught in an intimate moment. It was just as well, Sybil would've pushed him aside had he not moved. She flung her arms around my neck in one of her signature hugs. "It's true, you are awake!"

She released me and stepped aside for Alistair. I still hadn't gotten used to seeing him returned and safe. He'd regained the weight he lost in captivity. His hand looked good as new, though I did notice its unnatural stillness.

"So you think you can sleep for two weeks and slack off work?" Alistair said with a smile.

"It's the only way to get you off my back. I've been telling you I need a vacation."

Alistair's smile broadened. "Well now that you've had one, I assume you're ready to get back to work. We need to debrief and get you caught up. Drake's waiting for us in a conference room across the hall. He says you already know about Julien."

Every eye in the room conspicuously turned toward me. They all seemed to hold their breath as if waiting for me to break down.

"Yes, I'm aware that he wasn't a hallucination. What I can't figure out is why he's here."

"Well, it wasn't for a social call. He came bearing news," Alistair said.

So definitely not a coincidence. "How come I get the feeling it's not good news?"

Alistair snorted. "Because you're not stupid. It's a whole new game now."

4

a pitcher of water and some glasses sat in the middle of the round conference table along with a vegetable tray and some cookies. I immediately grabbed a napkin and three chocolate chip cookies, not caring how it looked. I needed sugar.

I sat between Sybil and Deacon, across from Alistair and Drake. Pint crawled in my lap. It was odd for him to be present during a debriefing, but he seemed to need the closeness.

I ate half a cookie while everyone got settled then asked, "So what's been going on for the last two weeks?"

Alistair took the lead. "Julien had some disturbing information when he showed up. It appears Queen Malev has decided to form an alliance with King Kelar."

"What? Why?" Kelar was king of the sorcerers. As far as I knew, at no point in history had the high fae formed an alliance with anyone.

"She's pissed that you saved me. You dared to defy her."

"So? What does forming an alliance with the sorcerers do for her?" I found it hard to believe that Malev would admit she needed help dealing with me.

"We're not entirely sure. That's why Deacon and I have been

running surveillance missions back in Elustria at the Starlight Palace and around Stardowns. We know she still wants Goffrey dead, but she might suspect that he's not her real rival. She wants whatever knowledge the Circle has. Right now, it's a standoff between her and Meilin. We have Gordon on the inside, and I'm still technically an officer of the Circle," Alistair said.

Alistair going to Elustria made sense. He still had access to the Circle, and with everything going on, Meilin may not be so eager to be rid of me. That would mean playing nice with Alistair as well. What I didn't understand was Deacon's role. I looked at him. "What's been your part in these missions?"

"One thing I have going for me is that, unlike you, no one knows who I am. That's the advantage of being the Dragon Companion. Hardly anyone even knows my name, much less what I look like. It's been easy to use a little bit of glamour and pose as an off-duty guard. I've kept my eyes and ears open, getting gossip, seeing what the general attitude is at court. The guards don't like what's going on, I can tell you that much."

That made sense. Deacon had a lot in common with the guards. Even if he didn't glamour his magic, it could easily be mistaken for a sorcerer's. It had the same strength and power. Only another dragon shifter would be able to definitively call him out, and there wouldn't be any at court. Even if there were, they'd be loyal to Deacon, not King Kelar.

"So what's going on at the Circle?" I asked Alistair.

"They're practically locked down. It's taken some of the heat off of you. Meilin is more concerned with defeating Malev at the moment. She resents this intrusion. The entire operation is at a standstill. All missions are suspended. I'm not in Meilin's inner circle, but she has bigger things to worry about than what to do with me. Gordon gets closer to her than I do, but he's not one of her closest advisors. He is a little tainted by how everything went sideways with you. Luckily for him, you made no secret of the fact that you weren't working with him, so he's been able to escape the worst of her ire. There's no intelligence coming in or going out of headquarters. Meilin doesn't want a single thing leaking to Malev," Alistair said.

At this point, Drake leaned forward. "So what did you gather on this last trip?"

Before Alistair opened his mouth, I could tell it wasn't good. He got this look in his eyes, and he sighed the way he did sometimes when he had bad news. "Malev sent some of her trusted advisors to get information from the Circle. She wants all the intelligence we have about her rival. She wants mission reports from Nadiya's latest missions as well as adjacent ones."

One of the adjacent missions would be the assassin sent to kill me. That report wouldn't make for interesting reading. He showed up, I killed him, end of report. However, we also knew that Meilin had sent other people to Norway. It wouldn't have just been the assassin. That meant there were reports somewhere.

"Do you know how much the Circle knows? Have you and Gordon been able to get your hands on the reports?" I asked Alistair.

"I haven't, but I'm not too concerned. The reason Gordon and I haven't been able to see the reports is because Meilin's not letting anyone see them. She's keeping them safe from us and from the fae. However, I don't get the impression that they're aware Goffrey isn't Malev's rival."

"If Malev goes digging into this, it won't take her long to figure it out," I said. "She's not an idiot. Any halfway decent agent would be able to figure it out, just as I did. Except they'd do it faster because they wouldn't be strung out on the nether. This is bad."

"I think you overestimate the other agents, but I take your meaning. We have to assume that if Malev gets into the Circle, it will be catastrophic."

I turned to Deacon. "What did you get?"

As he'd listened to Alistair, he'd leaned in, resting his forearms on the table. Now he sat back in his chair. "The general mood is that the people are pissed. They don't want an alliance with the high fae, and they don't want high fae in their territory. I don't know what the mood is out among the general population, but the denizens of the Starlight Palace are taking it as an offense to their pride."

That sounded about right. In those elite circles, bloodlines, purity of magic, they were all important. Every race felt superior to every other, especially when old money and old blood were involved. Out among working people, they didn't care so much about the differences between races. Sorcerers, shifters, elves, fae, they all worked together, but even the working class would chafe at one race attempting to interfere with the leadership of another.

Queen Malev was generally hated among the common people because she kept hidden away in the fae realm. People took that to mean she thought herself too good for Elustria. That didn't sit well. All of this negative attitude would work in our favor. We just needed to help it along and call on it when it would benefit us.

Drake spoke up. "Sybil, what happened at the summit?"

Sybil had been unusually quiet. Whether it was her professional side coming through or she had something solemn to share, I didn't know.

"I met with Jaygar, the priestesses, and a few other influential followers at the temple. They're concerned. They don't doubt the Dragon Fae, but word has gotten around about what happened at Bubbles and Brews." Sybil looked down at her hands, not meeting my gaze. "The priestesses and Jaygar kept the nether sickness secret, but word still managed to get out. Dorran figured it out himself, and others did too. I conveyed to them how important it is that they quash these rumors. They can undermine us."

I refused to lower my gaze in shame. The only people whose opinions mattered to me were in this room. Let the others think what they wanted. "It's all right, Sybil. It's my fault. I shouldn't have kept going to the nether, but I did it anyway. We need to stay focused. We'll win back support."

Sybil looked up into my eyes and nodded. "You're right. And on that topic, the story of how you saved Alistair has been making the rounds. Rumors of your illness may be more fun for gossip, but people are taking hope in the rescue story. You saved a lifelong friend. You did it by humiliating the fae queen whom nobody likes. They all wish it had been them."

"And how exactly did the story get out?" I asked. Alistair's capture hadn't been widely reported. He was a covert agent captured by an adversary. That kind of thing usually didn't see the light of day. The only people who knew what happened were those directly involved in the mission and the dragon shifters. Drake had a firm grip on his people. None of them would've leaked.

"Oh, that one was me," Sybil said. "For you to do what needs to be done, you need the support of the people, and that's a great hero story. Even though we're not thrilled about the rumors of nether sickness, it does add a little something to the story. You were willing to drive yourself mad to save your friend. That's the kind of heroism people like."

Reckless heroism. If that's what people wanted, I could give it to them in abundance. "We need to find a way to get more intel. I can run missions with you now. Is there any obvious way you can think of to prevent this alliance from going forward?"

"That's something I've been trying to figure out, but I don't have anything yet," Alistair said.

Before we could discuss any plans, Dorran appeared in the corner of the room across from me. The gem in his staff glowed, and his cowl hid his face. The druid was always one for a grand entrance. His sudden appearance shocked the others in the room, but not me.

"I was wondering how long it would be until I saw you. I'm guessing the little birdie outside my window quite literally told you I was awake." If so much as a fly had seen me, I was sure word would've gotten back to Dorran.

"It's good to see that you're up and about," Dorran said with a respectful tip of his head.

"I take it this isn't a social call." In my experience, Dorran did everything for a reason.

"No, I came to tell you that Cassalina is in residence at her court. You should see her while she's there. I don't know how long she's staying. It's been more than a week since she was last Earthside."

I ate my second cookie and fed the third to Pint. It was a little too much sugar for me so soon after getting up. I wished I had more time to get my bearings before seeing Cassalina, but I couldn't pass up this opportunity. She was a close friend and confidant of Queen Malev. She was also setting up a rival court to depose her. Cassalina could give us more information about this supposed alliance between the fae queen and sorcerer king.

Deacon took my hand underneath the table and looked at me. "Are you sure you're ready to go on a mission right now?"

Instead of making me feel weak, the concern in his eyes gave me strength. Something about knowing how deeply he cared made it easier for me to keep going. "This barely qualifies as a mission. After two weeks in bed, I'm dying to get out."

I couldn't tell if he believed me, but he wouldn't contradict me in front of others. Besides, I was sure he felt he could protect me if need be. There was a nice security in finally having a partner who was a real match for me.

"Then you need to get going," Dorran said. "She could leave at any moment."

Getting my bearings would have to wait.

5

When I stepped through the portal Sybil created, the crisp Norwegian air burned my lungs. The cold perked up my skin and my senses. I felt more alive than I had in a long time.

I wished we could fly again. I wanted to soar on the back of Deacon's dragon form, but the portal put us close to the entrance of Cassalina's court. I didn't know exactly how we would enter without Dorran. We'd have to rely on the guards recognizing us and allowing us inside, so that meant no glamour.

We approached the stone face of the mountain that served as the entrance to Cassalina's court. This time, I could clearly feel the strange magic Deacon had mentioned before. It had a distinct scent, like wet rocks, that stood out among the earthy, sour smell that I'd noticed previously. Without the nether clouding my mind, the foreign magic seemed obvious.

"Was the other magic this strong before?" I asked Deacon as he examined the rock face.

He looked over his shoulder at me. "Yes. It hasn't changed intensity. You notice it?"

I nodded. "The nether must have dulled my senses earlier."

I didn't like the presence of a strange magic neither Deacon nor I could identify, but that would have to wait until later. Perhaps Dorran knew what it was.

"I can't detect anything here that'll trap us. It's safe for us to try to enter," Deacon said after he finished his inspection.

I removed my cuff and placed my hand on the rock next to Deacon's. I didn't know what else we should do, but I performed a spell I normally would to open a trapdoor, even though I didn't expect it to work on fae magic.

The rock shimmered then disappeared. Only, it wasn't the rock that disappeared, it was us. We found ourselves standing alone inside Cassalina's court, in a private antechamber off to the side of the throne room. The strange magic hummed in the background, too distant to discern anything from it, especially when there were two much stronger magics headed our way: Cassalina and Dorran. If he was coming too, why didn't he just port us all directly here? What had he said to Cassalina in this time? He had too many secrets.

Cassalina strode into the room. She commanded every inch of this mountain, and it showed. She carried herself with the effortless confidence of someone who knew her own power. It amazed me that anyone could believe Goffrey was the one in charge. He played his part of decoy well, but his authority was borrowed from Cassalina. I worried that if Malev did much digging, she'd uncover the ruse.

Dorran followed Cassalina and nodded to us as if we hadn't just been in the same room together.

"Dorran here told me you were on your way, so I had the gate let you in and bring you here. I'm glad to see you're finally up and going again," Cassalina said, her voice heavy with judgement. She gestured for us all to take our seats.

"How fortunate for us that your visit here coincides with my recovery," I said as I sat next to Deacon on the sofa.

"Yes. I have important news to share. I just found out that Malev is planning to sign a formal alliance with Kelar."

"We already knew that," I said.

Cassalina shook her head. "I'm sorry. I'm not making myself clear. She's going to sign it in person at the Starlight Palace. She wants to make it a spectacle. Any and all sorcerers who want to attend are welcome. She's eager to have an audience so the sorcerers know that she's tied to them now."

I sat back, my mind turning over this new information. Could she really be that stupid? I leaned forward. "You're telling me she's going to leave the fae realm knowing I'm out here?"

Dorran spoke up. "The fact that you've woken up is not widely known. We want you to keep it that way."

"We can't have Malev back out," Cassalina said. "This is your chance. You need to assassinate her at the signing."

I looked at Deacon to see what he thought of this. I wasn't objective on the matter. Neither was Deacon, but in this room, I trusted him to be the most objective.

I knew Deacon could see in my eyes the desire to kill Malev. The only thing stopping me up until now was that she was ensconced in the fae realm. It would be suicide to try to kill her there.

Deacon faced Cassalina. "Why should we assassinate her for you? It's not really our place to get in the middle of fae politics."

Dorran answered before Cassalina could. "It is imperative that Malev not find out the location of Cassalina's court."

Dorran wouldn't say anything more on the matter. He wasn't one for elaborating on his point.

"The Circle has a lot of information about my court that I can't allow into Malev's hands. I know this sounds self-serving coming from me, and I don't dispute that it is, but trust me when I tell you that it would also be catastrophic for Earth. If she finds the location of my court, she's not just going to kill me. She's going to take over.

Then she'll have a presence in all three places: the fae realm, Elustria, and Earth. I can't even imagine what she'd do then."

Meilin wouldn't let Malev get information from the Circle. Her knowledge of Cassalina's court was power, and she would never turn any of it over to Malev, even if there was an alliance. As far as I knew, Malev was still under the impression that Goffrey was her rival, not Cassalina. Meilin would protect the knowledge of the rival court's location with her life. I didn't worry about that, but Cassalina had just given me cover for killing Malev. I'd take it.

"When is she going to be there?" I asked.

Cassalina smiled in a self-satisfied way. She would gain the most from Malev's death. "The signing is tomorrow. It's going to be followed by a banquet. In the aftermath, I will step forward and take charge. I told you I have a legitimate claim to the throne. You have my word that my court will leave the sorcerer court in peace. Now, I need to get back. We're so close, I can't let her start suspecting me now. Dorran, will you be so kind as to port them back home?"

Dorran nodded and lifted his staff. When it hit the ground, all three of us appeared back in Drake's conference room.

"I'll leave you to plan," Dorran said. "Just remember, keep your condition a secret. I'll quash any rumors I come across."

"Wait," I said. "Why do you care so much about Cassalina's court?"

His cowl was pushed back farther than usual. I saw a little twinkle in his eyes. "That's for me to know. It's in the best interests of Earth that Malev doesn't ever step foot here." He disappeared.

"What now?" Deacon asked.

"We need to round up everyone. I'm not killing the fae queen unless we're all in agreement."

🜂

It didn't take long for everyone, including Pint, to get back to the conference room. I quickly relayed what had happened with Cassalina.

"I obviously have my own motivations for wanting to kill Malev, and there's nothing pure about them. I'm out for vengeance. So if I'm going to do this, I want the support of the people in this room." I wasn't used to making decisions by committee. Usually the Circle told me who to kill, and I did it. The decision was completely out of my hands. This time was different. I turned to Alistair first. I trusted him completely, but he was just as biased as me, even more so in this instance.

"I wish I could watch the life drain from her eyes," Alistair said, his voice colder than I'd ever heard it before. "However, if you want to know what I think as an officer of the Circle, I'd say it's crucial that she die. She can't be allowed to interfere in the sorcerer court."

I turned to Drake. He may be an ass, but I respected him as a leader. "And what do you think about this?"

"I think killing her now will save lives in the future." I could see in his eyes that he worried how all this would affect his shifters. Malev had her focus on the sorcerer court now, but how long until she decided to meddle with the dragons?

"Sybil, are there any concerns with the prophecy we should be aware of?" I asked.

"I say kill her. It's in line with the prophecy. It's your job to protect people. She's a monster."

I turned to my right. "Deacon?"

"This may be our only chance. We need to take it."

Pint stirred in my lap. "I agree. Take her out."

I scratched his neck in thanks for his contribution.

"Looks like we need to come up with a plan," I said and looked at the faces around me. We didn't have much time. It would be a miracle if we could pull it off.

"I'm going to order some food be brought up here," Drake said. "I'll also get the word out that your condition is to be kept secret.

Not that my shifters are prone to talk with outsiders anyway, but I'll make it clear that it's a direct order."

"Thank you, Drake." I met his eyes and nodded to him. I could see in his gaze that he understood my meaning. I wasn't just thanking him for the food or the order to his dragons. I was thanking him for his support to kill Malev.

Once the door closed behind Drake, I looked around the table at Sybil, Alistair, and Deacon. "So, any ideas on how we kill the most powerful fae in the world?"

6

$\mathcal{I}$ felt more in my element now than I had in a while. This was just like an assignment. I had a target, a clear mission, and it was up to me to figure out how to do it. Usually the Circle would come up with the basics of the plan, but I'd been doing this long enough that I didn't need that guidance. Besides, missions seldom went according to plan.

"The first thing we have to do is figure out how to get you in," Alistair said. "We don't have the time or the resources to do more recon. We can figure out a rough sketch of how we think it might go, but it's going to be up to you to think on your feet."

"That's how it always ends up," I said.

Deacon poured me a glass of water and urged me to drink before he spoke. "It seems like getting in is going to be the easy part. We just have to glamour ourselves as sorcerers. That won't be difficult."

Deacon must've somehow noticed that I'd weakened slightly. I hadn't been awake for long, but it would take time to build up my stamina. I didn't realize how bad off I was until the water replenished me. "I've never spent much time at court. I've always been in the field. What kind of security do you think they'll have, Alistair?

Will they be checking imprints, identities? Or can we get in just appearing as random people?"

While the Circle headquarters was located at the Starlight Palace, it operated separately from court. Alistair would have a better idea than any of us how court security operated, but it wasn't exactly his specialty.

"My guess is they'll be checking identities. If the fae queen's going to be there in addition to King Kelar, they have to take precautions."

Dealing with Elustrian security was different than security on Earth. In a world of magic, weapons weren't as great a threat. "Is there any chance Gordon can get us information about the security protocols?"

Alistair thought about it. "It's a really tight timeframe. We can try, but I don't want to push too hard and show our hand. I trust him, but there's always the chance that someone will catch our exchange. I don't want to risk word getting back to Malev and her changing her plans. Not if we don't have to."

"I've been to a few formal events as the Oracle," Sybil said. "I don't think you have to worry about much security from the fae. For one, Malev is too arrogant to think she needs any. Secondly, Malev isn't used to security outside the fae realm. She has so many things built into her realm that she's connected to that she doesn't know any other way to do security.

"That just leaves the sorcerer security. I think they'll focus mainly on verifying identities. It'll only be sorcerers and high fae allowed in. I can also see the court not wanting to subject the sorcerers to much security. They're already going to feel irritated with the high fae there. They won't take kindly to being treated like outlaws in their own court with fae walking around."

"So you don't think I have to worry about my void blade getting through?" I asked.

Sybil shook her head. "They won't be looking for weapons.

They'd expect that only from mages, and there won't be any mages attending."

"So the main thing we need to worry about is glamouring as a couple who both won't be there and won't trip alarms. Any suggestions?" I looked around, but Sybil and Deacon were unlikely to know of anyone who would meet that criteria. I didn't even know if Deacon knew any sorcerers. Alistair was our best bet at coming up with good candidates, and he sat shaking his head. "What is it?" I asked.

"Oh, I just can't wrap my head around the fact that you can glamour now. It's strange and wonderful."

I had forgotten that he would've never seen me glamour before. So much had happened while Malev held him captive. "It is a useful tool."

I wished glamouring our imprints didn't require that I wear the cuff. Then again, I didn't think I'd ever heard of someone being able to glamour their magical imprint. It made sense that it came with some sort of sacrifice. I just liked the thought of going to Elustria with my magic unbound. At least now I had the temple to go to if I really needed to stretch my magic. There I could take off the cuff and remain safe, hidden from those who would hunt me. I'd occasionally gone to the desert and used my magic without the cuff on, but it wasn't the same. In Elustria, magic hung in the air. It created an electric atmosphere for performing magic.

Deacon got a look on his face like he'd come up with an idea but was reluctant to share.

"What are you thinking?" I asked.

"We have Julien. He seems to think the high fae really want to talk to him. If one of us goes in as him, there's a good chance we'd get close to Malev."

I could understand his reluctance to share that idea. Neither one of us was eager to appear as Julien. "But there's just as much of a chance that at the sight of Julien, she'd capture him and take him to the fae realm. We can't risk that. It's a bold idea, but I don't think it's the right one. We need someone whom Malev won't recognize, a couple who can walk about without getting a second glance."

"I have the perfect couple," Alistair said. "My sister and her husband. He actually used to work as a guard at the Starlight Palace years ago."

Sybil looked stunned. "Why didn't you mention that earlier? He could help us."

"Because we don't bring family into work," I said, maintaining eye contact with Alistair. Families were sacrosanct in our business. That's why Julien hadn't known what I did for a living. That's why I had never met Alistair's sister or his sweet niece before she was killed. "You don't have to do this, Alistair. We can find another way."

"I appreciate that, but it's time. Things have changed, not just for us, but for them. They don't have anything to live for anymore. They'd want to help."

Deacon leaned forward on the table. "Will they be on some sort of watchlist because of their connection to you and your connection to Nadiya? After all, they have their sights on Julien."

"I don't think so. They've been out of the public eye for a long time. When they had their daughter, they retired to the countryside. They don't know anything about my work. Julien was targeted because he would know something about Nadiya. The same can't be said of my family. The Circle doesn't know about them. In the beginning they did, but as soon as I got high enough in the ranks, I purged any mention of them from Circle records. They have no connection to me officially."

It was moments like this that reminded me how good Alistair was at his job. He was ruthless in his own way, always in protection of others.

"So how do you want to do this?" I asked. "Are you going to read them in or leave them in the cold?"

"I'd like to read them in. They need something. They need to know that there are people fighting for a better world. I have to give them hope."

This was a huge step for Alistair. I respected it. I couldn't imagine the pain of losing a child. If this would make living even a tad bit easier for them, then I was all for it. I had never met Alistair's sister, but I had heard so much about her that I felt as if I knew her. She and her husband could be trusted to keep our secrets.

"We'll have to meet them," Deacon said. Seeing a picture wouldn't be enough to do a convincing job with the glamour. We needed their imprint.

"I understand. I'll go now and come get you when they're ready." Alistair stood and made a portal to his sister's garden.

When he was gone, I faced Deacon. "I need to see Julien."

7

I tried to read Deacon's eyes, but I couldn't decipher them. We had time before we headed to Elustria, and I wanted to see Julien before everything got crazy with this mission. For all I knew, I wouldn't come back. It wasn't fair to Julien for me to not see him after he traveled so far and brought such valuable intelligence.

Pint flew from my lap onto the table, clearly wanting to be part of this conversation.

Deacon said in a calm, measured tone, "I'd like to be in the room with you when you talk to him."

"Yeah, me too," Pint said, much more animated than Deacon.

"There's no reason for that. I don't need you two there intimidating him. I need to hear what he came here to say." Deacon was intimidating under the best of circumstances. I couldn't imagine how someone he didn't like would feel under his gaze.

"I don't trust him," Deacon said. "He's hurt you, and he knows it. You're vulnerable around him. I don't trust him not to take advantage of that." He had his arms crossed over his chest. It made his biceps fill out his shirt in a way that was both sexy and menacing in this instance.

"I'm not vulnerable around him." I didn't know where Deacon had gotten that from.

"Yes, you are, because you still think you deserve the way he treated you. That makes you vulnerable. He's a blind spot for you. You don't see him how he really is."

"Oh, and you do? We were engaged. I lived with him. He certainly knew me a lot longer than the two weeks you have. Oh, excuse me, four weeks. Gotta make sure we get the two weeks that I was unconscious in there." I wasn't being fair to Deacon, but he wasn't being fair to Julien.

Deacon's eyes looked like I had slapped him. He stood from the table without a word and left the room.

Sybil put a hand on my shoulder. "He's just worried about you. When you passed out and then didn't wake up…" She shook her head. "I've never seen him like that. It really shook something inside him. He wouldn't leave your bedside. I thought he'd drive himself crazy with worry. He's not the type who's used to being ineffective, and there was nothing he could do to help you. I finally convinced him that doing missions in Elustria would help you more than staying and driving himself insane."

I turned to meet Sybil's gaze. "Thank you for telling me that." It didn't surprise me. It fell in line with everything I knew about Deacon.

"You're welcome." Sybil stood from the table. "I'm going to Elustria to round up some followers. We'll keep vigil at the temple for our ailing Dragon Fae who is still unconscious on her sickbed."

"Good idea," I said. We needed to make sure Malev was confident that I was incapacitated. I didn't know if her hubris was great enough to appear at the Starlight Palace if she thought I might be conscious.

"Don't worry, Sybil," Pint said. "If Julien says anything rude to her, I'll burn off his eyebrows."

Sybil laughed and ported away.

"You're not coming in either, Pint," I said.

"What?" He jerked his head back and stared at me with incredulity. "That's not fair. I've been waiting this whole time to get in with that worm. Deacon won't let me or anyone else in to see him."

"That's because he's smart, and he knows I want Julien protected. We're not in the habit of harming innocent people."

"Pfft. Julien's not innocent."

"We have to treat him like any other person who approached us with information."

"Oh really? Then you need to have someone else in the room with you. I know I act like I take no interest in your work, but there's a reason why you work in pairs. You send two people to question someone because one partner might pick up something the other one misses."

Pint had me with that one. I knew it, and he knew it. I could feel Deacon right outside the door, so chances were he knew it too with his exceptional hearing.

This whole thing was messy. I never claimed otherwise. My personal and professional lives couldn't mix. They couldn't even coexist. I had learned that lesson from Julien. In this line of work, the personal didn't take a backseat. It was left waiting on the side of the road.

I needed to get this over with, to move forward. We had our hands full with Malev's machinations.

With no good answer for Pint, I stood and left the room. It was time for me to see Julien.

When I emerged from the conference room, Deacon had a little smirk on his face.

"The walls are thin here, I see," I said.

Deacon shrugged. "I always knew I liked something about that little dragon."

"I suppose you'll be listening in on my conversation with Julien from outside."

"I won't pretend like I don't want to, but if you ask me not to, I won't. I can respect that you need privacy."

"Thanks." Deacon got a look on his face, like he had something to say, but he didn't know how. "What is it?"

He sighed. "Are you sure about this? There's really no need for you to see or talk to him. We've gotten all the relevant information. I worry that he only wants to talk with you to torture you about the past."

"And if he does? I owe him."

Deacon shook his head and looked away. "You don't owe him a damn thing."

I liked the version of me that Deacon saw. But if I was blinded to parts of Julien, then Deacon was blinded to parts of me. To him, I was a myth. He met me knowing that I was the Dragon Fae. That altered the way he would forever view me.

"I'm sorry for what I said in there. It wasn't fair to you. But I'm sure I want to see him. I want to get it over with."

Deacon nodded and led the way to Julien's room. He took me down a back staircase all the way to the basement. It turned out Julien's room was only a few doors down and two floors below mine. A shifter stood outside his door, and Deacon gestured with his head for him to leave. The shifter nodded and walked to the other end of the hall.

"You're keeping him here like a prisoner?" I asked. Sure, Deacon may not like Julien, neither did Alistair, but that didn't justify this treatment.

"He's not a prisoner. He's free to leave at any time. As long as he's here, he can't roam freely. He has an escort. That would be true for any outsider who came to Syndicate headquarters. You have my word on that. You can ask Drake."

I didn't need to ask Drake. Deacon never had to defend his word to me. "No, I understand. According to Drake and Pint, you're the one who's been making sure he's treated fairly."

"I just tried to think about what you'd want. Now, are you ready?"

I took a deep breath and nodded.

"Okay, I'll be at the end of the hall with Daniel."

I assumed Daniel was the guard. Deacon left me there in front of the door. This was it. The last time I'd seen Julien in person, the hatred and betrayal in his eyes had drilled a hole in my heart. I'd seen him since then, though without his knowledge. He hadn't changed the security I'd installed at our shared home. So I was still able to use a viewing portal to see him. I hadn't wanted to invade his privacy, but I did need to make sure he was all right. As far as I could tell, he hadn't gotten into another relationship. He still lived in the house all alone.

Three years ago he'd seen me as a liar. Two weeks ago he saw me as a strung out nether addict who couldn't stand on her own two feet. I was determined that now he would see a better version of me.

I opened the door and went inside.

8

Julien stood when the door opened. In the years we'd been apart he hadn't changed. His blond hair still hung to his shoulders. In his hand he held the book he'd been reading. He'd always been a blend of academic and artist. He came from an old family with money, and he had the slender build of a man who never had need of physical strength. The most time he spent outdoors was sitting on the bank of the lake we'd lived on, sketching the scenery.

The one thing that had changed was his blue eyes. The last time I'd seen them in Elustria they had been cold and hard. Now they looked at me with, not warmth, but at least recognition.

I closed the door behind me to give us privacy. The room was nice like every other place I'd seen in Drake's home. I'd half expected to find him in a bare room with stark white walls and a small bed. Instead, he had a fully furnished room complete with a reading nook. I bet he loved that.

I didn't know what to say, but one of us had to speak. The silence grew unbearable.

"It's good to see you up and about, Nataliana."

I hated hearing that name from him. Nataliana was dead. His

comment stabbed me with shame at him having seen me in my condition at the bar. I quickly brushed past it.

"Are you comfortable?" I asked. Pleasantries seemed so trite given what had transpired between us, but I couldn't think of anything else.

"Oh, yes, quite. The Dragon Prince has a nice library. I've been catching up on my reading," Julien said in that refined voice of his.

This room didn't have a table with chairs in it. Probably for the best. I didn't know if I wanted to be that close to Julien. Instead, there was an upholstered bench at the foot of the bed. I sat there, and Julien resumed his seat in the reading nook, a nice distance between us. It would be awkward to get closer.

It was strange to smell Julien's magic after my enhanced senses from the anointing. Deacon was right: as a sorcerer, Julien did have an electric smell to his magic. I couldn't quite describe it. It smelled like a musty library with a current of electricity through it. My magic did not leap in recognition of his.

"So why did you come here?" I asked.

"They didn't tell you?"

"No. They only told me what I need to know from a mission standpoint."

Julien leaned back. "Oh, interesting. Well, after the Feast of the Dragon, word got out about you, and strange things started happening. Security at the house picked up mages—you did an exceptional job with it. They came from the Directorate. So I went to court to report to the Circle. They had their own questions for me. They were very interested in the fact that we used to be engaged." Julien laughed. "They seemed to think that I knew you better than they did. Little did they know, I barely knew you at all."

His words cut. Yes, I had kept my job from him. I knew that was wrong, that my job wasn't like other people's jobs. It was part of my identity. So he had something of a point, but I had never been dishonest with him outside of that. My hopes, dreams, fears, insecurities that I shared with him were very real. I couldn't let him get to me. I had work to do. "I'm sorry I hurt you."

Julien leaned forward and wiped his hand over his face. "It's all in the past."

He moved from the chair and sat next to me on the bench. His magic so close to mine was uncomfortable. It had been intimate at one time and now felt like a stranger's.

"I don't want to rehash the past. I shouldn't have said that about not knowing you. This is all just so confusing. I mean, now you're saying you're the Dragon Fae. It's a lot. People with the Circle started questioning me, and I didn't know what I could say that could be useful. It all felt very strange.

"They kept me at court. At first they said it was for my protection, and I believed them. I didn't feel safe at home. Over time, they seemed increasingly upset with you. Then that last day, things changed. There was a flurry of activity, and the next thing I knew, a fae was trying to get in to question me. I didn't know what was happening. All I knew was that I didn't want to be used as a pawn in this game. I didn't feel safe anymore. It felt like the sorcerers in the Circle were after me, mages in the Directorate, and now the fae. I couldn't stay. The only person I could think to go to was you."

His eyes softened as he looked at me. His demeanor changed. For the first time, I felt familiar around him, like being back in time. "I realized that it had been your security at home that kept me safe."

"So you came here for protection?"

Julien smiled. "Well, I also wanted to see about this Dragon Fae business. I mean, what is it? Another one of your covers?"

To him, everything I did was a lie, so this would be no different. Not long ago, I would've laughed and agreed with him. It was some cosmic joke that people were saying I was the Dragon Fae. But I couldn't do that anymore, not after everything I'd been through. "No, it's not a cover."

Julien sobered and nodded. "Oh, I see."

I could tell from his eyes that he still thought it was bullshit. While I didn't like the insinuation that I would lie about something like this, it was hard to fault him. It had taken time for me to believe that there might be some truth to being the Dragon Fae.

"You know," he continued, "even after I found out who you really are, I didn't stop loving you. I just…I didn't know if the person I loved was real."

His magic reached out to mine, and I stood, backing a few steps away. This couldn't happen. I had loved him and hurt him and now that life was over. "I'm glad you felt safe coming to me. You are well protected here."

Despite what Deacon said about Julien not being a prisoner, I realized he had to be. We couldn't let him go for his own safety. There were too many people who could harm him in a bid to get leverage over me. It wasn't fair. This was why I hadn't fought to stay with him after he'd found out I was an assassin. My job would always put him in danger. If he wanted out of that, then I had to let him.

"I'm sure you've been told this, but if there's anything you need, just ask. It's not fair that you got dragged into all this. The least we can do is make you as comfortable as possible."

"Thank you. As I said, I'm being well taken care of. This is something of a nice vacation for me actually, a change of scenery."

Without a word, I left his room. The sound of the door shutting alerted Deacon. He'd been leaning against the wall at the end of the hall, talking to Daniel. Deacon came toward me, concern in his eyes. Daniel followed.

"Are you all right? How did it go?" Deacon asked, searching my eyes for answers.

"It was fine." I wouldn't tell Deacon about Julien's sharp jabs that still had the power to cut me. It was weak, pathetic. "Thank you for handling this so well."

Deacon nodded to Daniel to resume his post, and we walked back upstairs. I waited until I knew Julien wouldn't be able to hear us through the door. "We can't let him leave. If people are searching for him, he's a high target."

"I thought the same. He's an innocent, so we need to keep him safe. He can also be used against you."

I could understand now why Julien's story had alarmed Alistair. Neither Deacon nor Alistair really cared about Julien's safety; it was the revelation that a fae had tried to interrogate him that had them concerned. For fae to be at the court of the Starlight Palace in and of itself was remarkable enough. The fact that the fae had access to the Circle to even request an interview with Julien, much less push for one forcefully enough that Julien would find out about it, was nothing short of earth-shattering. It signaled Queen Malev's direct interference with sorcerer affairs. Now, only two weeks later, she had declared a formal alliance. I would have never thought something like this would happen.

When we reached the second floor, Pint and Alistair approached us. "My sister's ready for us," Alistair said.

"I'll get my void blade, and then we'll leave." I went to my room, Pint following. "Are you going to be fine here?" I asked him as I went inside. "I don't want you to worry about me while I'm gone."

"I don't worry about you," Pint said as he landed on my shoulder. "You're like a weed: you just keep coming back."

I laughed. I grabbed my void blade from the nightstand and spotted my phone charging. Two weeks ago, I'd promised Trevor that he'd see me again. I'd really freaked him out by taking my go-bag. Even though he knew that bag was meant to make me disappear, I'd assured him that wasn't the case this time. He had to be worried. I picked up my phone and sent off a quick text to him.

I'm safe. Will come see you when I can. –N

I put the phone back. I wouldn't need it in Elustria, and it would only raise suspicion if someone saw it.

Pint flew off my shoulder. "Now, if you'll excuse me, I have some young dragon shifters to play with."

I sighed in relief as he left the room. It was nice to have this little bit of normalcy back. Pint never said goodbye before missions. His clinginess after I woke had worried me. This was a good sign. He never really had other dragons to play with, and I could imagine the young dragon shifters had fun with him.

With my void blade secured in a sheath at the small of my back, I met Deacon and Alistair in the conference room. He already had a portal ready to go.

Time to meet his family and the next identity I'd assume.

9

couldn't help feeling it was reckless, revealing this kind of information to Alistair's family. I trusted Emma and Philip, but I worried about the danger it put them in. However, looking across the dinner table at their hollow eyes accentuated by dark circles of grief and sleeplessness, I almost wondered if they'd welcome death if it came calling. Little Adalyn had been their entire world. When she died, she took every spark of life with her.

Over dinner, Alistair caught them both up on everything that had happened.

"So you're really the Dragon Fae?" Emma asked after we finished our meal.

I noticed she had barely touched her food. Her wafer-thin appearance declared her grief. The woman in front of me bore no resemblance to the vivacious creature Alistair had told me about.

"Yes, I am. I was anointed a few weeks ago."

"We heard the rumors," Philip said. "But it didn't really register. It was right when Ada…" His voice trailed off, and he didn't need to finish.

"Of course. I understand."

"So if it weren't for you, the same thing that happened at the Academy would've happened elsewhere in Elustria?" Emma asked.

It was strange to talk about my work this way. I didn't understand why she asked. Did she want to thank me for saving others? Curse me for not saving her daughter? "It was all of us. We did what we could, but I'll forever bear the shame of not preventing the attack at the Academy. I went there as a child."

"Don't blame yourself. You'd have to be a monster to think they'd attack children," Philip said, his voice hot steel.

The spark in Philip's eyes when he spoke about those monsters, it was the first spark I'd seen in him all evening. He had a fire in him, a rage that burned. He kept it smoldered most of the time, likely to prevent burning his wife. To compound injustice on top of injustice, he not only had to bury his daughter, but the world told him he had to bury his anger, his fury. Maybe this mission could give him an outlet, however small.

Emma turned to her brother. "So that I understand, you want to have the Dragon Fae and her companion disguise themselves as me and Philip in order to go to the alliance signing?"

"That's right," Alistair said.

"But we won't do it without your permission," I assured her. "The things we're going to do there aren't legal, and we'll be doing them with your faces on. If we get caught, we'll reveal ourselves, but if not, people still might see us and assume we're you."

"You're going to kill her, aren't you?" Philip said. That spark lit in his eyes again.

They wouldn't tell anyone our plans, and it wouldn't hurt them to know. We did the damage as soon as we entered their house. It didn't matter how much they knew at this point.

"Yes," I said.

Philip got up from the table and left the room. I didn't know what that meant. I looked at Deacon, but he just shrugged and shook his head. Emma and Alistair seemed equally confused.

A minute later Philip returned, levitating a giant book in front of him. He plopped it down on the table and opened it to the middle. Several large maps unfolded from the center of the book.

"You might find this helpful. I worked at the Starlight Palace when I was younger, before I met Emma. I was a guard there. It was a fun experience for a young man, but I didn't have the personality to make a career out of it. I got this book a few years ago for Adalyn. She loved the Starlight Palace, and this book is all about its history."

The pages I could see were full of beautiful illustrations. The maps that unfurled were likewise intricate with beautiful detail and full color. I could imagine a little girl loving it.

Philip selected one of the maps and leaned over it. "Now, this is where I suspect they're going to have the actual signing. It's the hall of state. It's where foreign ambassadors are welcomed."

"You don't think it'll be in the throne room?" Alistair asked.

Philip shook his head. "I don't think so. That room is all about King Kelar's power. I don't think the fae queen would tolerate signing a document in front of him while he sits on his throne. The hall of state has all the grandeur she'd want for this event without the very visible reminder that she's in his territory. Treaties and trade agreements have been signed there.

"Now, of course, things could've changed in the many years it's been since I worked there, but I was present for a few trade agreements, and this was how the room would be set up for it." He used magic to draw a diagram of where he thought the actual signing would take place, where Kelar and Malev would be, how the audience would be situated, and where the guards would be posted.

"Given how much of a to-do they've made about this, inviting any sorcerer who wants to attend, it's likely the room will fill up. In that case, overflow is usually handled in the courtyard, and a viewing portal is established so that people can see what's happening."

"They wouldn't use one of the other rooms in the palace?" Deacon asked.

Philip shook his head. "No, not when the people in overflow are likely to be commoners who are coming just for this event. It's quicker and easier to herd them into the courtyard. Then they can just as quickly leave afterward. It's too much of a security nightmare having a bunch of people wandering around the palace."

I didn't like the thought of being in the overflow. We had to be in the main room, but I also didn't like the thought of getting there too early. It left too much time for us to dodge questions, chitchat, and blend in with the crowd. The less time on-site, the better. "How many people does the hall of state hold? Are they just going to let people in until it gets full, or do you think they'll have some type of ticketing system?"

"If they're doing seating, it'll hold a couple hundred. If they do standing room only, quite a bit more than that. It's hard to say if they'll ticket. They'll want all of the high-ranking nobles right up front. I imagine there will be spots reserved for them, but I think it'll just be first come, first served for the rest of it.

"However, you don't have to worry so much about that, and here's why. What these maps don't show you are all the secret passages throughout the palace. Since the palace is enchanted to prevent teleporting, the passages are a way for the royal family to get around unseen. When I worked there, they were rarely used."

He proceeded to show us entrances we could access discreetly from the courtyard and secret passages we could use to end up in the hall of state. I committed everything to memory.

"If you like, I can mark all of these with disappearing ink. If you're caught, you can make the markings disappear."

"That won't be necessary," Deacon said. "We can't risk being seen with a map at all. It raises too many questions. We have excellent memories. We've got it all."

Philip gave us more intel than I could've hoped for. While he described all the ins and outs of the security and the secret passages, he came alive for the only time that evening.

"Emma, how do you feel about all this?" I asked. She had stayed quiet during her husband's presentation. "We will be doing this wearing your identities."

She startled at the sound of her name. I wondered where her thoughts had been. She met my eyes, and I saw that hers were not only haunted by her daughter's ghost, they had a ferocity to them, as if the grief wanted to claw out of her and consume the world. Her husband was fire, and she was cold ice. "That bitch took my brother's hand. I only wish I could be the one to kill her."

Well, that settled that.

Tomorrow, if all went well, Malev would be dead.

10

The line inched forward. Deacon and I stood together outside the gates of the Starlight Palace. The glamour felt itchy against my skin, thick and heavy. There had to be a psychological element to it.

Our previous glamours had always been fictional people. All we had to do was appear other than we were. In this instance, we had to pass for someone else. We had identity papers with us that would be checked. If our glamour was off or slipped for a millisecond, the game would be over.

Imprints were complex things, as multifaceted as fingerprints. Deacon and I would both have to produce one that matched the imprint on the identity papers. While appearances could change, the nuances of an imprint didn't. We had to be perfect.

"Calm down. It's going to be fine," Deacon said and took my hand in his.

I took a deep breath. I never felt this way before a mission. This time it was personal. It wasn't an assignment. I wasn't doing my boss's bidding. In the past, if I failed, the Circle would send someone else. No one else would come now. It was just me and Deacon.

I didn't look at him. If I did, I'd expect to see Deacon and be disappointed to see Philip.

There were only eight people ahead of us in line now.

I counted how many people weren't wearing traditional robes. At an event like this, flowing robes were common, but they didn't make for easy movement. Both Deacon and I had forgone them, opting instead for an equally traditional though less formal outfit of tight-fitting trousers and loose blouses. A few people in line were dressed similarly, but the majority were in robes. I had hoped that wouldn't be the case. We didn't need anything to differentiate us from the crowd.

This morning we'd practiced until we could fool Emma and Philip. We separated the couple and tested to see if they could expose us. According to them, we had the appearance perfect. They could only tell we weren't the real deal because they didn't feel a mate bond with us. If it was good enough for them, it had to be good enough for palace security.

Deacon and I went to separate guards and produced our papers. Identity papers were virtually impossible to forge, so as long as we matched them, no one would doubt us.

The guard looked at the picture of Emma and looked at me. He nodded in satisfaction. "Imprint here, please." He produced a square clay imprint tablet. I performed a regular identification spell, just a little bit of magic to get a clean imprint.

The guard took the tablet and placed my identity paper on top of it. Both the tablet and the paper glowed purple. I passed. "Enjoy your visit to the Starlight Palace."

I walked inside the gates, but Deacon was nowhere to be seen. I moved out of the way of the incoming people. Through a break in the flow of sorcerers, I caught a glimpse of Deacon still at his guard post. He and the guard appeared in serious conversation as the guard held Deacon's identity paper.

I casually made my way closer. I didn't want to draw attention, but I needed to be close enough to act. If worse came to worst,

Deacon could shift and fly away. He didn't need me, but I wanted to be nearby just in case.

The serious conversation continued. Deacon reached for his identity paper, and the guard snatched it back, holding it slightly higher and out of reach. I slipped my hand under my blouse at the small of my back and curled my fingers around the hilt of my void blade. I withdrew an inch of it from the sheath.

They exchanged a few more words and then burst into laughter. I sighed, replaced my blade, and relaxed. The guard handed Deacon his identity paper back, and Deacon waved to him as he walked inside the gate.

"What was that about?" I asked Deacon as he came up next to me.

"Out of all the guards here, I got one who actually knew Philip when he worked here." Deacon's face was grim. I could see the exchange had taken a toll on him.

"You're shitting me."

"I assure you, I am not. If that's the kind of luck we can expect today, I don't know if we should proceed."

"How did you handle it?"

Deacon shrugged. "I know his type. I've worked with men like that when guarding the dragons. They all have the same stories to share, the same sense of humor. I just acted very sure of myself. I figured it'd been so long ago—and they clearly hadn't kept in touch because he didn't offer condolences—so I figured I didn't need to pass myself off as a believable Philip, just a believable guard from that time. It's likely his memories of everyone that far back are all blurred together."

I was impressed. "That's a good tactic." We didn't need to present a truth, just a believable version of reality.

The courtyard was a spectacle of people. Colorful, sparkly numbers glittered in the air, counting down the time until the big event. We had seven minutes left, not enough time for anyone to notice us or strike up a conversation. We subtly walked to a section of the courtyard near a secret entrance, making sure it looked as if the crowd had pushed us that direction.

By the time we were situated, the countdown showed only five minutes left until the signing. The plan was to wait until everyone was distracted by the viewing portal then go through the secret passage. However, more fae appeared as the start time approached. The place was crawling with guards. Was Malev this afraid of me? Or was something else going on?

"Are you seeing this?" I asked Deacon.

He gave a quick nod. "I think we should move now."

Before, it had been less likely we would be seen once the event started and everyone's attention was elsewhere. The addition of so many guards changed that. If they were any good, they wouldn't be distracted. Our better bet was to move now, try to blend in with the crowd as much as we could, and then enter the secret passage when the guards weren't looking.

I gave Deacon a nod, and we started making our way to the entrance Philip had told us about. It was hidden where the curve of a turret met the straight line of the wall.

Deacon and I situated ourselves with our backs to the entrance. My hands felt around for a loose stone. When I found it, I nodded to Deacon. He used his superior height to look around the crowd then looked at me. "Act like I just told you something funny."

We both broke out in laughter. He looked around again. "All right. The guards aren't looking. Let's go."

I leaned back on my hands, and the secret door gave way. When we were inside, it snapped shut behind us, leaving us in darkness.

"Can you see?" I asked Deacon.

"Yes, take my hand." The passageway was only wide enough for one person, so Deacon stuck his hand out behind him, and I took it. The darkness boded well for us. It meant the passages really were rarely used. They may even be forgotten now.

After a few minutes, Deacon stopped and felt the wall. "I think this is it."

I shimmied in front of him and pushed lightly on the wall. It gave just a bit. I pushed a little more until I could see inside the room.

Deacon had done a good job navigating. We were right where we wanted to be, behind Malev and Kelar. They sat at a table with the treaty in front of them about twenty feet from the wall. We'd expected them to be closer. Similar to what we saw outside, there were far more guards present in the hall of state than we'd expected. A line of high fae guards stood between us and Malev.

As Malev and Kelar moved, there was a slight shimmering around them: a shield. It would deflect magical attacks and any projectiles, but I could still pierce it with my void blade. There was no hope of using magic against her. The shield would be difficult to penetrate—not impossible, but difficult. Difficult enough to give all those guards time to catch me.

I shut the door to talk to Deacon. I didn't want to use magic unnecessarily and possibly draw attention to our hiding spot, so we contented ourselves with the darkness.

"What did you see?" Deacon asked.

"It's not good. She's not as close as I wanted, and the security's tighter."

"We always expected it would be tougher at the beginning. I think our analysis is right. Once the signing is over, things will relax as they mingle with the nobles. That's our moment."

I hoped so. With everyone mingling, it would be easier to slip near Malev and void her. A luncheon was being served afterward in the banquet hall. During the transition between the hall of state and the banquet hall, there'd be opportunities as well. We just had to wait it out.

I cracked the door just enough to watch the ceremony. Deacon leaned against the wall next to me, listening.

King Kelar stood and welcomed the crowd. The cheering from the courtyard was so loud that it could be heard in here. The people loved their king, largely because they didn't have to deal with him.

Kelar had a wicked temper. It led to him being surrounded by sycophants. He didn't show that face to the world, though. He was a kind and loving ruler to his people.

Kelar went on to say that he thought the sorcerers would be stronger in an alliance with the fae. There were no cheers at this. Perhaps the people did have a better understanding of his temper than I thought, because there was also no booing. He signed the treaty with a flourish and sat.

Malev stood and gave a little speech about her admiration for Kelar and platitudes about how good it would be for the fae and sorcerers to work together. She signed the document as well and sat. She beamed at Kelar, and he seemed besotted with her. He took her hand in his and lifted it up in the air. Polite clapping answered the gesture, but there were no cheers.

Kelar lowered their hands then shyly looked at Malev. "Shall we share our news?"

"Well, I think they have a right to know." Malev smiled and deferred to him to decide to share whatever news they had.

Kelar stood to address the crowd. "When Queen Malev approached me with the idea of forming an alliance just a couple of weeks ago, I, like you, didn't know much about her. But during this short time, I have grown increasingly impressed with her. The way that she expertly negotiated this treaty, her honesty and forthrightness with me and her willingness to put the welfare of both our peoples first, moved me in a way I hadn't expected."

He looked down at her adoringly. My stomach swirled, and I had to fight the urge to puke. I did not like where this was headed.

"I knew a woman like this didn't come around twice in one lifetime, so I proposed to her. I'm happy to say that last night, in a private ceremony here in the garden of the Starlight Palace, we were bonded."

The crowd gasped. We could even hear the people outside. The room stirred as everyone started talking.

"What is he thinking?" I said to no one in particular.

"It explains the extra security," Deacon said.

Deacon was right. I was no longer the only person in the room who wanted to kill Malev.

"Silence!" King Kelar bellowed. "She is now not only the fae queen but your queen as well. You will show her all due respect. Now, I knew it would be difficult for you to understand because you have not had the chance to get to know her as I have. So I want to show you one of the many reasons why she has not only my love but my trust and faith." He looked to the guards standing at the door. "Bring in the Chancellor."

The doors opened, and everyone's head swiveled to see Meilin escorted between four guards, magic binding her arms to her sides. She walked with regal grace, her chin held high, fire in her eyes.

"This isn't good," I said to Deacon. "They have her bound."

"Many of you know that the Chancellor schemed her way into power. I let it slide because I had confidence in her abilities. It took Queen Malev to show me that my generosity was being repaid with treachery. Little did I know that the Chancellor was mishandling affairs in my name. When I became aware of her gross malfeasance, I wanted to banish her to the Vortex. But Queen Malev, merciful as she is, convinced me to execute her instead."

Kelar nodded to a sorcerer who I realized now was a netherwalker. He stepped forward and performed the execution, violently sucking Meilin's soul from her body. The magic that bound her voice silenced her screams and suppressed her magic. Deacon leaned over me to watch through the crack in the door.

"Shit," I said.

"I can't believe he really did it." Deacon shook his head.

"And now, with that unpleasantness out of the way, I invite you to our wedding luncheon," Kelar announced, oblivious to the discord in the room.

Pandemonium broke out, the guards between us and Malev closed ranks around her. There'd be no way for me to get through.

"Shit, shit, shit."

A sorcerer rushed the table, hurling fire at Malev, but it bounced off her shield effortlessly and right back onto the would-be assassin. He was quickly seized. The guards surrounded Malev so completely that she couldn't even be seen. One group of guards faced inward, guiding her out of the room, and a second ring of guards surrounded the first, facing outward, challenging anyone who moved. There was no way I could kill her now.

"Do you want to try the banquet hall?" Deacon asked.

Part of the job was knowing when it was time to step back, regroup, and plan for another attack. "No, even before this there were too many guards for my comfort. Now we know they're not just for show. No matter how quickly I take them out, it won't be quick enough. Malev will know, and she'll kill me before I can get close." I shut the door and leaned against the wall. "Dammit." I slammed my fist against the stone.

"If you're not going to make a move, we should get out of here. We need to let Sybil and Alistair know what's going on."

I nodded, and Deacon led us out the way we came. As we wound our way through the passage, I vowed that Malev wouldn't escape me. I had a perfect kill rate. She wouldn't be the one to ruin it.

11

After we'd returned the clothes Emma and Philip lent us, we relayed what had happened to everyone. The disappointment in Emma's eyes when we told her of our failure would haunt me until I fulfilled my mission. Malev had kidnapped and tortured Emma's brother, the only family she had left outside of Philip. My failure cut deep.

"Alistair, we need to go back to the compound," I said. "We need to figure out a plan with you and Sybil." I wanted to get out from under Emma's sad eyes. Sitting around here commiserating wouldn't change anything. We needed to act.

"You're more than welcome to stay here," Emma said. She had an eagerness to her expression that broke my heart. How lonely and sad her life must be to want us to stick around.

"We couldn't impose on your hospitality," I said.

"It's no imposition, really." Emma's eyes shone, full of hope.

Alistair took his sister's hand in his. "Our very presence puts you in danger. We only came here because we were desperate."

"Maybe I'm desperate too," Emma said.

Philip came up behind his wife and placed both hands on her shoulders. He looked over her head to meet Alistair's gaze. "I appreciate your caution, especially when it comes to my family." His voice caught on the word family. "But we want to be part of this. There's precious little we can do. Let us do this."

A kind of understanding seemed to pass between the two men, and Alistair nodded. "Very well. I'll go fetch Sybil and be back soon." He turned to me and Deacon. "In the meantime, you two should eat."

Emma ran into the kitchen, happy to have something to do. She was a woman who did not enjoy idleness, and in the wake of her daughter's death, she'd spent too many idle hours. It wasn't good for grief. Now that she had something to do, she clung to it like a life preserver, as if she hoped it would pull her out of the abyss.

🔥

While we ate, Deacon told Philip about his encounter with the guard.

Philip whistled. "What are the odds? I have no idea who you're talking about, but it sounds like you handled yourself well."

"When I protected the dragons on Desolate Ridge in the Spineback Mountains, I often rotated shifts with other guards. It doesn't take long to figure out that the people drawn to this life all have the same stories."

"And I suppose there's a type that would stay in that position without being promoted out. I guess it's flattering that he remembered me after all this time," Philip said as he mopped up the last of his stew with a hunk of bread.

The meal filled both body and soul. At Moonlark Academy, we had often eaten the same type of stew and bread Emma made. They were classic staples, not so different from Earth fare but with a distinct Elustrian flavor. It was working-class food, meant to sit on the stove until a free moment allowed for a meal. It filled my spirit with strength and reminded me of who we fought for. It wasn't for the fancy people at court. We fought for the average people of Elustria and Earth, those who knew the value of a hearty meal shared with friends. I missed this sense of community.

"Thank you, Emma. This was delicious," I said when we'd all finished. Her cheeks colored slightly at the public praise.

"It's an old family recipe. I'm glad you like it." She levitated all the dishes to the kitchen and left them for later.

We retired to the living room, and Emma brought hot tea out for us. It was a cozy and comfortable space, with the warm feel of a family home that had been lived in for years, such a stark difference from the conference room at the Syndicate compound. Philip was in the middle of a funny story from his time as a guard when Alistair and Sybil appeared.

Emma brought them tea, and we all settled around the coffee table sipping from our mismatched mugs. Sybil tucked her legs under her and hummed with delight at the taste of the tea. "I haven't had tea this good since I left for Earth."

"I imagine the plants there are quite different," Emma said.

Sybil nodded. "And there are hardly any plants where we're at. All desert. Don't know why anyone chooses to live there."

I didn't disagree with her.

Alistair put an end to the chitchat. "We need to fully debrief so we're all on the same page now that Sybil is here."

Deacon relayed what had happened in as much detail as possible. I occasionally jumped in with my own impressions of the events. We needed everyone to have as comprehensive a picture of what happened as possible. Alistair didn't question my call not to make a move, which I appreciated. No one wanted Malev dead more than I did. If there'd been any chance for me to kill her or even void her, I would have.

"So, now we need to figure out how to get another shot at this," I said when Deacon was done.

"Access is going to be your biggest problem," Alistair said. "How do we get you close enough? Only courtiers and nobles have regular access to the palace. Security will slacken a bit without so many strangers on palace grounds, but she's still going to be heavily guarded. We don't even know how often she'll be at the palace or when."

"The other issue is that I'm not familiar with the high fae," I said. "Until the last few weeks, I'd never faced them. I'm not familiar with their tactics. I don't know how they react in a given situation. I've spent a lifetime learning how to kill mages, but not the high fae."

"Maybe our friend can help us with that," Sybil said as she side-eyed Emma and Philip. They didn't know about Cassalina or any of the other people working with us. Part of this job was compartmentalizing intelligence. Everything was on a need-to-know basis.

Alistair nodded. "Yes, maybe. We'll have to check. We have a few friends who might be able to help in that department."

Cassalina would be our best chance, but if for some reason she didn't want to cooperate, we had Dorran, Farawyn, and the shade. I was in over my head, but I also had a larger support team than ever.

Emma refreshed all of our mugs while Philip spoke. "Why don't you do what you did today? Glamour yourselves. You could go in as staff members. In my experience, everyone ignores the staff. They're invisible. You'd be able to come and go and gather intelligence that way."

I did like the idea of glamouring ourselves to get access. It was a tool I wasn't used to having, but it had worked remarkably well today.

"It's a good idea, but staff won't work," Sybil said. "Things operate differently in the fae court. Queen Malev is served only by high-ranking courtiers. It's the same throughout the fae ranks. The rank directly below serves the one directly above. Staff members may be able to get gossip, but they'll never get close enough to Queen Malev. I highly doubt she'll tolerate any sorcerer staff."

"So you're saying they need to go in as a high fae couple?" Alistair asked.

Sybil started to speak, but I cut her off. "I can't go in as high fae.

We can glamour like them, but I don't know enough about fae magic or fae customs. There's too great a risk that we'd be found out. We're going to have to go in as a sorcerer couple."

"In that case, I think the only chance to get near her is to go in as a high-ranking sorceress," Sybil said.

I remembered the few times I'd been to Malev's court. Cassalina had served her, getting her drinks and taking them away when she was done. Cassalina was one of the highest ranked fae outside of Malev. Sybil was right, we had to go in as members of the court.

"It will have to be the right couple," Alistair said. "People who have access but aren't incredibly well known. You may be able to fool acquaintances, but we don't want to depend on you fooling close friends. Who has the kind of access we need while still being somewhat forgettable?" Alistair looked around the room.

I never spent time at court. I didn't know who any of the people were.

"There are plenty of sorcerers who have the right to be at court but don't come," Philip said. "Not everyone enjoys it. There's a lot of gossiping, intrigue, backstabbing. That just isn't for some people. I'd pick one of those couples."

"Right now, there's a perfect excuse to come to court: the curiosity around Queen Malev. I suspect there are a lot of people coming back," Emma said.

I made eye contact with Alistair. "We should use our contact at the Circle. It'll help to get his read on the situation as well. We need to know as much as we can about what we're going into," I said.

Alistair nodded. "I'll contact him and set up a meet."

"The sooner the better." I'd wanted to go to bed tonight with Malev no longer existing in the world. I thought I'd be back in Arizona, in the hot dry air and sun. Instead, the cool air around me hung humid with moisture and magic, an interesting mix that could only be experienced in Elustria.

With our next steps settled, Sybil went back to the temple. It seemed she kept the Dragon Fae followers together all on her own.

Given her stature and demeanor, it was easy for people to underestimate her, but she was one of the strongest women I'd ever met.

Deacon and I went for a walk in Emma and Phillip's garden. In the few weeks since their daughter had died, weeds had overtaken it. No matter how carefully they'd tended it, all it took was a little time for all of it to fall apart.

I'd saved the people of Elustria from the Directorate's planned attack on the Feast of the Dragon. I'd rescued Alistair. All that and it only took one lapse—getting nether addicted and passing out for two weeks—for it all to fall apart. If I'd been awake, would I have been able to stop Malev from forming this alliance? I didn't know. No one could know.

Deacon walked by my side, and he broke the silence. "You'll get her."

"How do you know? I've never killed a high fae before."

"Because she took Alistair. The moment she did that, she signed her death warrant. You've killed so many on other people's orders, never failing. This time, it's personal. You won't stop until you kill her."

"Even if it's the last thing I do?" I stopped walking, and Deacon refused to look at me. "You think this is it, don't you? You think this is how I die." His jaw clenched, and his cheek twitched, and still he looked steadfastly ahead. "If you think that, then why are you helping me?"

"Because I know this is something you have to do. The other thing…" his voice drifted off. He looked down and shook his head. "I just want to focus on being with you. I refuse to live in fear of this prophecy."

He finally looked at me. His intense green eyes had a way of piercing right through me. He leaned closer. "Besides, I'm holding out hope that we can cheat fate." He looked into my eyes for a moment and then turned and continued walking.

12

*D*eacon and I sat at a table in the back of the Rusty Spigot, a seedy bar in a shady part of Stardowns, the city surrounding the Starlight Palace. We wore the faces of strangers conjured from our imagination. We were both redheads this time, like Gordon, and that's how he would recognize us. We'd ordered some traditional Elustrian bar food, intent on taking advantage of the opportunity to eat our native cuisine.

Halfway through our meal, Gordon appeared. I'd thought that his youthful round face and spiky red hair would stick out in a place like this, but he had somehow made himself look like he belonged. His guarded eyes kept him from appearing as young as usual. His shoulders rounded in a slight hunch, a far cry from his regular immaculate posture. It was easy to forget that handlers were trained in field operations. They usually stayed behind the scenes, but Gordon could clearly take up the work of a spy any time he wanted.

We waved to him, and he joined us. Once he sat at the table, he cast a clear privacy bubble around us. A trained spy could use magic to break through such a bubble and listen in, but it would keep casual eavesdroppers away.

"I would have never…" he shook his head as he looked between the two of us. "This is incredible. You can stay like this indefinitely?"

"I don't see why not," I said. "It's uncomfortable, but not tiring."

"Congratulations on your success rescuing Alistair. And thank you. He's been a good friend to me," Gordon said.

"Thanks for your help." I would have never thought when Meilin assigned Gordon as my interim handler that I would ever have friendly words for him. "What can you tell us about the current situation?"

A waitress came to see if Gordon wanted anything, but he waved her away. "Things are a mess. In general, no one at the Circle wants to share intel with Queen Malev. But in reality, it's only a matter of time before someone breaks. Everyone's going close hold. I'm protecting all the intel I can. Usually we trust one another, but given the situation, everyone's keeping their own counsel. You don't know if the person you trust today could break beneath the fae tomorrow."

"So she's actively interrogating people?" Deacon asked.

"Not interrogating so much as demanding access. She wants her people inside the Circle archives. Right now, we're bogging them down with useless stuff. Old mission reports, status briefs, that sort of thing. We just sent her all of Broderick's reports."

Broderick was an old field agent who refused to retire. The Circle kept him stationed at the most boring posts hoping to force his retirement or at least keep him where he couldn't do any damage. Currently he was stationed in Canada outside of Casper Dinathion's old lair. Casper had been a Directorate mage and was killed by a CCS agent, the mage's covert service. There had been so much magic around Casper's base that the Circle thought it prudent to keep an agent nearby, especially when we needed a place for Broderick. He spent his time coming up with elaborate, verbose ways of writing reports that all said the same thing: nothing's happening here. The fae would have a frustrating time reading through all of them.

"What is she looking for?" I asked.

"She's not being specific, likely to keep us from destroying what she wants. My guess is she's looking for information about her rival and the intel from your last missions. So far, my identity as your handler at the time has remained secret. I don't know how much longer that's going to last."

"Do you have a bug-out plan?"

"Don't worry, they won't break me. I have a few contingencies. If it comes down to it, I'd rather die than end up in the hands of the fae," Gordon said. The steel in his voice and eyes said these weren't idle words. I would've never thought Gordon had it in him, but I didn't doubt it now. "At first, I thought she was mainly interested in her rival, wanting all the intel we have on the new court. But I'm starting to think she's more interested in you. She'd been working with Meilin and went behind her back to try to secure some type of alliance with the sorcerers. But it wasn't until you rescued Alistair that she committed.

"The Circle's completely cut off from court right now. There's no mingling between the two. Socially, we've always kept to ourselves, but there was natural mingling that happened. Now there's a hard line. No one from the Circle has any contact with courtiers. She knows that if we talked with them, we'd be able to turn them against her."

"So how did you get away to meet us?" Deacon asked. I wondered if Gordon noticed the hint of suspicion in his voice. If he did, his tone didn't give it away.

"We have a secret location in the archives where we can port in and out. A small group of us have been covering for each other. We let one person go, and when they get back, another leaves. The rest of us cover for the absent person. We'll be found out eventually, but we're doing what we can. I can't stay long."

I finished my last bite of food and pushed my plate back. "We're thinking now might be a good time to impersonate someone who hasn't been at court recently. With everything going on, we don't think it would raise many eyebrows for a couple to return to court after some time away."

"You're right. That's a smart move," Gordon said.

"We want your help picking the right couple. We need people who have good access, who could potentially get close to the king or Queen Malev, but they can't be too social. We'll have to pass ourselves off as them. Can you think of anyone?"

Gordon leaned back in his chair and crossed his arms, thinking.

"There are a few options. There's the Count and Countess of Strathorn. People like them because they're beautiful, have sufficient rank, and the count's father went to school with the king. They have excellent access, but they prefer the quiet life. It's been about a year since they've been to court. They currently spend all their time at their estate."

"That sounds like a good option."

"Then there's the Duke and Duchess of Claybourn."

"A Duke and Duchess are too high ranked. People will know that we're imposters," Deacon said.

"Normally, but not with them. They're an older couple, quite eccentric. They spend all their time at their estate or traveling. They have no children, and everyone's pretty much waiting for them to die so the king can gift their duchy to someone else. They have access due to their rank, and the duke has always been friendly with the king, but they're one of the holdover duchies from the Great Rift."

A thousand years ago, the royal family had changed. Holdover titles were the ones from the previous dynasty. They were allowed to keep their title and lands in exchange for agreeing to acknowledge the legitimacy of the new dynasty. Even though it happened a thousand years ago, people generally didn't like the holdovers. I imagined the court eagerly awaited the demise of this couple so the duchy could be given to a longtime supporter of King Kelar's family.

"The couple is generally well liked. From what I understand, they're very fun-loving, and no one can fault them, but they do have that rough-around-the-edges quality that a lot of the holdovers have. They don't spend much time at court, but if they appeared, they'd have access to the king himself."

The previous dynasty was not quite as formal and fussy as the new. "All right. Anyone else?"

Gordon glanced between me and Deacon and then settled on me. "There are the two Barons of Westchester."

My eyebrows shot up. "I don't think I'm ready to impersonate a man. I know I can get the glamour right, but I don't know that I can get the mannerisms. It'd be too risky that someone would see through me."

"Fair enough." Gordon shrugged. "If I had more time, I might come up with a few more options. When do you want to do this?"

"Immediately," I said. "Can you send us dossiers on suitable candidates?"

"I'll get back now and do it. Just give me a few hours. I'll use the outskirts dead drop location. Alistair knows where it's at." He stood, but before he dispelled the privacy bubble, he said, "Good luck, Dragon Fae. You're going to need it. I'll keep an eye out for you and make contact if I can once you're at court. But this may be the last time we see each other. If it is, it's been an honor working with you."

13

We leaned over the dossiers spread out on Emma's coffee table. Deacon and I had looked at them with Alistair, Philip, and Emma. Now it was time to make our choice. Gordon had given us six options, but we all seemed to gravitate toward the two he told us about. The others were either so entrenched in court politics that it would be nearly impossible for us to pass as them or they didn't have anywhere near the access we would need to get this job done.

"I think the Count and Countess of Strathorn are your best bet," Philip said.

"I don't know." Alistair shook his head slightly as he thought. "They're a little too popular for my taste."

"I can see how that would be a concern," Philip said. "But they're the court's golden couple. Everyone loves them. For that reason, no one will ever suspect them of anything. People will make excuses for anything strange they see."

Emma turned to Alistair. "I agree with Philip. Everyone wants to be like the countess. If she walked into court wearing a boot on her head, no one would question it, and the next day all the women would be doing the same. I think the fact that they're so private makes them alluring. It doesn't hurt that they're gorgeous. They know the court loves them, but they have this shy modesty about them that would be annoying except it's genuine. It makes people like them even more."

I wanted to point out that I did not have a history of being likable, so this might not be the best idea. But that wasn't my job. My job was to take the assignment and make it work. Alistair was my handler. He made these tactical decisions, and I went along with them.

Deacon, who had never really been an agent, obviously didn't get the memo that Alistair alone made these decisions. "I agree. The count and countess are the closest in age to us. I think they'd be the easiest for us to imitate."

He wasn't the one who had to be little miss golden child. I'd rather play the older eccentric couple. It sounded like a lot more fun. But if I wanted fun, I should've gone into a different line of work.

"All right then, the count and countess it is," Alistair said. "Commit their dossier to memory, and then I want you to to conduct surveillance. Make sure there's nothing significant that the dossier missed or anything that could disrupt the plan. If everything checks out, abduct them and take them to our base Earthside."

Given the high stakes of this job, we couldn't risk keeping them in Elustria while we worked. If they decided to go to court or communicate with someone at the Starlight Palace, it could blow the whole mission. Once we had them back at the Syndicate compound, we'd ask some questions and gather more information that would help us mimic them. I didn't like involving innocents, but this was the only option we had. I'd make sure they weren't hurt.

☞

The Strathorns lived in what would be called a cute cottage if it weren't so large. They had a simple flower garden, nothing ornate or overly fussy, and a kitchen garden that looked like it grew enough vegetables to provide well for two people. A bubbling brook ran behind the cottage. The scene was idyllic in every way. It wasn't their family seat, that was a much grander house that they allowed people to tour. This, according to their dossier, was where they preferred to spend their time.

No one was home when we arrived. They had virtually no security. Deacon and I could've easily broken in, but I didn't think it necessary. Instead, we took positions in a tree to await their return.

"This is quite a change from your car," Deacon said. He sat comfortably on a large branch and looked like he could recline there all day. Up until now, our stakeouts had taken place in my Corvette.

I laid on my stomach on a branch, my eyes focused on the house. "One of my earliest memories is climbing a tree. I used to do it all the time. It drove my mother crazy." Sadness pinched my heart at the memory of my mother. I couldn't believe I'd mentioned her so casually. I'd never done that before. I rarely thought about my time before Alistair took me from school.

"I bet she loved that, worrying about you falling out of trees all the time," Deacon said.

I smiled at the memory. "Actually, she did love it. Her biggest fear was that I'd turn into a simpering woman. Every scrape and bruise I came home with she took as proof that I'd be able to handle myself in the world. What drove her crazy was me being in a tree instead of where I was supposed to be." I didn't mention how rare it was for me to see my mother. No need to taint one of my few nice memories of her.

"Shh," Deacon said and leaned forward. It took me about ten seconds to hear it too, rustling in the woods across the way. About a minute later, the count and countess emerged from the trees. They wore broad smiles, as if they had an audience, but it was just the two of them. The countess held a bundle in her arms. When she looked down at it, her eyes filled with adoration as my stomach filled with dread.

A baby.

They had been absent from court for so long because they were busy having a baby. The three of them looked perfect, a happy little family. I wouldn't have been surprised if songbirds came and tied ribbons in their hair. When fate saw fit to give two people such a wonderful life, it wasn't our place to mess with that. I grabbed Deacon's hand and ported us to Emma's garden.

"Why'd you do that?" Deacon asked, his eyebrows furrowed in frustration as he looked around to get his bearings.

"We can't do it. I won't put them through this stress when they have a baby to worry about. Who knows how going through trauma like this would affect the child. We can't do it. It's not our place. I won't." I didn't have many lines in the sand, but this was one. To mess with innocent adults was one thing, but I couldn't take the innocence of a child. Not even the Dragon Fae could do that.

Deacon nodded, understanding in his eyes. "Fine. We'll move on to the next couple."

"The duke and duchess?" I asked.

"I think the consensus was they were the second choice," Deacon said.

I took a deep breath. I didn't like changing the plan last minute, but it was a bit of a relief after seeing the countess. "It's probably for the best. I think I'll make a much more convincing eccentric old woman than I would a perfect porcelain doll."

"She wasn't a perfect porcelain doll," Deacon said.

I glared at him. "Go on, tell me more about what she was."

Deacon's eyes widened slightly. "Oh, nothing. I didn't notice a thing. So, about this next couple. Old and eccentric, that sounds fun."

꧂

The duke and duchess currently resided in the seaside village of Aljorn. They didn't travel with an entourage and didn't use servants, more reasons why they were a good pick. By all accounts they were utterly plain down to their names: Jane and Michael. Their current house was one of dozens they owned around Elustria. It didn't seem like they spent more than a few months at a time in one location.

Deacon and I strolled along the beach. We watched Jane and Michael splash around in the sea, giggling like little children. By human standards they only looked around fifty years old, but they were each pushing a hundred and twenty. They ran around like five year olds.

"We'll wait for them at the house and grab them when they come in," I said to Deacon. When he didn't respond, I turned to see him completely entranced by this couple. I recognized the look in his eyes, the longing, the amazement. "I know, it's hard to believe there are people like them in the world. So carefree, having fun, laughing, playing. Is that how life's supposed to be?" I asked.

"Maybe, but not for people like us," Deacon said and turned away from the scene, making his way to the house.

People like us. He didn't just mean the Dragon Fae and her companion. Even if the prophecy hadn't happened, that life had never been meant for us. We were guardians. We handled the threats and protected the people. We fought and we killed so that other people could have carefree days. But never us.

It didn't take much to break into their house. It amazed me that people felt safe enough to not have security. What must it be like to know that no one was ever coming after you?

I went upstairs to pack their things. Some of their stuff might prove useful for our mission, plus they would need a change of clothes or two. I levitated a chest with their belongings down to the first floor and placed it next to the sofa. While I'd packed, Deacon had gone through their belongings downstairs. He held some letters and books.

"I found a journal," Deacon said. We needed anything that would help us imitate the couple. Handwriting samples would also prove useful. "I also found their contact book."

Quite a good haul. This would be more than sufficient for the mission. "Excellent. Put them in the chest. I packed some things for them and for us to use."

I took a few minutes to simply look around the house and get a feel for who this couple was. Their aesthetic could best be described as eclectic. Little trinkets from their adventures filled the space. They could've easily afforded expensive art, but they preferred mementos.

"They're on their way," Deacon said.

I could hear them talking as they walked up the path to the house. I created a portal to Drake's. The plan was a simple grab and go. We didn't anticipate using magic. I levitated the chest through the portal. Then we took up our spots, one of us on each side of the entry, flat against the wall.

Jane and Michael walked through the door, and as soon as they saw the portal, Jane squealed.

"This is it, honey." She squeezed her husband's hand and jumped up and down as if excited. Deacon looked at me confused, and I shrugged my shoulders.

I nodded to Deacon to proceed with the plan. As soon as the door shut, we sprang from behind them and placed our hands over their mouths. They didn't struggle at all. Jane clapped her hands in apparent glee.

This was the strangest abduction I'd ever taken part in.

Deacon went with Michael through the portal, and I followed. Alistair waited for us along with some shifters. Once through the portal, we removed our hands from their mouths. Jane and Michael stared wide-eyed at their surroundings.

"Ooh, this is even better than I thought," Jane said with a grin so wide I thought it might actually crack her face.

"Now, now, darling, don't ruin the fun. Remember, we've just been kidnapped," Michael said with an obvious wink to his wife.

She calmed down and took on a sober expression. "Right you are. Please, please don't hurt us," she said to the waiting dragon shifters while clearly trying to contain a smile.

"Take them to the room we set up downstairs," Alistair said to the shifters. When they left, he turned to us. "What was that all about?"

"I have no idea." It was one of the oddest things I'd ever seen.

14

Someone had enchanted Jane and Michael's room so they couldn't create portals, teleport, or communicate with anyone outside the room. Other than that, their magic was unrestricted. I didn't want our guests to feel like prisoners. They were innocent, and there was no reason to suspect they'd get violent. Even if they did, it wasn't like they could hurt me or Deacon.

A shifter had brought Jane and Michael's trunk down for them. Deacon and I waited until they had time to change out of their wet clothes from the sea. I also wanted to give them a little bit of time to sit and let their situation sink in. Hopefully it would make the next part go quicker.

After about twenty minutes, Deacon and I visited them. My cuff made sure they wouldn't recognize the Dragon Fae's magic. We still wanted to keep my condition secret. Even though escape was virtually impossible for Jane and Michael, there was no sense giving them knowledge that would be dangerous for them to have. The less they knew, the better for everyone.

When we entered the room, they were seated at their table. They looked at us, and Jane got that same crazed smile on her face that she had earlier. She squealed and started jumping in her seat. "This is it!"

Michael reached across the table and placed a calming hand on her arm. "Darling, don't ruin it."

Jane settled down and tried to compose her face, but her lips kept twitching, trying to break free into a smile.

This was better than her being scared, right? I'd been so concerned about traumatizing innocents that it never occurred to me that they might be...excited to be kidnapped? The whole thing was weird, but I didn't care as long as I got the information I needed.

"I just have a few questions to ask you," I said. "The sooner you cooperate, the sooner this is all over. I need to know the last time you attended court at the Starlight Palace."

Michael sat still, as if he hadn't heard me. Jane smiled and shook her head.

I tried again. "Can you tell me the last time you saw someone who regularly attends court at the Starlight Palace?"

Jane shook her head more vigorously.

Deacon stepped forward. I didn't know what he thought he could do differently, but maybe they would respond better to him. Jane was the more engaged of the two, and it would be difficult for any woman to resist Deacon.

"Why don't you tell us about your home in Stardowns?" Deacon asked.

Still nothing.

"All right, why don't you tell us some of your favorite things? What foods do you like? What activities? When you're at court, what do you like to do there?" Deacon's line of questioning was smart, but we still got nothing from them.

I had no clue what to do. This was unlike any interrogation I'd ever conducted. Normally, it didn't take much to get someone to talk, especially when dealing with someone who wasn't trained to resist or who didn't have a strong personal belief that prevented them from answering. Usually the disorientation from being taken somewhere new built up a sufficient amount of fear in the person's mind. It didn't matter what I did, they would see it as sinister. It kept me from having to do anything cruel to get answers. However, I'd never had anyone appear to enjoy being kidnapped and interrogated.

Maybe I should have Alistair conduct the interrogation. He had more experience than me. Deacon and I had decided to do it ourselves because we were the ones who had to impersonate these two. The more time we spent with them, the more convincing our impersonation would be. If Alistair conducted the interrogation, the information would come to us filtered through him. It wouldn't be ideal, but at this point, I didn't know what other option we had.

When Deacon didn't get any answers, he looked back at me, and I jerked my head toward the door. In the hallway, he spoke. "I don't understand it. I think we should threaten them."

"No," I said, my voice strong and short.

"We don't need to hurt them. I think we should just introduce a little fear."

"They're innocents. I don't want to traumatize them."

"Traumatize?" Deacon raised his eyebrows and leaned toward me, gesturing with his arm to the door. "Are you seeing the same two people I am? They're acting like this is a vacation."

Their demeanor was bizarre. I didn't have an answer for it. "How about we let Alistair give it a try?"

"I don't know how helpful it will be for us to get the information from him. And we might need follow-up questions, clarification. I'd just feel more comfortable if we did it ourselves," Deacon said.

I wondered if he had a trust issue with Alistair. He didn't have the long relationship with him that I did. But, it didn't really matter. I agreed with Deacon. I just didn't know how to go about getting answers.

"All right. We can keep trying, but scaring them is off the table.

We don't get physical, we don't use magic, and we don't play mind games. We have to find out what's going on and get them to want to give us information."

It sounded simple, but there was a reason people studied for years to learn how to interrogate. It was an intricate skill, one I hadn't mastered. I knew how to get answers under normal circumstances, but these weren't normal circumstances.

Deacon nodded his understanding of my terms. I grabbed the doorknob, took a deep breath, and went back inside.

"Why don't we start over?" I asked. "We just have a few simple questions for you. We want to get to know you better. We're not going to ask you about any deep dark secrets. We don't need any secrets about your friends. Just some basic information. You answer our questions, stay here for a little while, eat some good food, and we'll take you right back to your beach house." I looked at both of them for some sign of agreement.

"She's not going to answer any of your questions," Michael said. "You might as well give up now and give us the next clue. It'll be easier for all of us."

Deacon looked at me at the mention of a clue. I was just as in the dark as he was.

"Why won't she answer any of our questions?" I asked. Maybe that was the question I should have asked earlier.

"You're not going to break me," Jane said and giggled.

"The fatal flaw in this whole setup is that we know enchanted scrolls can't actually hurt us," Michael said.

"That's right, so you might as well give us the next clue and let us go. You won't break me. I'm going to win," Jane said.

I had to stop myself from rolling my eyes. We really had abducted a couple of eccentric ones. "We'll leave you to think over your position."

I led Deacon out of the room. In the hallway, I leaned against the wall, shaking my head. "What the hell are enchanted scrolls?"

"I have no idea," Deacon said. "Whatever they are, she's right. She's winning."

Despite everything, we both cracked up.

15

We found Alistair, Sybil, and Drake sitting in the upstairs living room. This situation had gotten away from us, and we needed their help.

"Done so soon? Did you get everything you needed?" Alistair asked.

We sat down with the group, and I shook my head. "We didn't get anything."

"You couldn't get those two bumpkins to talk?" Drake asked, incredulity in his voice.

Deacon took offense at his tone. "It's not like what you think. Besides, Nadiya's insistent that we not hurt them or even threaten it."

"Really?" Sybil asked as she cocked her head. "That's interesting."

Behind Sybil's cheery exterior, she had something of a sadistic streak. She enjoyed scaring the shit out of people. Out of everyone in the room, she was the one I'd least want interrogating me.

"They said they know enchanted scrolls won't hurt them and that they're going to win. Does anyone know what that means?" I looked around the living room at a bunch of blank stares.

The only circumstances under which I could picture the Claybourns being kidnapped was if they owed someone money. But if that were the case, they wouldn't be so sure of their safety. Were they involved with a cult? I couldn't rule out anything.

"If you feel you need to understand this in order to proceed, I can go to Elustria to research," Alistair offered.

"If we can't threaten or hurt them, then I feel our best option is to understand them," Deacon said.

Everyone in the room looked at me. "Yes, we need to understand them to proceed. It's the only course I'm comfortable with. Deacon and I can go do some digging."

Alistair stood. "No, you two need to stay here and eat something. I'll go to Elustria and make some inquiries. The Claybourns don't strike me as savvy clandestine types. Whatever they're talking about can't be that difficult to find. If it is, I'll come back and update you."

It felt good having Alistair back and working. I wouldn't be able to do this job without him. Case in point: the first time I tried I got so nether addicted that I passed out for two weeks.

When he was gone, Sybil took his spot next to me and leaned forward. "You know, while you two are eating, I could just slip in there and—"

"No! Absolutely not," I said. I couldn't believe I had to reiterate this to her.

Sybil leaned back and winked at me. "I understand."

I sighed. I had too much on my plate to also rein in Sybil's weird fascination with mental torture. "I'm serious, Sybil. I forbid you to go anywhere near them." She leaned forward and held up a finger, but I stopped her. "And no using any weird fae magic to mess with them from outside the room. Forget they're even here. As far as you're concerned, we have no one here from Elustria."

She fell back in her seat and crossed her arms over her chest in a little pout. "Fine."

6

We were about halfway through our meal when Alistair appeared. I expected him to be gone a lot longer. He tossed a stack of brochures on the table.

"This is Enchanted Scrolls." He sat down next to me. "I didn't even get a chance to ask Gordon. When I appeared at Emma's, I told her about the little kink in our plan. She laughed and handed me these brochures they'd gotten."

I tore open the seal on a brochure, and a little holographic-type image floated in front of me. A sorcerer with slicked back hair walked in front of my face. "Do you crave adventure? Are you tired of the same thing day in and day out? Do you feel like you were born for more?"

I was beginning to get a cult-y vibe, the same as I'd gotten from the Be Your Best Self movement.

"Well then, we at Enchanted Scrolls have the solution for you. For a low monthly subscription fee, our team of immersive story-tellers will send you on the adventure of a lifetime. Each month you'll have a challenge that you must complete in order to get the next clue to solving the mystery. What mystery? That's up to you. Do you want to solve a murder? Find a lost treasure? Uncover a scandal? Choose your adventure and be whisked away today! I have a feeling once you've done one, you'll want to do them all. So what are you waiting for? Respond today. Adventure awaits!" The man disappeared in a puff of smoke. This kind of enchantment was one-time use. Elustrian junk mail.

"So they think this is something they paid for?" Deacon asked.

"It appears so," Alistair said. "You'll have to play along to get them to talk."

This explained Jane's excitement. She and Michael were the type of couple to travel, experience life, do things. That was why they were never at court. They were too busy living. I wondered what it would be like to have a life where being kidnapped and interrogated was just another great adventure. Well, it was time for me to continue the story.

When I entered the room, Jane and Michael stopped talking and gave me their full attention. This all made so much more sense now. Deacon shut the door behind us, and I took the lead.

"It's clear you won't break. Good job! You now advance to the next challenge. This is a difficult one. Many people don't pass. For the next challenge, my associate and I are going to impersonate you at a dinner party full of your closest friends. If we're able to fool them for the entire night, you get the next clue."

"I don't think you can fool Laura Beth," Jane said.

Laura Beth. I made a mental note to stay away from her. "My associate and I are very good at this. The key to success is you telling us as much as you can that'll help us convince your friends that we're you. Do you understand?"

Jane narrowed her eyes. "How do we know this isn't some sort of trick?"

Deacon must've sensed I was about to lose it with these people. He stepped forward. "You don't. But why would we trick you?" He shrugged and turned his back on them, walking toward me. "It doesn't matter. You'll find out by the end of the night. If we don't go to this dinner party as you two and fool your friends, it's all over. You'll go home, and I guess you can try one of the other adventure packages." He turned and eyed the couple.

Jane and Michael shared a look. An entire conversation passed between them. Michael nodded to her, and Jane looked at me. "All right. What do you want to know?"

16

This time, we didn't have to wait in line to get through the gate to the Starlight Palace. The main entrance wasn't busy, but we used a private gate for those of higher rank. When we presented our identity papers, the guard bowed in respect and ushered us through. He didn't even confirm our imprints. A simple glance at the words *duke* and *duchess* was all it took.

No wonder the fae queen had her own security. Identification documents were nearly impossible to forge, but the guard didn't seem interested in verifying the identity of such high-ranking nobles. He likely didn't want to cause offense by not immediately recognizing us. I imagined some of the nobility would take umbrage at that.

The courtyard looked quite different today. The ornate landscaping and sculptures that dotted the area were easier to appreciate without the throngs of people. There were only a few who strolled around, enjoying the nice weather.

We headed directly to the great hall. Dinner wouldn't be served for a little while yet, and the nobility would mingle there until it was time to eat. More importantly, the Lord Chamberlain would be there. We needed him to see us and notify the king of our arrival.

When we arrived at the great hall, a herald announced us. "The Duke and Duchess of Claybourn."

When we entered the room, most everyone went back to their business of gossiping, but a few people did watch us or glance our way. A sorcerer controlled a string and woodwind sextet by himself in the corner. He produced lively music that filled the air, but it couldn't force cheer into the atmosphere. No laughter sounded in the room. Everyone spoke in subdued tones. An undercurrent of anger bubbled just beneath the surface.

"Your Graces," a man said from behind us. We turned just as he rose from his bow. The Lord Chamberlain. "I wish I'd known you were coming. But no worries, I will have your seating arranged near the table of honor. I'll alert the king to your presence." He bowed his head and left the hall.

That was the advantage of impersonating such high-ranking people. During dinner, we'd be seated close to King Kelar and Queen Malev. Afterward, we'd be able to drink and mingle with them. It would be simple enough to get close to Malev and cut her with my blade. Then killing her would be easy. Once the deed was done, I'd take on a different appearance and make sure everyone saw my face change. I didn't want the Duchess blamed for the crime. Then I'd escape.

"I see even you two couldn't resist the curiosity. Come to see if it's really true?" a woman asked. The contact book Deacon had found at Jane and Michael's contained pictures of every noble in the court of the Starlight Palace. Michael apparently lacked a knack for names, and Jane just didn't care enough to, according to her, remember the names of people who bored her. So Deacon and I had studied it before we left, and I racked my brain to match this face with a name. I came up with the Marchioness of Jeun.

"We could hardly believe it," I said. "We had to come see for ourselves."

"Whatever you heard, it's all true. She's married our king, and he executed the Chancellor. He didn't even give a reason, not really." The Marquess seemed scandalized. It wasn't just the usual reaction to shocking gossip. Fear lurked in her eyes. If the Chancellor could so easily be killed on a whim, what did that foretell for the rest of them? Meilin had been greedy and power-hungry, but as far as I knew, she never had any aspirations for Kelar's throne. The king had never seemed interested in the tediousness of ruling. The only thing that had changed was Malev.

"Has the Circle said anything?" The Circle was the council of sorcerers who actually ran things. I worked for their covert service, which was colloquially known as the Circle. Meilin, as head of the council, had been the Chancellor, but that still left a dozen other members. "Has a new Chancellor been appointed?"

"No, not officially. Rumor has it that Queen Malev is involved in choosing the replacement. Some people even think she'll try to put a high fae in." The Marquess shook her head and took a sip of her drink.

Queen Malev couldn't be stupid enough to try to put in a fae, could she? That would never happen. The king would have a revolt on his hands. Even his most loyal courtiers would speak against him.

A gong sounded and the lights above us flashed. A herald announced, "Dinner is served."

I had hoped the king would summon us to meet him before dinner. The Claybourn's rank and history with the king warranted it, especially after such a long absence from court, so I had to assume the oversight was Malev's doing. It would've been simpler and cleaner to kill her before dinner. But at least this way we would get a meal out of the deal.

We followed everyone into the banquet room. I mentally checked the location of my void blade. All around me the words *Meilin* and *chancellor* bubbled along in the stream of conversation.

Inside the banquet hall, the tables were set out in a standard horseshoe pattern. The table of honor stood at the far end of the hall on a dais. Normally, the king would be joined by close advisors, honored guests, or simply the highest-ranking people in the room at the table of honor, but only two places were set.

The regulars went to their usual places, and the Lord Chamberlain approached us. "Please, follow me to your seats."

He gave a little bow, and we followed him. We were seated at the first table to the left of the table of honor, closest to the king. Deacon sat to my right, and to my left sat an older gentleman. I searched my brain for his name and came up with Gwilsham. He gave me a little nod then went back to talking to the companion on his left.

Artwork telling the story of the birth of Elustria covered the walls. In all my time on Earth, I'd never seen any art that could compare with what we had here. Behind us, a stone mosaic illustrated the great turmoil of the world before the sorcerers harnessed and controlled the Vortex. The colored stone matched the harsh conditions of our history. The wall opposite the mosaic had a mural painted with vibrant colors showing the evolution of our people as we advanced our magic and built cities. Behind the table of honor, an enormous tapestry showed the establishment of the current dynasty. The opposite wall stood as a blank canvas for a visiting artist to do their work.

At the moment, a sorcerer splashed magic of different colors across the canvas. When the magic hit, it exploded in color and sparkles drifted slowly down to the ground and disappeared, leaving a mark in their wake. By the end of dinner, the entire wall would be covered in a masterpiece that would be cleared away in time for tomorrow's dinner.

A few minutes after everyone took their seats, the herald announced the arrival of King Kelar and Queen Malev. A door at the back of the banquet hall opened, and everyone stood as they entered. Before they took their places at the table of honor, a dozen guards lined up in front of the dais forming a shield, once again foiling any attempt I might have made during dinner to get close to her. The heavy-handed show intrigued me. Malev clearly wanted the people to fear her or at least fear making a move against her. It also displayed a certain amount of weakness and vulnerability that she needed to rely on others for protection.

Kelar and Malev made their way to the table, and Kelar gestured for everyone to sit after we all curtsied or bowed. The king gave a toast to start the meal, but I didn't pay attention to what he said. Instead, I observed those around me. No one even made an effort to appear happy. Everyone went through the motions of curtsying, bowing, raising a glass, but there weren't even any nervous smiles.

Our food appeared, and as we all ate, conversation died to hardly anything. There were a few attempts at casual conversation, but no one wanted to risk being overheard by Malev or her fae guards. There didn't seem to be many safe topics of conversation.

Kelar spoke only to Malev. With the guards between his table and the rest, it didn't facilitate any talking between us and him.

The performer from the previous room continued playing in the banquet hall. The music only served to emphasize the awkward atmosphere. Kelar couldn't be this stupid. Even if he had somehow fallen head over heels in love with Malev, he couldn't be this blind to the feelings of his court and his people. Meilin may have been power-hungry, but she wasn't seeking to overthrow him. No one was. But Kelar was creating the perfect environment for an uprising. I couldn't figure out what would've possessed him to make this alliance with Malev.

After dessert appeared, Kelar raised his hand for the room's attention. It didn't take long for the little conversation to stop.

"I know my actions of late have confounded some of you. I've heard the talk around court. I understand your frustrations. After all, you are only working with some of the information."

This crowd wouldn't let him off that easily. They all expected this was just a ruse, a play to make them feel better about what the king had done to Meilin.

"Now, as king, I don't believe I need to justify myself to anyone. But, I understand that you all are having a tough time with this. So

I wish to put your minds at ease. I did not have the Chancellor executed on a whim. It was a difficult decision, one I wrestled with. I knew she had overstepped her place, but I was hesitant. I was merciful. I didn't want to take action unless the situation became untenable. The situation reached that point when the Chancellor endorsed a fraud as the Dragon Fae."

Confusion swept across the faces of those present. A few whispers popped up.

"Her offenses toward me I could forgive. But I could not overlook her blasphemy. She took our sacred traditions, our hallowed prophecies, and turned them into a mockery by declaring that one of her own agents—an assassin, a spy—was the Dragon Fae." Kelar shook his head and looked down at the table as if gathering himself then faced the room again. "This I could not abide. No matter how much it pained me to do so, I had to order her execution. Nataliana, the assassin, is not the Dragon Fae. This deception I cannot forgive. I only wish we could bring the pretender to justice as well."

My entire body went cold as Kelar looked right at me.

17

As my blood turned to ice, I concentrated on the feel of the glamour against my skin, like thick makeup concealing my identity. The king couldn't possibly know he was looking at me. I kept my face up, meeting his gaze head on. Deacon didn't make a move of recognition, not even a hand on my knee under the table. His control impressed me.

Kelar's gaze passed by me and on to others in the room; then he resumed his seat. I couldn't say how long he had looked at me, but I guessed it was only a second or two. I kept my breathing steady and focused on the reactions of those around me. The whispers at his announcement turned to murmurs and then open conversation.

"That's not what I expected," Deacon said next to me.

"Looks like we came back to court at just the right time." Not speaking would be the most suspicious thing we could do right now, but neither one of us wanted to express a strong opinion. Neutrality would serve us best.

The initial confusion that filled the voices around me turned to anger, hurt, betrayal, and shock. No one seemed to know what to make of this announcement. Since arriving at court, I hadn't heard much talk of the Dragon Fae. Malev presented a much more enticing topic of conversation. Kelar had successfully shifted the interest away from her.

I glanced at Malev while chitchatting with Deacon, making sure my face and tone displayed support for the king. If Malev thought we were against her, it would make my job that much harder. A hint of glee lit her eyes. She enjoyed the chaos she sowed, especially when it doubled as an attack against me.

Dessert went virtually untouched as everyone digested this new information. The man next to me, who seemed old enough to have one foot in the grave, came to life at the announcement.

"Was the attack on Moonlark Academy a lie too?" he asked his companion.

"No, I know families who lost children," the woman replied, offended at the suggestion.

The king's statement threatened to undermine the shared cultural foundation of sorcerers. If people doubted the Dragon Fae and therefore started doubting the truth of the horrific attack on Moonlark Academy, it could lead to internal strife in the kingdom. He couldn't have thought this through. All he wanted was cover for killing Meilin and to get people to stop hating Malev. Did he even believe what he said?

The target on my back grew several sizes. I was used to Malev and mages hating me, but I'd never been hated by my own people before.

The conversation in the hall went from shocked to strained. Speaking freely here amounted to foolishness. The real talk would happen away from this room. A few minutes later, Kelar and Malev left the way they had come, the row of guards following them. Even if I performed perfectly, there was no way I could kill Malev. Any attempt would require I sacrifice my life in the process. That didn't deter me, but the almost guaranteed failure did.

"Let's go join the others," Deacon said, jarring me from my visions of the ways I might have attempted to kill the fae queen.

I shouldn't have lost myself in my thoughts, and Deacon's eyes said as much. I didn't see judgement, just concern. "Of course."

Instead of going back to the great hall, people gravitated to the gardens where there were fewer ears to overhear any potentially treasonous talk. In times like these, the ears of guards and servants —the invisible people of the palace—could not be trusted.

We needed to overhear as many different conversations as possible. The people in this garden may not represent the regular sorcerers of Elustria, but they would be the people who spread the news. The way they chose to frame this latest revelation from Kelar would influence what the public thought of it. If I wasn't going to kill Malev tonight, I needed to at least gather some worthwhile intelligence.

I sought out the Marchioness of Jeun from earlier. She'd already proved that she had no problem gossiping with virtual strangers. We met her near some topiaries outside the entrance to a hedge maze. She brightened as soon as she saw us, welcoming us into her little group of five chatting courtiers. When we approached, they fell silent for a moment, waiting to see if we could be trusted. The Marchioness of Jeun gave us our in.

"Well, you two certainly chose the right night to come back to court," she said. That's all it took for the others to relax around us.

"I don't recall dinners being quite that eventful," Deacon said. Even with the outward appearance of the Duke of Claybourn, he still had his regular charm. It would take more than a change of appearance to rid him of that.

"Yes, well, like her or hate her, the fae queen certainly has spiced things up around here," one of the women said.

"Like her or hate her? I never agreed to that. She has no business being here," said another.

One of the two men replied. "But what about what the king said? If Meilin really did endorse a fraud as the Dragon Fae—"

Before he could finish that thought, Gerald, the Lord Chamberlain came running over. "Your Graces," he said. "Pardon me for interrupting, but the king has extended an invitation for you to join him for some after-dinner drinks."

Of course he chose this moment to acknowledge us, when there was good gossip to be had. Our main mission was to kill Malev. I didn't think she'd be at this little cocktail hour, but even so, getting in close with the king got us that much closer to her. No matter how much I wanted to hear what was being said, the mission came first. Always had and always would.

"Oh, wonderful." I clapped my hands together in delight as Jane would have in this situation.

"It was nice seeing you all again." Deacon nodded to the little group before we followed Gerald back inside.

The Starlight Palace had always stood as a monument to the beauty of sorcerer culture. Magical art danced along the walls. Twinkly lights lit the halls. Intricate wood carvings decorated the doors and window frames. Rare gemstones imbued with the magic of Elustria decorated metalwork. The palace itself elicited joy from those present, which made the current atmosphere that much more disturbing.

Tense silence stilled the magic in the air. To the untrained eye, the guards we passed seemed suspicious of everything and everyone. But I caught the subtleties in their eyes and body language. They weren't wary of lurking threats. They worried about the spying eyes and ears of the fae.

The Lord Chamberlain led us to a cozy sitting room that would be considered large anywhere else. When we entered, the king was speaking with the only other sorcerer in the room. The other half dozen occupants were all high fae.

"Your Majesty, here are the Duke and Duchess of Claybourn, as requested." The Lord Chamberlain bowed and left.

Kelar turned from his conversation to look at us, and I sank into a deep curtsy. When I rose, I recognized the sorcerer next to him: Tarelle, the Marquess of Dimbledy. He'd been the king's best friend since childhood. I'd never met him personally but had seen his picture with the king plenty of times when I lived in Elustria. His presence was somewhat reassuring amid all the fae.

"Ah, the Claybourns. So good to see you!" Kelar said when he saw us. He extended his hands palms up, as did Tarelle. "It's been quite a while since you've been to court. I thought I must have misheard when Gerald said you were here."

"When we heard our king had taken a queen for himself, we had to come congratulate you in person," Deacon said as Tarelle handed us each a drink. We raised our glasses in a little toast.

I wouldn't drink anything prepared by a fae, but I'd watched as Tarelle made the drinks, and he and Kelar each had one. Refusing would appear rude, and we needed Kelar's trust. Still, I looked to Deacon and smiled as we raised our glasses. He returned the smile and nodded. If he detected any negative magic, he'd come up with some excuse. Following his lead, I took a sip and tasted a simple liqueur.

The smell of all the different magics in the room overwhelmed me. I didn't have the experience Deacon did in separating them from each other. All the fae magic overtook Kelar's and Tarelle's. It left me uncomfortable.

Kelar gestured to a group of chairs and the four of us sat. The high fae talked among themselves, putting on a show of giving us privacy. I wondered if Kelar thought he could trust them.

"Perhaps it would be nice if the four of us could talk alone," Tarelle said pointedly to the king.

"Oh, yes, of course." Kelar loudly cleared his throat. "Thorassil, give us the room." The high fae who I assumed was Thorassil nodded to the king and led the rest of the fae out of the room.

I couldn't get a clear read on Tarelle. Did he send the fae away because he didn't want them here or to gain our trust? I had a diffi-cult time believing Malev would allow him to remain close to Kelar if he didn't support her. Or did Malev not have that level of control? No, she'd gotten Kelar to execute Meilin. She wouldn't allow an exception for the king's best friend.

"Did you enjoy tonight's dinner?" Kelar asked. It was easier to feel his and Tarelle's magic now, but the scent of the fae still hung in the air.

"It was delicious. Exactly what we expected," Deacon answered. Something about being glamoured must've made it easier for him to lie. Maybe it wasn't a lie. The food had tasted quite good.

"When the queen first came to the palace, she mentioned wanting to bring her own chef, but I assured her that wouldn't be necessary," Tarelle said. "It took a little cajoling to get her to try Maurice's food. She didn't think a sorcerer could make dishes a fae would like. All it took was one meal for her to realize that he could satisfy even her elevated taste."

I suppressed a shudder at even the thought of having a high fae as chef in the palace. No sane sorcerer would eat food prepared by one. Why did Tarelle volunteer all this information? To show us that he was the one who saved us from fae food? Or to show how influential he was with the royal couple? Or perhaps he was simply making conversation.

"So what do you think of my new queen?" Kelar asked. "I'm eager to get your opinion."

Something in Kelar's eyes unnerved me. Their focus didn't match the rest of his expression. I didn't understand it. Tarelle's gaze didn't have the same strangeness. I didn't recall seeing or feeling it earlier. When we first entered the room, Kelar had appeared natural.

The fae. With them gone, Malev had lost her eyes and ears. I didn't know how precisely, but I felt she'd done something that allowed her to see through the king's eyes. I had no way to communicate this to Deacon. Any movement on my part could give us away. The Claybourns wouldn't have noticed something so subtle.

I did have one avenue of communication, crude as it was: our bond from the anointing. Deacon and I could feel each other's emotions to an extent. While remaining engaged in the conversation, I let myself feel overwhelming fear. It had to be strong enough for Deacon to notice. I could only hope that he'd understand my meaning.

My fear soon subsided in a wave of warmth. It hadn't worked. I didn't need Deacon's comfort. I grabbed onto fear again and let it push away the warmth. This time the comfort beat back the fear before it could even take root. The strength of his emotion stirred a memory. This was the feeling I got when we confided in each other. It was the feeling of being seen.

It wasn't comfort he was sending. It was understanding.

"We think it's absolutely marvelous that you've finally done something for yourself," Deacon said with a cheery, congratulatory tone. He'd have to bear the weight of this conversation since his persona, Michael, was an old friend of the king's.

"And what of my choice of bride?" Kelar pressed for specifics.

"Only a queen would be good enough for you." Deacon had to tread a fine line. An obvious lie at this point would serve no one.

"I'm disappointed she's not here," I said, looking around quickly as if I might find her. "I'd hoped you'd invited us to get to know her better. We don't know much about the high fae, but she seemed as glamorous as the stories led us to believe. I heard she holds court in a hall made of diamond. Is that true?" I asked with wide eyes, playing the part of country bumpkin awed at the splendor of fae royalty.

Kelar chuckled. "I'm not sure about the diamond part, but I'll let her know you asked after her. Unfortunately, she's busy at her own court tonight."

"Speaking of which," Tarelle interrupted, leaning forward and looking at the king, "you have some work to do yourself. Why don't we let the Claybourns catch up with some of their other friends?"

"Ah, yes, quite right." The king stood, and the rest of us followed suit.

"It was a pleasure seeing you both. I hope you'll stay at court for a while before jaunting off again," Tarelle said. His tone made it seem like he was good friends with the Claybourns, but they hadn't indicated as much to us, and we'd found no evidence of it. If he did know them well, did he suspect the truth? Surely he would reveal us to the king if he thought we were imposters.

"We have no immediate plans to leave. You know us, we go and stay wherever the mood takes us," Deacon answered.

The king looked down, and his face twitched. I didn't let on that I'd seen it, but Tarelle clearly did. He ushered us to the door, his face showing nothing but comfortable friendship. He didn't have a hint of concealment or impatience.

"Yes, you always had that wanderlust lurking beneath the surface. It just took Jane to bring it out. I'm glad the mood has brought you here. It would have been a shame for you to miss out on this happy time."

Behind Tarelle, the king brought his hand to his head as if he had a headache.

"Thank you for the drinks," I said and nodded to him as Deacon and I left the room. The door shut behind us, and I led Deacon back the way we came.

"Back to the garden?" Deacon asked.

I ignored his question and instead pinched his ass. The surprise on his face, even if it was Michael's face, was priceless. To erase any question of my intentions, I giggled. Comprehension dawned on his face. Deacon knew me well enough to know that even though I might pinch his ass, I would never giggle like that.

I pulled him to me in a deep kiss, wrapping my arms around his neck. With my eyes closed, it was easy to forget our glamours. We may look like Jane and Michael, but we kissed like Nadiya and Deacon.

I broke free before I could forget myself and wagged my eyebrows playfully. Taking hold of his shirt, I pulled him into an alcove. When I kissed him this time, I kept my eyes open. Once we crossed the threshold of the shadows, hidden from sight, I felt around the wall behind me until I found the right spot. A little pressure and we were inside a secret passage.

18

"I don't think anyone saw us, but if they did, you put on a nice show," Deacon said, his voice all business as he stepped away from me. In the darkness of the passage I could only feel his presence.

"You weren't too bad either."

Deacon snorted in reply. "Kissing you isn't exactly difficult."

I didn't dwell on that comment. We had too much work to do to get distracted. "I want to see if we can find the fae. Something wasn't right with Kelar. We can pick up court gossip later."

Deacon took a deep breath. In my mind, I could see him clear as day, the way his face relaxed and his eyes closed when he tried to pick up a scent. Of course, he wouldn't look like that now. If I lit the passage, I'd see Michael Claybourn opposite me. I couldn't wait until we no longer needed the glamour.

"Let me get by you," Deacon said as he put his hands on my hips and turned me so he could pass. "I'll see how close I can get us. The scent is faint."

He took my hand and led the way. In the darkness we could easily become separated. But it wasn't sight that informed me of Deacon's position. Our bond made me hyperaware of his presence.

As we made our way through the labyrinthine passageways, I could feel all the changes in Deacon's emotions. Uncertainty when we came to intersections, surety when he got a strong whiff of the scent. Our close proximity made the bond so strong that I couldn't be sure if I smelled the fae or if the scent was a phantom echo from Deacon.

After a couple of minutes, the smell solidified in my nose. The mix of scents from the fae who had been with Kelar almost masked the scent of dead flowers that set off alarms in my head. "It's her. She's here."

"Yes, but there are too many with her." Deacon squeezed my hand as we walked, and I released the grip my other hand had around my hidden void blade. Without thinking, I'd grabbed it at the first hint of her smell. My patience wore thin with this mission.

Kelar had specifically said she was at her court. Did she really fear so much for her life that she wouldn't be in a room with a couple of Kelar's most loyal subjects? It didn't make sense. She must have spied through Kelar's eyes as I'd suspected, seeking to catch our true feelings.

As we arrived in the passage outside the room, a burst of magic flashed and then disappeared, along with Malev's scent.

"She's gone back to her realm," Deacon said.

The other high fae remained. I could still smell and feel their magic, but I couldn't hear anything. "What are they saying?"

Deacon paused a moment before answering. "They have a shield up so they can't be overheard. Can you penetrate it?"

Their paranoia knew no bounds. "Yes, but I've never done it to a fae shield before. They might be able to tell that their conversation's been breached." Even though I could leave behind an unidentifiable imprint, I didn't want them to know that their paranoia was warranted. They likely weren't saying anything that would be worth tipping them off. "I don't think it's worth it."

"I agree. We'll remember this location for the future, though."

I could only recall how to get here from where we entered the secret passages. But Deacon's sense of location was good enough that he likely knew exactly where in the palace we stood.

A new, familiar scent entered the pack of fae. Cassalina. I found a peephole and watched as the group of fae turned toward her.

"If Her Majesty wanted you all loafing around together, she'd have you back at her court. You're here to perform a mission. Get to it," Cassalina said with the authority of the queen's favorite.

The shield came down, and we could hear the groaning of the rest of the fae. "But it's so dreary here."

"What does the queen want with all of these sorcerers anyway? Who cares what they do? She'll get bored of this soon enough."

"How come she gets to go back to court?"

Cassalina tilted her head to the side and raised her eyebrows. "I wouldn't be so eager to go back. The queen has returned to execute Goffrey."

My stomach tightened at the news. Cassalina did a good job of concealing her own feelings on the matter.

"What did he do?" one of the fae asked. Fearful unease filled his voice. The eyes of the rest of the fae looked as if they hoped there was a good reason for Goffrey's demise, more than simply Malev's bad temper.

"She was sick of him complaining about doing his duty," Cassalina said, her eyes piercing the offending fae.

The man blanched underneath her gaze.

"Come on, Cassalina," one of the other fae said. "You don't have to be like that. You know this is a shit assignment."

"I only know that it's our job to do as the queen asks. Those who don't obey, end up like Goffrey. If she wanted our opinion on the matter, she would ask for it. Now, the quicker you all get on with it, the quicker we can be done with this shit assignment." Cassalina smirked and winked.

She played her part beautifully. She appeared the ever loyal advisor to Malev while at the same time increasing the unrest among the queen's subjects. When the time came for her to depose Malev, she'd have the support she wanted.

The other fae present nodded in camaraderie with Cassalina, a bunch of workers united in a shared sense of exasperation with their boss. The group left the room, off to do whatever tasks Malev had set them to. Only Cassalina remained.

"Take off your glamour," I whispered to Deacon. The magic of the other fae had disappeared to nothing. I couldn't smell or feel anyone else near. We had to take this opportunity to talk with Cassalina, but I didn't want her knowing our assumed identities.

Deacon's glamour fell away. His familiar physical presence loomed over me. When mine disappeared, it felt like my skin could breathe for the first time in ages. I felt along the wall until a section gave way under my hand. I pushed through, and Deacon followed, our magics still cloaked by the dragonhide cuff.

Cassalina whirled around at the sound of the secret door opening and closing. Her startled eyes shifted to surprise. "Fancy seeing you two here."

"We could say the same about you," I said.

Cassalina laughed and walked over to a group of chairs off to one side of the room. She sat and gestured for us to join her. The sigh she gave as she sat was one of true weariness. "I don't want to be. None of us do. The sorcerers don't want us here only slightly more than we don't want to be here. No one's very happy with this turn Malev has taken. I assume you heard everything?"

"How did Malev find out about Goffrey?" I asked.

"Does it matter?" Cassalina countered. "He's dead regardless."

"It matters a great deal. Did she find out about him from a sorcerer source? From the Circle?" Cassalina was right in one sense. Whatever her answer, it wouldn't change my mission to kill Malev. But I needed to know how far Malev's tentacles reached into the sorcerer world.

"Oh, no." Cassalina waved away my worries with her hand. "Nothing like that. She suspected him for other reasons."

"So she thinks he was establishing a rival court?" Deacon asked. "Is that the public reason she's giving for his execution?"

"Yes to your first question, no to the second. Things are a little different in her court. She doesn't need to give a reason, but she did say that he didn't follow orders. She doesn't want to give any ideas to those who don't know about my breakaway court."

Cassalina didn't appear at all worried. Anyone who had already followed her wouldn't be scared by Goffrey's execution. They all knew Malev's capabilities. Goffrey's entire purpose was to serve as a scapegoat. He knew it and so did everyone else involved in Cassalina's court.

"Have you sealed whatever leaks led to his execution?" I asked. If Cassalina took the correct precautions, this could buy her a good amount of time. Malev would assume she had eliminated the head of the dragon and the body would likewise die.

"Don't you worry. I know what I'm doing." The cold ruthlessness in Cassalina's face reminded me of a more controlled version of Malev.

Cassalina had Malev's ear, and she would bend it to her will. She might even be Goffrey's betrayer. I had a difficult time believing anyone as dedicated as Goffrey would make a mistake. Still, he knew the risks when he took on his role. I could only hope that his death would be quick, but knowing Malev, it likely wouldn't be.

"In fact, it appears that I know what I'm doing more than you do, given that Malev still walks among us, able to kill my followers," Cassalina said, not even trying to diplomatically hide the blame in her voice.

I knew better than to fall into her trap. I wouldn't take the blame for Goffrey's death. He wasn't an innocent bystander. "If you don't like the way I'm doing things, you can always kill her yourself."

To be honest, I didn't want Cassalina to deprive me of the satisfaction. Avenging the harm done to Alistair drove me on this mission more than anything else.

Cassalina shifted in her seat, and the severe expression left her face. We both knew she couldn't kill Malev. It was a fine line she walked. As Malev's closest friend, the queen would notice any moves Cassalina made to kill her and would either stop her or make sure she died with her.

"What is it you need to get the job done?" she asked.

"She keeps herself surrounded by fae guards. I haven't had a second of opportunity to get close enough. That's all I need is opportunity."

"She's paranoid about being away from her own realm." Cassalina rolled her eyes. Could it really be called paranoia, though, when Cassalina knew there was good reason for Malev to be worried? "I don't know how much I can help with that, but I'll try."

"What do you have the other fae doing here?" Knowing their intent would make it easier to stay clear of them and find ways to manipulate them if need be.

"Malev has them searching for the Circle's covert headquarters. She's obsessed with knowing everything the Circle does, both about you and her rival court. For her, this is a game that she must win. She hasn't had anything to occupy her like this in quite a while. She thought by killing Meilin everything would fall into her lap. It isn't working out that way, and it's enraged her. The fae she has here are her best. She's kept me out of her plans with them. She doesn't like showing weakness to me, and she sees this obsession and her failure to succeed as a weakness."

"I suppose just getting over it isn't an option for her," I said.

Cassalina laughed. "No. We fae don't simply get over things. We bide our time if we have to, but we always get our way in the end or die in the pursuit."

I wondered what Malev had done that Cassalina couldn't get over. I didn't believe for a second that she wanted to depose the queen for altruistic reasons. A friendship that had lasted as long as theirs would be rife with disagreements and offenses. Which one had lodged like a thorn in Cassalina's heart to turn her against her friend? I doubted she'd tell me, and I didn't need to know.

"What has she done to Kelar?" I asked instead. "He doesn't seem himself in private."

"She's cast a spell on him that allows her to see through his eyes. She wants to keep a constant watch on him, make sure that no one can poison him against her. She has to be in this realm for it to work. So if you have any planning that needs to be done in his presence, make sure she's in the fae realm first."

That was something at least. I'd hoped for a little more help, but this would have to do. "When will Malev return?"

Cassalina sat back in her chair, tired. "I'm hoping tomorrow. That means I'll be here all night if you need me. When she returns, I'll go back to her court."

"It seems all the time without her there would be to your benefit," Deacon said. I could sense the accusation in his words, though he did a good job of keeping it from his voice. Cassalina wanted Malev dead, but she might not be eager to help us get the job done quickly if she benefited from Malev's obsession with the sorcerer court.

"Not really. It makes it difficult for me to get away to my own court. The sooner Malev is dead, the better for me. Once she's eliminated, I'll be her natural successor. With Goffrey gone, I have even more to do with little help. None of my other lieutenants are as good as he was. Her putting me in charge while she's here also isn't endearing me to the high fae. I'd like my tenure as her de facto regent to be as short as possible."

I couldn't detect any deception in her words. Out of everything she'd said, this rang with the most truth. The weariness in her face showed that she wanted this over. I imagined part of it had to do with her relationship with Malev. They'd been best friends for a lifetime, which for a fae equaled many human lifetimes. The longer this dragged on, the longer she had to wrestle with what little bit of conscience she had. It couldn't be a great feeling, especially when she had no intention of changing course.

"Do you know if she's planning on joining the king for dinner tomorrow night?" I asked. Possible plans formed in my mind for how to get close to her this time.

"If she's here, yes. I doubt she'll be back much before then. Killing Goffrey will take a while, and she'll want to savor everyone's response to it." Cassalina didn't so much as shudder at what she said.

Through our bond, I could feel Deacon perk up a split second before he said, "There's someone coming."

We all stood, and Deacon and I made our way back to the secret entrance.

"I hope the next time we meet we'll all have better news," Cassalina said in farewell.

"If you know of anything that can help us, pass it to Dorran. He has ways of getting in touch with us," I said. I didn't trust her with the knowledge that we glamoured ourselves as the Claybourns.

The scent of another's magic reached me as Deacon grabbed my hand and pulled me through to the secret passage. We watched through the peephole as an unfamiliar sorcerer entered the room and invited Cassalina to speak with the king.

Odd that it wasn't Gerald delivering the message. The servant seemed a mixture of scared and indignant at having to converse with a high fae. The tension all around the court couldn't last. Something would have to give, and I didn't think it would be Malev.

Once the sorcerer and Cassalina left, Deacon reapplied his glamour. I followed suit.

"Back to the garden?" Deacon asked in Michael's voice.

"Yes, though I wish we knew how the fae are planning to get into the Circle's files. I doubt anyone at court is stupid enough to speak unguarded around them." Which meant they likely used their fae magic against the sorcerers in the palace. To perform fae magic undetected meant these were formidable agents.

Deacon led the way to the garden. He watched through a peephole, and when no one was looking, we appeared outside of the palace wall. In the time we'd been gone, the conversation had muted and the crowd had thinned. With the fae around, people likely retreated to their city homes to continue their more serious conversations. Now that it seemed this mission would last longer than we'd anticipated, we would have to consider entertaining at the Claybourn's home as well.

"Your Grace," Gerald said from behind us. When we turned, he handed a note to Deacon. "I'm so glad I found you before you left. I've been looking all over. I was asked to deliver this to you personally." He bowed his head and turned on his heels, walking back the way he'd come.

Deacon unfolded the note, read it, then passed it to me.

Let's talk. I'll be in touch.
   -Tarelle

20

*B*ack at the Claybourn's Stardowns townhouse, I sent a coded message to Emma. She would act as our go-between with Sybil and Alistair. They needed to know that we hadn't made the kill yet. We'd stay here until the job was done.

The Claybourn townhouse was unlike anything I'd ever seen. It stood five stories and was the largest private residence I'd ever been in. It didn't take long looking around to realize that Jane and Michael didn't use much of it. Heirlooms filled much of the space, priceless art, antiques, magical oddities. The place could double as a museum. Only a few rooms held personal items of the couple.

A house this large normally had a full-time staff, but the Claybourns didn't like to be waited on. Their staff remained at the family seat whenever they traveled unless they planned to do large-scale entertaining. During my short time with Jane and Michael, it was hard to believe they had this much wealth. It must irk others at court that they had such a prosperous duchy when they seemed not to enjoy any of the lavishness and opulence their station afforded. There'd be quite the fight over their titles after their deaths.

In a house like this, it was almost impossible to not use magic. For instance, instead of dust covers on all the furniture, a spell kept them guarded against dust and sun damage. The spell could be left in place, but it made all the furniture feel odd to the touch. The only way to remove it was to use magic.

Deacon and I decided we'd use the same rooms Jane and Michael did. That meant opening up the sitting room, library, dining room, kitchen, and their bedroom. Deacon went with me room to room to make sure I didn't accidentally trip any security measures. A security charm at the front door had allowed us passage because of our imprints, and that seemed the extent of the security. Granted, it was foolproof against anyone else, but it still seemed too little given the size of their home and the possessions inside. For our convenience, I also put in place a shield to protect our conversations. Anyone watching would be able to observe us, but they wouldn't be able to hear us.

"Let's order something to eat. There's no way you got enough at dinner," I said once we were done.

A stack of delivery menus sat prominently on the kitchen counter. Thumbing through them, it looked like Jane and Michael had great taste in food. They were almost all from the spice quarter. You'd never catch a titled person there, or so I thought. It was loud, dirty, and full of the best food in Stardowns. One dish from there would contain more spice than an entire banquet at the Starlight Palace. The upper classes thought that an abundance of spice was only used to cover up an inferior product. Fools. I hoped they never learned what they were missing. It meant more for the rest of us. And right now, that included me.

Deacon came up behind me. As his hand reached around for one of the menus, I had to remind myself that he wasn't Deacon, he was Michael Claybourn, at least in appearance. We couldn't let our glamours down in case someone saw. It felt especially strange to wear them in private like this. We'd have to get used to it.

"Sure. I'm up for anything," Deacon said as he read through some of the menus.

The menus themselves served as teleportation portals for

customers to both place and receive their orders. I picked up the most worn of the menus and went with a hunch. The menu would communicate our location, which based on the condition of the menu, the restaurant would know as the Claybourn's house. I placed an order for "our" usual.

"We're at the mercy of the Claybourns now," I said as I put all the menus back.

"They really are something," Deacon said, admiration in his voice.

Jane and Michael led a life completely foreign to ours. In fairness, it seemed foreign to most people. They certainly didn't live like other members of the court. But neither did they live like the working class of Stardowns. They were truly their own people.

It didn't take long for the food to arrive, just enough time to change out of our court clothes and get more comfortable. Our order appeared in the middle of the dining room table with a note sitting on top.

So nice to see you're back in town! It's been too long. I threw in some extra poof candies to welcome you home.

    -Karson

"Figures they'd have a sweet tooth," I said after reading the note aloud.

One of the advantages of magical food delivery was the use of actual silverware. After we finished our meal, the dishes would go back to the restaurant. Deacon and I each filled our plates with a bit of everything. There was spicy fish stew, noodles tossed with vegetables in a sour sauce, and fried dough balls with hot meat filling inside. The poof candies ended up being puff pastry filled with fruit and topped with powdered sugar.

"Mmm," Deacon moaned with his first bite. I laughed as his eyelids slid down and he savored the bite of stew.

"Miss real Elustrian cuisine?" I asked. I'd been Earthside for so long that I'd grown accustomed to their food. Elustrian food would always have a nostalgic affect on me, but I didn't crave it regularly.

Deacon opened his eyes and smiled. "Yes. I didn't think I would. I've always been an eat to survive kind of person, but this reminds me of childhood."

"You didn't eat like this as an adult?" I popped one of the fried dough balls in my mouth and savored the rich broth that squirted out with the meat.

"I spent most of my time in dragon form. Even if I was in human form, I'd usually shift to eat. It's more convenient than cooking, especially since I was usually in the mountains away from civilization."

Deacon, ever the practical one. Why waste time making something delicious to eat when you could just eat a raw animal?

Everything tasted as good as I'd expected it would. Once we'd laid waste to the food, Deacon leaned back in his chair as he licked the last of the powdered sugar from his fingers. "So what is it you wanted to butter me up for?"

Lying wouldn't do me any good. He could feel my emotions through our bond, and a lie would only damage our trust. "What gave me away?"

"We ate at the palace, and as much as you enjoy a good meal, you're an eat to survive person just like I am. You hardly eat when you're on a mission unless it serves a purpose. You wouldn't have thought to order food unless you needed it for something. The only purpose I can think of is to get me in as good a mood as you could."

Damn, I missed having partners who couldn't read me. None of them had gotten to know me. Deacon had advantages over the sorcerers I'd worked with in the past: better senses, a magical bond with me, and he was the first one I'd let get close.

"We need to talk about our options and our next moves." This mission had stalled, and we both knew it.

Deacon shrugged. "The way I see it, we just have to be patient. The only thing that's changed is the timetable."

Every day Malev stayed alive grated on me. "We can't wait out a fae. We'd be here the rest of our lives, and it would be a blink of an eye to her."

"She'll slip up. She's too cocky."

I shook my head. "She may be cocky, but she's also paranoid."

"Killing Goffrey should calm that a bit."

"Only if she thinks she got the right person. I'm not convinced she thinks Goffrey's death will put an end to the rumors of a rival court. Even if she really thinks he's the culprit, the rumors damage her as much as the real thing."

"So you're suggesting we force her into a situation that gives us an opening?" Deacon's right eyebrow quirked up in an adorable way that spoke of interest and admiration at my daring.

"I can't think of anything we could do that would get her away from her guard. And we can't kill her in her realm. There's too great a chance that she'd kill us before we could get her."

"What then?"

"I kill her the next time we see her."

Deacon caught my meaning. His face shut down and he leaned forward over the table. "No. Absolutely not."

"I know I can find a way to get next to her. I can be fast enough to draw blood with the void blade. All it takes is a single nick. Even if I don't kill her, she'll be as good as dead." I genuinely didn't know if I'd rather she survived in a meaningless existence without magic or died on the spot. With my luck, she'd find a way to get her magic back, so the best bet was a sure kill. "If my aim is to kill her at all costs, I can use sheer speed and surprise to do it."

"And you'll be dead in the next second." Angry storm clouds covered his eyes. I'd never seen him like this. A shiver of fear went down my spine. I'd hate to be there if he ever unleashed this fury I glimpsed.

I couldn't let him see me waver. "So? This is as good a mission to die on as any. At least this mission is for me, not my masters at the Circle. It needs to be done, and I'm the only one who can do it. So why not?"

"You can't," he growled.

"I can't? I assure you, I can."

"Nadiya, don't. This isn't how it's supposed to happen."

"You saying that doesn't make it so. We both know the prophesy says I'm going to die young. Why are you against it happening now? Why are you against me exercising a little bit of control over it? It's my death we're talking about. At least we're not mate bonded. You can move on. The sooner it happens, the better for you and everyone involved."

Deacon looked so stricken that I wanted to take back my last words. Something about us not being bonded devastated him. My hand twitched, eager to reach out and comfort him, to assure him that I didn't mean it. I knew he wanted to bond, but he had to see the practicalities, didn't he? As much as I wanted to, I couldn't comfort him. This issue loomed too large for me to sweep it away with a touch or soft words.

"You can't." His voice sounded strangled. Desperation darted in his eyes. He grabbed my arm on the table so tightly it hurt. "Please. I'm begging you."

The naked vulnerability in his eyes hurt more than his grip on my arm. It all confused me. "Why? What are you scared of? You've known from the beginning I wouldn't be with you long. The prophecy—"

"The prophecy says that we'll be mate bonded before you die."

"So? Doesn't this make it easier?" I knew my death would hurt Deacon, devastate him even. But it could only get worse after we bonded. The severing of that bond with death was a whole other kind of pain.

Deacon shook his head and closed his eyes. He lowered his head, thinking about what he wanted to say. When he looked up, I saw determination to sway me. "I'm not in this for easy, Nadiya.

The prophecy says we'll be bonded when you die. You have decided you don't want to bond."

"You should be happy then. According to the prophecy, I'll survive killing her." I smiled, trying to lighten the mood.

"Nadiya, stop behaving like a child," Deacon said, his voice raising to a volume I'd never heard from him. I removed my smile. "The prophecy is to guide us, not act as an excuse for suicidal behavior. If you do this, if you die before we're bonded, it could ruin everything."

I didn't have any idea what he was talking about. "Ruin what?"

He pressed his lips together in a firm line and looked to the side. Whatever it was, he didn't want me to know.

"You have to tell me if you want me to change my mind."

"I can't." He faced me, and I could see past his glamour to his real face. "I can't mess with prophecy any more than you can. I wish I could, but I can't risk it."

Through our bond, I could feel his heightened emotions. When I focused on them, our anointing ceremony flashed in my mind. I could see it clear as day, Deacon coming back from the nether, looking to Sybil. "What did the original companion tell you in the nether?"

Deacon's eyes widened the slightest bit. He stood from the table and walked away, his back to me.

Now that I'd found my target, I could attack with precision. "The Origin spoke to me. I told you what she said, but you never told me what her companion said to you."

"Yes," Deacon said so softly I had to lean forward to hear. "And what did she tell you?"

"To trust you."

He nodded his head, his back still toward me. Slowly, he turned, but he wouldn't lift his head. He didn't want me seeing his face. I could feel his sadness and desperation. Something about those heightened emotions allowed me to peer past his glamour and see him, his glamour flickering like a ghost around him.

His eyes on the ground, he lowered himself to his knees. I stood, my chair scratching the floor behind me. The sight of him on his knees twisted something in my gut, and I felt sick. It was the same feeling I'd had when he bowed to Drake. A dragon prince humbled himself before me, and everything about it was wrong.

"I'm begging you, Nadiya."

The sickness climbed up my stomach and burned my throat. I couldn't do this to him. I fell on my knees in front him. "I won't. I promise, I won't."

I would say whatever it took to stop this. I reached out with both hands and raised his face to mine. "I'm sorry. I shouldn't have been so flippant. I'm not used to having a partner like this. I've had quite a lot of time to accustom myself to the idea of dying on a mission. Please, don't think about it anymore."

"You won't try to kill her without a plan to get yourself out?"

I shook my head. "No. I won't. I swear."

He wrapped his arms around me. "Thank you." The relief in his voice only served to emphasize the panic that had engulfed him.

When we finally separated, I could no longer see through his glamour. Michael's eyes and slender face looked back at me. Somehow, the Origin's magic had worked to bring me around. The cool breeze of fate raised goosebumps on my arms. Was the command to trust him meant for this moment?

The Origin's voice laughed in my ear.

21

*C*andlelight danced across Deacon's naked chest. His broad shoulders and muscled abs—not an ounce of fat in sight—lowered down on top of me. My hips reflexively moved to meet him. The feel of his skin against mine ignited something inside me, but I couldn't help missing the view of that beautiful chest.

His lips brushed the delicate skin behind my ear, and I moaned. I didn't know if I'd ever been kissed there. I moved my head to the side, tilting my chin up, giving him more access.

Instead of the soft brush of lips I expected, he pecked at my neck. *Knock, knock, knock.* Strange, but I didn't want to break the mood, so I ignored it. *Knock, knock, knock.* His nose pecked on my neck.

The world shifted beneath me. I opened my eyes to see that Deacon, as Michael Claybourn, had risen from the bed and opened the door to the bedroom. Then I heard it, a knocking on the front door.

It had been a dream. A lovely, wonderful, spicy dream that I wanted to close my eyes and sink back into—*knock, knock, knock*—after I killed whoever knocked on our door.

It likely wasn't an adversary, but I grabbed my void blade in its sheath from under the mattress just in case. I slipped it into the waistband of Jane's pajama pants and joined Deacon at the top of the stairs.

"We'll talk about whatever had you moaning in your sleep after he's gone." Deacon winked, and I used every bit of self-control to keep myself from turning red. Asshole. I could feel his mirth through our bond.

Shit. The bond. He'd have felt all my emotions through it. His mirth grew, and no amount of self-control could keep the flush from my neck now.

Deacon laughed and led the way downstairs. When we got to the first-floor landing, I smelled what Deacon already had: the visitor's magic. It was a sorcerer, so likely a friend. Even if they wished us harm, I'd have no problem going against a sorcerer. With Deacon, I could defeat any sorcerer at court.

The knocking persisted, undeterred by our lack of acknowledgement. Deacon waited for me at the door and nodded to the viewing portal next to it.

Tarelle.

He'd warned us he wanted to speak, but I'd assumed he'd pull us aside at court. Deacon and I made quite the sight in Michael and Jane's pajamas, but it wouldn't be in keeping with our cover to change into normal clothes. The darkness of night still blanketed the street outside.

Deacon opened the door and yawned, rubbing pretend sleep out of his eyes. "Tarelle?"

I stood behind Deacon, peering groggily around his shoulder to see who interrupted our sleep.

"Sorry to wake you, old friend. This was the only time I was sure I wouldn't be missed. May I come in?"

"Of course." Deacon opened the door wider and gestured for Tarelle to come inside. I lead him into the sitting room with Deacon following.

"Can I get you something to drink?" I asked as I gestured Tarelle to a seat.

"No, thank you. I won't be here long."

Deacon and I sat next to each other on the sofa facing Tarelle. Anxious nerves crawled around the sorcerer's eyes. He leaned forward, and his gaze darted briefly to the side before focusing on us.

"I know it's been a while. I should have kept in touch better."

"Don't worry about it. We could have done better too. We've been off living our lives while you've been mired in court," Deacon said, waving away Tarelle's concerns.

"You're far too generous. It was I who stopped replying to your letters, though it is true that I didn't want to burden you with matters at court. Now I fear it's too late. Tell me, are you still believers in the Dragon Fae?"

The shock in our bond told me Tarelle's question took Deacon by surprise too. How had we missed that Jane and Michael were believers? It would have come in handy. Maybe it still would.

"Yes, especially after recent events. Isn't it happening as prophecy foretold?" Deacon said.

Tarelle nodded. "Good. I'm hoping you'll help me. I want to see who else believes at court and how willing they are to back up that belief with action."

Deacon looked to me to answer. We hadn't expected anything like this. Our plan hinged on being apolitical and the potential access that gave us at court. If we did what Tarelle wanted and Malev got a whiff of it, this cover would be useless. I couldn't pass up this opportunity, though.

"What exactly do you want from us?" I asked.

"I want you to host a dinner party here at your home tonight. You've just come to court. It makes sense that you'd have people over, get to know them. It'll also be easy to get people here. You two are an oddity and have the biggest townhouse in Stardowns. They'll come just to get a look inside."

"So you want us to invite a bunch of strangers into our home, feed them, and then see where their beliefs lie?" I asked.

Tarelle smiled. "Basically. I'll take care of getting the invitations out. All I need from you two is your house, food, and your good company. I want to gauge how people are feeling away from the palace. You can't like the fae queen being here any more than I do."

"But what has this got to do with her?" Deacon asked.

"No one likes her, but there's nothing much anyone can do about her. Who the king chooses to take as his queen is his own business. But for her to denounce the Dragon Fae is another thing entirely. We all heard what the shade said at the Feast of the Dragon. We were saved by the Dragon Fae that day. The fae queen can't take that away. People aren't willing to speak up against our king, but they may be willing to take action in defense of the Dragon Fae."

"But the king denounced the Dragon Fae too. How is this not a betrayal to him?" I asked.

Tarelle scrunched up his face and shook his head. "No, he only did that because of her. Before she got her claws in him, he'd been excited about the return of the Dragon Fae. I thought maybe he'd written you and that was why you came to court."

Michael and Jane hadn't shown any inclination to return to court. When we had taken them, they weren't anywhere near Stardowns.

"He didn't write us. We came out of curiosity," I said. "Does it have to be tonight?"

Tarelle nodded. "The queen isn't coming tonight, so the king is going to take dinner privately. It's our best chance."

Deacon and I looked at each other as if this were some big inconvenience we had to agree on. "It's up to you. You're the one who's going to have to do everything," Deacon said.

I tilted my head side to side as if I were considering. In reality, this wouldn't be difficult. I'd hire a catering company to take care of everything, maybe some staff to help clean up and get the place presentable. I'd seen a flyer for the service the Claybourns usually used when entertaining.

"I guess we've got ourselves a party," I said with a smile, but then I took a stern expression and pointed a finger at Tarelle. "I'm willing to host your dinner, but I don't want you to take it as more than it is. We're not committing to more than that." I lowered my finger and smiled again. "But we can always help a friend."

Knowing Jane and Michael, they'd probably jump at the chance for some covert adventure, but since we actually were spies, I couldn't risk Tarelle finding our eagerness suspicious. However, this could be the jump-start our stalled mission needed.

"Thanks. That's all I'm asking." Tarelle slapped his hands on his knees and stood. "I've got to get back. I'll see you tonight at six."

After Deacon shut the door behind Tarelle, he turned to look at me and wagged his eyebrows. "You know, if you want to get back to your dream, we could probably get an hour or two more sleep."

It had been too much to hope that he'd forgotten. "Ha, ha. Very funny. We've got too much to do."

Deacon shrugged. "I'm just saying, your needs are important. If I can be of any service, even just in your dreams…"

I cocked my left eyebrow. "And who said it was you I was dreaming about?"

That sobered him, and I went to get dressed with a smirk.

2 2

The twelve guests mingled as everyone took turns dishing up a plate for themselves at the buffet. The formal dining room sparkled in shades of blue and gold. A giant chandelier made to look like stag antlers crawled above us. Flames danced along the antlers, giving a warm glow to the room. I didn't know a private home could look so fancy. It didn't seem to match the personality of the owners, but looks were deceiving.

The staff we'd hired to take care of the evening had worked here before. They got the house open and ready for entertaining in record time. I had them layout the food buffet style and then dismissed them. We didn't need any listening ears present during the actual dinner.

There had been a short bit of time where I'd had the room to myself and discovered some of its secrets that spoke to Jane and Michael's personalities, such as the large chair in the corner with a moose embroidered on it that would huff with indignation if someone sat on it.

Tarelle had introduced each guest as they arrived. None of the names or faces were familiar as being close friends of the Claybourns. They seemed an interesting lot as I took in the sight of them around the large dining table.

Once everyone was seated, Tarelle eyed Count Petofsky, one of his oldest friends, and gave him a nod. The count returned it and looked at the other guests. "Thank you to our hosts for allowing us to intrude upon your hospitality." He raised his glass, and the rest of the table followed suit in toasting us. "It's nice to have a dinner away from the palace."

"Hmm. That's an understatement," Baroness Silvadra said then laughed as she took a drink. She had magical tattoos of silver snakes that slithered over her skin, up her arms and onto her face, curling around her violet eyes.

Everyone present either laughed or eyed each other knowingly. Tarelle had chosen his guests well.

"What? You mean you don't want to have dinner with the fae bitch who has ensnared our king?" the Marquis of Hagmor said, hand mockingly on his chest and his slender jaw open.

Viscountess Lanaway's upper lip curled into a sneer. "Have you seen the way he is now? I haven't been able to spend much time with him, but when I do see him, he seems completely under her spell."

"Do you mean literally or figuratively?" Baron Shanks asked in a thick guttural accent. He lived in the north and sported a shaggy rust-colored beard.

Uneasy glances passed between the guests.

The viscountess bit her bottom lip and nodded her head from side to side as she considered the question. "I'm torn." She looked around the table. "Could she actually have some sort of magical hold on him?"

"What do you think, Tarelle?" Count Petofsky asked. "You're the only one who gets close to him these days."

Every eye in the room turned to Tarelle. Did he know about the spell Malev had on the king? He hadn't said anything to us, but he had to know something was going on, otherwise he wouldn't have taken so many precautions in contacting us, would he?

He took a moment before he spoke, letting the silence that settled in the room give weight to his words. Whatever he said, the people here would believe it. That was a heavy power and a great responsibility. "The thing that has concerned me the most is his denunciation of the Dragon Fae."

He used his moment to turn the conversation to the Dragon Fae. Interesting and smart. If word did escape this room about the goings on here, he couldn't risk his relationship with the king. Making this about the Dragon Fae insulated him.

My faith in Tarelle increased. If he were to alienate the king, there would be no one we could trust at Kelar's side. So he didn't speak out about the king or about the hated fae queen. He kept his comments about the Dragon Fae who Kelar himself believed would return.

Petofsky nodded in agreement. "That concerns me too. When word first came that the Dragon Fae had returned, I was there with you and Kelar. He believed. He was excited. What happened?"

"She never actually showed up is what happened," Silvadra said, pursing her lips.

"Are you saying you don't believe? Even with everything in the prophecy pointing to it being true?" Count Gilipin, a short round man with wild tufts of hair, asked.

"I'm saying if the Dragon Fae has returned, much good she's done us. She comes back and the only person she interacts with is a shade? I'm saying it's either not true or we're better off without her. All her supposed appearance has done is get people excited over nothing. And who knows? Maybe without all that excitement and Meilin's involvement, Malev wouldn't have gotten her claws into the king."

My heart clenched at Silvadra's words. She couldn't be the only person thinking them. I couldn't blame her. I hadn't done anyone any good except for Alistair. And I'd only helped him because of our personal connection.

Silvadra's speculation about what would have happened if the Dragon Fae hadn't come back also held some truth. If I weren't part of the picture, would Malev had gotten involved with Kelar? My appearance had nothing to do with Cassalina forming a rival court, but would the Circle have gotten involved if Malev hadn't acknowledged me as the Dragon Fae to Meilin?

Countess Gilipin shook her head. She sat a few inches taller than her husband, and her elaborate updo gave her even more height. "This whole thing with Meilin is what has me baffled. She's been the glue that's held the court together for years. Why would the king suddenly turn on her?"

"That's my point," Baroness Silvadra said. "Why would he unless he knows she was part of this Dragon Fae deception?"

"But did it really have anything to do with her?" the countess asked.

"Of course it did," the Marquess of Marchand, a plain woman with a no-nonsense attitude, said. "If Meilin wanted to fake the return of the Dragon Fae, she could. The fact of the matter is she got cocky and overreached."

"That's not fair." Her husband, the Marquis of Marchand, raised his eyebrows and eyed her reproachfully. "Kelar let her. It's no secret that he's taken no interest in running the kingdom. If it weren't for Meilin keeping things together, he would have been ousted in a revolt because of his incompetence."

Tarelle couldn't let that last comment slide. "He's not incompetent, just uninterested, mainly because he knew Meilin did a good job and he trusted her."

"So why turn on her?" the marquis asked, demanding an answer.

Tarelle shrugged. "Who knows?"

The implication was clear. If he thought there was just cause for Meilin's demise, he'd say so. The reason for Meilin's downfall was obvious: Malev.

"Is the Dragon Fae somehow a threat to the queen?" Viscount Lanaway asked. "What does she have to gain in undermining the public's confidence in her return?"

"Aye, of course she's a threat to the queen," Baron Shanks said. "She has the power of myth on her side. If the Dragon Fae has returned, it'll be her the people give their loyalty to, not the queen."

"If she's returned." Baroness Silvadra nodded.

Everyone present, even those who hadn't taken part in the conversation, nodded their agreement. They believed in the Dragon Fae, but they needed more than blind faith to guide them. If the Dragon Fae appeared, they would rally to her side.

Deacon caught my eye at the opposite end of the table and nodded. He wanted me to take in the support of these people who were oblivious to my real identity. Not breaking eye contact, he rose his glass. "To the Dragon Fae. May she know how eagerly we await her return."

23

About an hour after the last guest left, we got the signal from Sybil to meet at Emma's. My brain was still processing the dinner conversation, and I was glad for the opportunity to get away. Deacon would want to talk about it, and I wasn't ready yet. Meanwhile, Sybil might have some useful information for us. At the very least, she might be able to tell us more about the spell Malev had on Kelar.

Inside Emma's home, we removed our glamour. I stretched out my limbs, relishing the freedom. Jane stood a good head shorter than me, and wearing her glamour cramped. The best part of being without the glamour was seeing the way Deacon looked at me. He made me feel beautiful in my own skin. And seeing him instead of Michael was certainly easy on the eyes.

Emma brought out tea and cakes for us while we waited for Sybil. Even though we'd just eaten, the cake was a sweet distraction. I hadn't been able to enjoy the food at dinner. The conversation had been too concerning.

"How's it going?" Emma asked after she set down the tray and took a seat.

I didn't know how to answer her. Obviously, Malev wasn't dead. Did much else matter?

So Deacon answered her instead. "We're finding out there's more support for the Dragon Fae than we had initially thought."

Emma nodded. "That doesn't surprise me. People want something or someone to believe in, especially now. Malev bonding with our king makes it seem even more likely that the Dragon Fae is returning. Who else could save us from her?"

Sybil appeared in the room, and her face lit up when she saw us. "Yay, you made it! What are you talking about?" She looked between the three of us.

"Just catching up," Emma said as she stood. "It's late. I'll leave you to it."

"Thanks," Sybil said as Emma left the room. She took a seat across from us. "So fill me in on what's happened."

I continued to eat cake while Deacon relayed recent events to Sybil. Of course, it was all quite one-sided. His rendition of events, including his opposition to my idea of a suicide mission as well as the events of tonight's dinner, were relayed differently than I would have done. However, I was much more interested in the cake, and none of the material facts were different.

"I'm glad you stopped her," Sybil said when Deacon told her about the other night. "The prophecy would not be best served that way."

"Really?" I said. "I thought the prophecy wasn't big on details. We know that I'm going to die young. I'd rather go down killing Malev than have a heart attack or whatever else the prophecy has in store for me."

Sybil laughed. "A heart attack?" She shook her head. "You don't have to worry about that. You wouldn't make much of a hero if clogged arteries were what felled you."

"So why are you and Deacon so sure that this isn't the way it happens?" I was tired of this mission. Not because it had been a long time, but because I didn't see an end. I didn't know how we could possibly defeat Malev. I didn't like being ineffective.

"I know it's not the way it's supposed to happen because you two will be mate bonded before you die." Sybil said it with calm confidence, as if she weren't speaking of my imminent death.

"If that's the case, then why don't we just never bond?" It seemed one way to cheat death.

Sybil shook her head vigorously, and her cheeks paled a little. "No. Staying un-bonded won't save your life. It'll just screw up the prophecy. It would be catastrophic. It is of the utmost importance that you two bond."

Everything about this prophecy seem to be a convenient way for others to get me to do what they wanted. Although, that wasn't entirely fair. I knew Sybil and Deacon only wanted what was best. Still, it seemed this prophecy had been stretched and manipulated until its shape bore no resemblance to the original.

I elaborated on what Cassalina had said. Deacon had skipped the details of that conversation, whether because he didn't remember or because he felt what happened afterward was more important, I didn't know.

"One problem we are running into is that Malev has cast a spell on Kelar. She can see through his eyes. According to Cassalina, it only works when she's in this realm, but it's still worrisome. We're going to have to figure out a way to get close to her without anything suspicious happening in front of the king. I don't know how much of him is aware when she's using the spell. For all we know, the king's mind isn't present when she's looking through his eyes."

"Did Cassalina tell you any more specifics about the spell?" Sybil asked.

"No, she just said that Malev can see through his eyes and that she can only do it when she's in this realm."

"And she and Kelar are bonded?"

I nodded. "Yes."

Sybil gnawed on her lower lip. "This isn't good. I should've known this was a possibility. That's why the priestesses teach about it."

"What are you talking about?" Deacon asked.

Sybil released her bottom lip and looked between the two of us, her gaze settling on me. "If you kill Malev, Kelar will die as well. The only way to spare him is to break the spell first."

My first thought was: so be it. Kelar had chosen to entangle himself with the fae queen. But I quickly quashed that thought. She'd taken advantage of him. For all we knew, she had used a spell to coerce him into bonding. He didn't deserve to die, no matter how much I might dislike him. "Do you have any idea how to break the spell?"

Sybil shook her head. "I don't. I can research it. The priestesses may know. We were taught that the high fae, when they bond, their life force melds in a certain way. She's melded their life forces together to be able to do this. It's a perversion of the mate bond, something only a truly evil person would do. You'll need to break the spell in order to keep him alive."

Deacon looked at me. "And I suppose just letting him die isn't an option?"

"A part of me wishes it were. But even if I got over my qualms about innocence, he is the sorcerer king, and he doesn't have a legitimate heir. His bastards are all over Elustria. He's refused to acknowledge any of them. If he died, especially at the same time the fae queen dies, it will cause a power vacuum. One"—a thought suddenly struck me, and everything became clear—"that I'm sure Cassalina would fill. In fact, it's curious that when she mentioned the spell, she conveniently left out this portion of it."

"Do you think she meant to leave it out or does she just not care if Kelar lives or dies?" Sybil asked. "Is it a power play or indifference?"

Good question. With fae, it was difficult to tell. Their motivations were often different than ours. "Initially I thought it was simply an oversight, the fae not caring who lives or dies. In fact, she didn't seem to care at all that Malev was going to kill Goffrey. Not even a hint of sadness. Now I think her ambition reaches higher than we originally thought."

Sybil sat back in her chair, contemplating the ramifications of this new revelation. "It could be possible that Cassalina wanted all this from the beginning. But why wait until now to make her move against Malev? They've known each other forever. She could've turned against her at any time."

"Instead," I said, "she waits until Malev has power over the sorcerers. She waits until all the pieces are perfectly in place, and then I innocently kill Malev for her and oops, the king dies too. He has no heir. It would cause mass confusion and crisis in the sorcerer kingdom. The perfect opportunity for the second in command of the fae to step in and take charge. She could even play it as being a temporary thing, her benevolently helping the sorcerers sort through the aftermath of such a tragic event."

"And then what happens to the Dragon Fae after it comes to light that she killed Malev which in turn killed the king?" Deacon asked.

Sybil gasped. "I hadn't even thought of that." Her eyes widened as she digested this possibility. "No, we can't let that happen. You absolutely cannot kill Malev until you've broken that spell. I'll get working on it right away. There has to be a solution."

"I don't like how twisted this has gotten," I said. "Do you know why Dorran is so insistent that we help Cassalina?"

"No, I don't know the specifics. I do know he feels strongly about it. It's very important that Malev not find the location of Cassalina's court. I'm not sure why. That's all I know."

"What are you thinking?" Deacon asked me.

"I'm thinking we need to pay Dorran a visit."

24

The next morning at the compound, I tested my theory of just how connected Dorran was to the natural world. Outside, I searched until I found an ant. I scooped it up and told it, "Let Dorran know I need to see him as soon as possible."

The ant didn't even stop crawling around on my palm. It didn't bite me either, so did that mean it understood? I set it back on the ground and waited. It wasn't much of a gamble. Even if the ant didn't get word back to Dorran, there were enough birds flying around that he would get the message soon enough. Still, it'd be interesting to know if the ant beat them all to it.

I wanted to go out to the enclave, search for Dorran there, but it was too risky. We wanted people to think that I was still incapacitated. We could glamour and go, but still, the sight of Dorran talking to two strangers might get tongues wagging. Best to stay put.

I walked back into the house and searched for Deacon. While I was sending my message, he was talking with his sisters. I found them all in the game room on the first floor. Deacon would sense me, and even if we weren't connected through our anointing, he'd at least smell me.

139

Still, I stopped at the doorway and watched, hoping he wouldn't pause his conversation for me. He had a young dragon shifter on his knee, a two-year-old boy. Deacon bounced his knee, and the child squealed. They were all laughing about something, a story one of the sisters had told. This could easily be my favorite sight in the world. It was the closest to family I'd ever been.

"You wanted to speak to me?" Dorran's voice came from behind me.

Deacon saw Dorran and passed off the toddler to one of his sisters to come join us.

"An ant?" Dorran smirked. "An interesting choice."

"I wanted to see how long it would take," I said as I led the way. We needed a private space to speak, so up to the conference room it was.

"And how are you doing, Deacon?" Dorran asked. "Does this new mission suit you?"

"I do my job," Deacon said. He offered no other hint of how he felt. His face was completely blank.

"Apparently not. Malev still lives," Dorran said after the door to the conference room shut behind us.

Even with all the chairs in the room, none of us sat. "Yes, about that," I said. "There've been quite a few hitches in the plan."

Dorran threw his cowl back to reveal his entire face. He eyed me with something bordering on disdain. "I thought you could handle anything."

"I've never been bested yet, but I am only one person."

"A person with a dragon shifter."

"Oh, so is that what you want?" Deacon asked. "You want me to shift and torch her? Watch the fire bounce off her shield? You'd be fine with the consequences of that action?"

Dorran bowed his head and sighed. When he looked back up, his face had a much more understanding expression. "I'm sorry. I'm just eager for this to be done."

"Well, it looks like it could be quite a while," I said. "There's a spell we have to break first, and after that spell is broken, we still have to figure out a way to kill her. So far, I haven't been able to get anywhere near close enough. She keeps herself completely surrounded by high fae."

"You have to see this through to the end. Malev has to die," Dorran said. "Failure is not an option. Everything hinges on her death."

Dorran had been alive longer than anyone I'd ever heard of. He was much older than Malev. He'd survived millennia. Druids like him didn't exist anymore, or at least not at his strength. "If it's so important, why don't you kill her?"

Dorran looked at me, then Deacon, and back at me. The corners of his eyes creased, forming even deeper wrinkles than normal. His mouth twisted to the side, trying to decide what to tell us. Whatever it was, he struggled with whether to trust us.

I didn't offer up any encouragement. Whether he trusted us or not was his business. I didn't care.

"Believe me, I would love nothing more than to kill her myself. I've wanted to so much that I almost..." his voice trailed off. Then he shook his head. "No, I can't risk it. I can't leave Earth. If I go to Elustria or the fae realm, I'll die."

"What?" Deacon asked. It was the same question I had. I'd understand if an Elustrian said they would die on Earth away from Elustria's magic, but a magical person not able to survive if they left Earth? It didn't make sense.

"Obviously I'm not eager for this information to get out. You're the only people alive who know. The reason I've lived so long is because of Earth's energy. It's what sustains me. If I leave here, I don't know how long I'd last, but I would quickly weaken and then eventually petrify."

Druids didn't die in the same sense as the rest of us, at least not when it came to natural causes. They could be killed the same as anyone else, but absent that, they would petrify over time, joining the nature that their magic sprang from.

I could understand now why he had struggled with the decision to tell us. Everyone assumed he was invulnerable, but that was because they knew him on Earth. It struck me that he would never again feel the magical air of Elustria, see any of her magical creatures or plants. He was forever sentenced to Earth. Even though I considered Earth my home now, the thought of never being able to return to Elustria made my chest ache. I couldn't imagine what that must be like for him.

"So why didn't you have us bring her to Earth?" I asked. "We could lure her here." There was still the issue of the spell she had on Kelar, but Dorran wouldn't care about that. I wanted to know his reasoning.

"Malev cannot step foot on Earth. It's vitally important that she never come here. That is why she must die, to keep her from Earth."

"Why? Earth is boring to the high fae. There's no magic here for her. Humans are dull and uninteresting. Why are you scared of her coming here?"

"I can't speak of it," Dorran said. Then a smile crept up his face. "But I can show you."

He brought his staff down on the floor and submerged us in darkness.

25

The darkness covered everything. I held my hand in front of my nose and couldn't see it. The smell of wet rock overwhelmed me. We had to be in a cave somewhere. My senses told me Deacon still stood a few feet away, but instead of feeling and smelling Dorran's magic, a strange magic throbbed in the space around me.

I recognized it: the magic from the rock face outside of Cassalina's court. This was the same magic amplified a thousand times. We had to be near the source. I reached out to Deacon. When my hand brushed against his side, he took hold of it.

Through the darkness, Deacon pulled me to him and whispered in my ear, "I can see a little. I don't know what that magic is. What do you want to do?"

He moved his head so I could whisper my reply into his ear. "Take us to the source. It has to be what Dorran wants us to see. I don't think it's a good idea to use magic until we know more."

Deacon nodded and led me by the hand. We took it slowly due to the darkness and our efforts to keep our footsteps as quiet as possible. The hair on my arms stood up, a reaction to the cold. I wished for Deacon's fiery breath. It would bring both light and warmth, but it wasn't wise to tip our hand so soon. From Deacon's reaction, I knew he had never encountered magic like this before. We had no idea what to expect.

The cave floor slanted downward and curved around, revealing a blue light. The light grew as we descended down a spiral ramp. Rock didn't form this way. Someone or something must have created this. The faint blue glow intensified into a darker blue the farther we went, eventually getting bright enough that I could see without any problem. I let go of Deacon's hand, preparing for whatever we might find.

The ramp ended, and we stood in a giant cavern filled with huge blue crystals, the source of the light. Each crystal jutted from the floor and stood between four and five feet tall. Fifty or so were lined up on each side of the rectangular cavern, leaving a walkway in between to the other end where it looked like another ramp lead farther down.

"Fuck," Deacon said on an exhaled breath, barely a whisper.

"What?" I asked. I followed him to one of the crystals. As we got closer and my eyes adjusted to the strange blue light, I gasped.

A man stood frozen inside the crystal.

He was bald with a beard braided down to his waist. A leather band encircled his thick bicep. I couldn't believe it. He was an Elustrian dwarf, here, on Earth. Based on his style of clothing, he'd left Elustria hundreds, maybe thousands, of years ago.

"How did they get here?" I wondered out loud.

"These are the crystal dwarves," Deacon said. His voice awed. "I thought they were legend, a story people told to pass the time." Deacon shook his head in amazement.

I didn't know much about dwarves. I knew that they tapped into magic from rocks, minerals, and gems. They lived almost exclusively in the mountains. In all my time in Elustria, I'd seen maybe one.

The dwarf king was one of the richest people in Elustria due to his control over all the precious gemstones. The dwarven capital, from what I'd heard, was a magnificent city woven into the Diadem Mountains. They didn't take kindly to outsiders and really only mixed with the other races of Elustria to trade.

"Let's assume I don't know anything about the crystal dwarves," I said.

"Of course, why would you?" Deacon examined one of the crystals without touching it. We didn't know how they would react to us or our magic. "Dwarven stories and legends were one way we passed the time when I was a guard. Besides, the story is so old, I doubt many people know it. I don't know what the truth is, but the way I heard it, these dwarves came to Earth thousands of years ago. They found some type of magic crystal and tried to bring it back to Elustria or something. I don't know the details, but it caused a rift with the dwarf king. So all of these crystal dwarves stayed on Earth and were never heard from again. I didn't imagine the story was true."

Earth didn't have much magic. That was why there was so little mingling between Elustria and Earth. Most Elustrians had no desire to go to what they viewed as a barren world. Did the dwarves actually find some magic that was native to Earth? Or did they somehow bring it or call it out with their own magic?

I didn't know much about history or the intricacies of magic. My education had been limited to how to blend in, overhear things not meant for me, gain the trust of strangers, and ultimately kill. If it didn't help me do any of those things, no one saw fit to teach it to me. "Do you know anything about the type of magic they were supposed to have found here?"

Deacon shook his head. "The stories I heard never got that specific. I don't know if it's because the dwarves don't want that knowledge passed down or if it's because no one really knows."

I walked among the crystals, admiring the perfectly preserved dwarves within. It looked as if a simple spell would free them and they would go about living as if no time had passed at all. It was extraordinary.

Deacon followed behind me. Together we walked down the ramp to the next level and came across an almost identical cavern. Down and down we went, through at least six levels of dwarves encased in glowing blue crystals. As fascinating as this was, I didn't quite understand why Dorran wanted to show it to us.

The dwarves had to be why Cassalina chose this location for her court. It had always seemed weird that she chose Earth at all, and even weirder that she'd chosen a place so uninteresting to a fae. She must have plans for this magic, plans that Malev couldn't be allowed to interfere with.

But what exactly did Dorran want? For us to destroy this? For Cassalina to rule it? Or simply for Malev to never find it? Did Malev already know that her rival had formed their court where the crystal dwarves had gone?

Coming here only brought up more questions. The source of the strange magic Deacon and I had felt outside Cassalina's court was the only answer these caverns gave us. Now that we had that answer, what should we do with it?

"How dare you?" Cassalina's voice thundered behind us. I turned to see her eyes lit with furious flames.

assalina teleported us to a small room in the mountain that we'd never been in before. I guessed it was far away from anyone who might casually walk by. She looked ready to yell and didn't want to be overheard.

"What were you doing down there?" Cassalina demanded.

"Don't get that way with them. I'm the one who sent them there," Dorran said, stepping out of the shadows in one of the corners of the room. I hadn't noticed him when we arrived.

"You!" Cassalina pointed at the druid, and I wondered if she was about to cast a spell. Seeing the two of them fight would be amusing, certainly more fun than getting yelled at by an irate fae. "You were sworn to secrecy."

Dorran tilted his head patronizingly. "I only swore not to speak of it. I didn't. In fact, I specifically told them I couldn't speak of it. I showed them instead."

"Grr," Cassalina growled. Her face contorted in rage, and she pulled back her hand. The gem in Dorran's staff glowed. Heeding the warning, she composed herself.

"Being a fae, I'd think you'd be better at making bargains. As it is, they were wondering why it's so important to me that Malev not come to Earth. So I showed them." He looked at us. "Do you know what you saw?"

Deacon nodded. "Yes. They're the crystal dwarves, aren't they?"

"Very good," Dorran said with a smile.

Cassalina stormed between us and Dorran. "This isn't a game. It endangers everything for me to be away unplanned. What if Malev needs me and I'm not there? We can't afford for her to become suspicious."

An alarm must have alerted her to our presence in the caverns. I asked, "Were you with Malev when you left?"

"Thankfully, no."

"Then why don't you calm down?" Dorran said. "We're all in this for the same thing: to see Malev dead."

"Which begs the question: why are some people keeping secrets?" I looked pointedly at Cassalina.

She smirked. "You must understand why I had to keep the dwarves a secret."

I stayed silent. Deacon crossed his arms over his chest. The silence settled thick around us.

"Dorran's right," Cassalina continued. "Malev can't come to Earth. If she found the dwarves or even a hint that they're here, she'd stop at nothing to get their power."

"And you're just here as their guardian?" I arched an eyebrow as I peered at her.

Cassalina shrugged. "I can't do anything with them. She can."

"What do you mean?" Deacon asked. He wouldn't let her shut down the discussion that easily.

"The spell that has the dwarves and their magic trapped is strong and ancient. There's only one way to break it, and it involves a talisman that she has."

"Why haven't you stolen it?" I asked.

"I don't even know where it is. Even if I did, it's too great a risk. She would know."

"Unless she's dead." I stared her down, daring her to deny that this was the real reason she wanted me to kill Malev.

"Correct." Cassalina nodded.

"So why should we give you this power? Malev is terrible, but at least she keeps out of Earth business. I can't say the same for you." Before this, we'd assumed that Cassalina kept her court here simply to hide it from Malev. Once she took the fae throne, we'd expected her to be on her way. This mountain held too much power for me to believe that Cassalina would abandon it now.

"I want the fae throne more than I want this mountain. When Malev's dead, I'll even destroy the talisman. It's in all of our best interests that she die."

"Yes, which brings me back to my question: why are you keeping secrets?" The dwarves hadn't been what I was referring to.

"I don't understand what you mean." Cassalina's brows furrowed as she shook her head, appearing genuinely perplexed.

"When you told us about the spell on Kelar, you conveniently left out that if we kill Malev, Kelar will die as well."

"Oh." Understanding dawned. Cassalina shrugged. "I didn't think it was relevant."

Of course she wouldn't. "Not relevant that killing Malev would also throw the sorcerer court into chaos?"

"I don't care what happens at the sorcerer court," Cassalina said. I tilted my head in disbelief, and she put her hand on her chest. "You can't possibly think that I have ambitions to take over." She laughed, a high tinkling sound. "Really, you must think horribly of me. I have no desire to ever step foot in the sorcerer kingdom again after this is all over. I'm completely uninterested. If you like, I can even back someone of your choosing to succeed Kelar."

That brought me up short. I had thought that Cassalina was making a power grab, or at least a bigger one than she had already confessed. If we did as she asked and Kelar died, whoever we picked would get the throne. In the chaos following the king's death, no one would have the strength to oppose whoever the new fae queen backed. It was a chance to write history, shape the future of my people. Who knew what that future would look like now that Meilin no longer pulled the levers of power? Without her, Kelar could be a disastrous ruler.

Still, that wasn't my decision to make. Kelar remained an innocent in this particular situation. Every effort must be made to save his life. "I'm not going to kill her until the king is safe."

Cassalina laughed. "You must enjoy making more work for yourself. Do you even know how to break the spell?"

"No, but you're going to tell me. Otherwise you can figure out how to get rid of Malev yourself."

"Telling you how to do it isn't going to make it any easier. You're going to need a spiritstone. And before you ask, I have no idea where to get one. They're rare, and I've never seen one. After you get the spiritstone, you need a netherwalker to perform the magic. Good luck finding one of those."

Netherwalkers could enter the nether at will and also shape it and command it with their magic. As I'd seen firsthand, repeatedly spending time in the nether led to madness. Netherwalkers were, by definition, at least a little mad. People who sought to learn that kind of magic weren't welcome in respectable society.

Cassalina continued, "You'll need the netherwalker to put Kelar's spirit into the spiritstone to keep it safe while you kill Malev. She'll know as soon as Kelar's spirit is in the stone, so you have to be ready. After you kill her, you'll need the netherwalker to put Kelar's spirit back into his body. Assuming his body is still in good condition, it should be fine."

"And that's the only way to do it?" Deacon asked, his voice gruff. "There's no way to simply break the spell instead of avoiding it?"

"I don't know of any other way," Cassalina replied. "There could be, but you'd have to research it for yourselves. This is the only way I know of to avoid the consequences of Malev's spell."

I looked at Dorran to see if he had any insight. There were a lot of failure points with the spiritstone plane, points at which it could all fall apart. Breaking the spell altogether might be easier.

"I wouldn't have the first idea of where to start looking for another answer," Dorran said. "This type of magic is dark stuff. Even if there were another way, it might not necessarily be easier. There aren't many people walking around who can break a high fae's spell."

I nodded. Most magic folk didn't learn any more magic than they needed to make their lives convenient. It would take a lifetime of study to learn how to break a high fae's spell. People with that kind of power weren't easy to find and were even harder to recruit. We'd have a hard enough time finding a netherwalker.

"Then it sounds like we need to get going." I braced for the pain from my cuff and created a portal to Emma's house.

In Emma's garden, Deacon asked me, "You don't believe she's really going to destroy the talisman, do you?"

"Not a chance. We're going to have to get to it first." Just one more thing to add to an already crowded—and deadly—to-do list.

27

We left a message with Emma that we needed to talk to Sybil and Alistair. Then we applied our glamour and teleported to the townhouse. A note from Tarelle waited for us.

Thank you for hosting our little dinner. It confirmed for me that the Dragon Fae is the answer to all of our problems. I'll keep in touch, and remember to be careful around the palace. There are eyes and ears everywhere.

-T

"In case I didn't feel enough pressure as it is." I passed the note to Deacon then headed to the Claybourn's library.

"Where are you going?" Deacon asked.

"To see if I can find out more about spiritstones. I don't want to make inquiries on the black market for something I know nothing about, and we don't want word getting out that someone's looking for one. I need to make sure I approach the right person the first time." I didn't have many contacts in Elustria anymore. Sybil and Alistair may be able to connect us to the right person, but until our next meeting, I needed to be as ready as possible.

Deacon nodded and left me to my research. It took me a second to remember how to get to the library in the labyrinthian house, and once I did, it took me another second to take in the space.

The Claybourns knew how to make a library. The room had vaulted ceilings, taking up two floors of the house. A giant window with an enticing window seat looked out on the back garden. In the corner, a lectern held a catalogue of the Claybourn's collection. I began there.

Unfortunately, using the catalogue required magic. I hated for Deacon to feel the pain of it, but I didn't have another option if I wanted to get the information I needed this century. The library was too massive to go hunting through books individually. I put my hand above the open catalogue, braced for the shock from my magic. "Show me books that mention spiritstones."

The pages of the catalogue fluttered, turning forward and then backward. The Claybourns had a flair for the dramatic. The catalogue could simply present my results without all the fluttering about if the owner chose. When the pages settled open to the middle of the book, the results of my inquiry appeared in elegant script. There were only four titles listed, which was four more than I'd expected. Next to each was a description of where the book was, including, "By the bed in Clay Cottage," and, "Loaned to Katie Nevilles and now in the possession of Baroness Silvadra."

Huh. That was interesting. Out of the four titles in the library, two of them were novels. The third was *Compendium of Magical Objects Volume 3.* That would provide general knowledge at best. However, the book currently in Baroness Silvadra's possession was *Walking With the Nether: A Guide to the Magic of the In Between.*

Since the Claybourns hadn't been in Stardowns for quite some time, there was no telling when they'd leant the book to Katie Nevilles and when she had passed it to Silvadra. Out of all the dinner guests, Silvadra had been the most interesting. Would she read a book like that out of idle curiosity? She didn't seem the type to enjoy something out of pure intellectual interest. She had too much of a sense of action about her.

I'd talk to Deacon about Silvadra's interest later. Rather than use magic to levitate the compendium to me, I decided to get it manually and spare Deacon the unexpected jolt. It was on the third shelf of the sixth bookcase.

As I searched the spines, a title caught my eye. *The Dragon Fae: Separating Myth From Reality.* Then next to it sat *Ushering in the Age of the Dragon Fae.* We knew from Tarelle that the Claybourns believed in the Dragon Fae, but I didn't realize it was a strong belief. Then again, the presence of the books meant nothing, especially in a library of this size. Still, I grabbed them on the way to my destination.

With the compendium in hand, I sat in the window seat overlooking the back garden. As I suspected, the compendium didn't give me any information we didn't already have, just a basic definition of a spiritstone and a bit of history.

A light knock on the library door preceded Deacon's entrance carrying a tray of food. "I ordered us something. You were in too much of a hurry this morning to get anything decent. You've got to be starving."

I hadn't noticed any hunger, but the smell of food made my stomach growl. "Thanks," I said as I stood from the window seat and went to the table where Deacon set the food. The fruit, cheeses, and sausages looked as good as they smelled.

We ate in comfortable silence. The scene must look like domestic normalcy from the outside, just a couple sharing a meal, no rush, no stress. I wished that were the truth of the situation. Together, Deacon and I would make a decent couple. We could have these normal mornings.

I laughed to myself. We could never be normal. We weren't an old couple. We were a bastard dragon shifter and a sorceress assassin with some fae blood thrown in generations ago.

And I was fated to die young.

No matter how much I wanted a normal life, it was never an option. My circumstances dictated my life, and I couldn't change it anymore than I could change the blood in my veins.

"What's so funny?" Deacon asked after I laughed.

I shook my head. I didn't want to get into it, but I could give him a sliver of the truth. "Us, an old couple eating breakfast together. No one would guess the truth."

Deacon finished first and went to the window seat to see what I'd been reading. "There's not much here about spiritstones."

"No. The catalogue didn't have many entries, and most of them were novels." I wiped my mouth and hands on a napkin and joined him. "Sorry for the bit of magic, but it's the only way to use the catalogue."

"Don't worry about it. Don't let our bond keep you from using magic. I've had worse."

Yes, he had, like the time a pixie took some skin from his chest to fashion a cuff for me. He'd had worse, but I didn't like being the source of anything negative in his life. He already had a great deal of pain ahead of him from tying himself to me. I focused my attention back on the books.

"What's more interesting is what's missing. The catalogue listed a book called *Walking With the Nether: A Guide to the Magic of the In Between*. It was loaned to someone named Katie Nevilles."

"Who is she?" Deacon asked.

"I have no idea, but more important is what she did with it. According to the catalogue, she loaned it without permission to one Baroness Silvadra."

Deacon's eyebrows shot up. "Really? That is interesting." He pointed at the two other books I had grabbed. "And you got these to see if you could find some way out of this whole prophecy?" He wore a sad smile when he looked at me for an answer.

I shook my head and lightened the mood with a genuine smile of my own. "No, actually, I thought I should learn more about the prophecy. I want to know what our dinner guests likely knew.

My family celebrated the Feast of the Dragon. I was raised to believe in the Dragon Fae, but I didn't study the prophecy. I don't know if intellectually my parents really believed it. If they knew it was to be me, they definitely wouldn't have." I laughed imagining my mother's shock at hearing her daughter would be the Dragon Fae. "My father told me the general myth but nothing more."

I'd never been one for academic study. I'd rather learn by doing and failing and trying again than reading a book. I'd gotten away with it because Alistair taught me everything I needed to know to do my job. If I needed information, he got it for me.

"You won't find what you need to know in a book," Deacon said as he picked one of them up and thumbed through it. He placed it back on the window seat and turned to me. "Everything you need to know was said at that dinner."

The look in his face mirrored the one he had when he toasted the Dragon Fae that night. Even though he looked like Michael Claybourn, his expression was all Deacon.

"Actually, I've been thinking that maybe I should make an appearance. Who knows how long this mission is going to take with all these new complications? We can't let people despair. We need them to know that there's something worth fighting, worth resisting, for. It might even keep Kelar from handing Malev more power."

Deacon's eyes lit up, but he held himself back. He looked like a hunter who'd spotted a deer but knew to proceed carefully lest he scare it off. "I think that would be wise."

I guffawed. "Really? You think it wise? Prudent? That's the extent of your feelings on the matter?"

Deacon suppressed a smile, not willing to give me the victory.

"I'd thought about looking through these books to determine what type of appearance would be most impactful, see if there's some part of the prophecy that I could give weight to."

Deacon shook his head and put his hands on my shoulders as he met my eyes. I swore I could see his glamour flicker and some of the real Deacon peek through.

"Those books were written by other people about the Dragon Fae. Have you forgotten that you're anointed? You are the Dragon Fae. You don't take your orders from old men who have written down their thoughts about you. You're writing the prophecy now."

My relationship with prophecy was different than Deacon's. In the beginning of this journey, those around me had manipulated events to make it seem as if I were the Dragon Fae. But Deacon was right, no matter my feelings or doubts on the subject, I'd been anointed. I'd walked through the nether and conversed with the Origin, the first Dragon Fae. Mistake or not, it was too late now. I was the Dragon Fae. It wasn't up to me to mold to prophecy. It was up to the prophesiers to mold to me.

I didn't know when or how yet, but I would give hope to the people. The doubt that had sat around my dinner table had disheartened me. These people needed me, but deep down, I knew I needed their belief in me even more.

28

*A*round lunchtime we got the signal to meet at Emma's. It felt like we were just there speaking to Sybil, but so much had happened since then. Yet we weren't much closer to achieving our objective: killing Malev. I longed for the simpler days when I tracked and killed mages. My entire career felt like child's play in light of my recent work.

We removed our glamour and let ourselves into the house. The sound of laughter led us to the dining room. Sybil and Alistair sat around the table with Emma and Philip.

"Don't let us spoil the fun," Deacon said when everyone looked at us as we entered.

It was a glimpse of happiness, but the light didn't reach Emma's eyes. It'd been mere weeks since she lost her daughter. I didn't know if a wound like that was capable of healing, but at least she had Alistair with her. One of the only good things to come from this mission was him getting to spend more time with his sister.

"Nonsense, we were just waiting for you two to get here," Emma said as she got up from the table and went to the kitchen. Deacon and I took the two remaining seats next to each other.

Emma returned, levitating a huge lunch. "My brother here let slip that he tries to meet with you over food whenever possible because you have a tendency to not eat otherwise," she said as she settled back into her seat.

"That's not true. I love food. The only good thing about living in that desert is the amazing food." I picked up a serving spoon and help myself to some type of casserole.

"You may love it, but you don't cook it," Alistair said. "And getting you to indulge and eat on your own is nearly impossible. You're an eat to survive person."

"That's what I said!" Deacon looked at me with satisfaction.

"I don't know how you survived before I moved in next door," Sybil said as she loaded up her own plate. "I'm not much for cooking either, but it seems like you lived off coffee, whiskey, and cereal. Poor Pint has to come to my place to beg for scraps."

I scoffed. "Scraps? You keep your fridge stocked with steaks! Excuse me for not coddling a dragon who should be hunting for his own food. Scorpions with the occasional meat from the store were fine for him before you came along."

"If it weren't for that dragon, I doubt you'd do any grocery shopping at all," Alistair said with a grin.

"Stop picking on her." Emma swatted Alistair's arm good-naturedly. "Not everyone likes to cook or should." She eyed her husband.

Philip laughed and put his hands up. "It's true. I should be kept well away from a kitchen."

Emma turned back to Alistair. "And I don't recall you ever cooking a meal in your life."

"Fair point. But I also didn't forget to eat for so long during a mission that I fainted on a source." Alistair stared pointedly at me.

"That happened *one* time. And it all worked out in the end. When I came to, he was so mortified thinking it had been some-thing he'd done that I milked that source for months." Everyone at the table laughed. I loved this easy banter around a dining table with friends. It was something I'd never had before.

During lunch, we kept the conversation light. Emma told us stories about Alistair, and he reciprocated. I couldn't quite imagine Alistair as a child. He seemed far too serious to ever bother with something as silly as childhood. According to Emma, he'd been serious his whole life, which had gotten him into a few funny situations growing up. But he always had a soft spot for his sister and learned to prank her back just to see her laugh. So much had changed over the years, sorrow and tragedy had taken away youthful innocence, but their joy at making each other laugh remained.

When the meal finished, Emma sent the dishes into the kitchen, and we shifted to business. Deacon and I told them what had happened since we saw Sybil the previous night.

"A mountain full of frozen dwarves? On Earth?" Philip sat back in his chair, shaking his head.

"I know. It's the last thing I expected," I said. Everything got more complicated at each turn.

"You don't trust Cassalina, do you?" Alistair asked me in a tone that said he didn't.

"Of course not. I trust that our interests align right now. I tried doing some research on spiritstones but didn't come up with much. Does Cassalina's explanation sound right to you, Sybil?"

She'd sat chewing her bottom lip, taking in every detail of our story. "Yeah. It sounds like it should work. In any case, it's our best option. I spoke with the priestesses and the general consensus is that there is no way to break the spell. Our knowledge of the nether is limited. What we do have is only to facilitate the anointing. You're going to have to find a netherwalker unless you plan to try to capture Kelar's spirit yourself."

It hadn't even occurred to me to try it. "No, I don't have the skill for it, and history shows that I should stay well away from the nether if at all possible."

Deacon grabbed my hand under the table and gave it a little squeeze. My nether sickness was still a sore point, but I knew he didn't hold it against me. "I don't suppose any of you know a netherwalker?" Deacon asked, looking around the table.

Alistair shook his head. "Even when Nadiya was based in Elustria, I didn't have any contacts like that. They're few and far between, and those who are netherwalkers don't exactly broadcast it. I can ask Gordon."

"No, don't do that," I said. "It's too risky. I trust Gordon, but there's too much uncertainty in the Circle. We can't risk word getting out that someone's looking for a netherwalker or a spiritstone."

"We'll make inquiries away from the sorcerer court," Sybil said. "We have allies all over Elustria. I'll consult the prophecy and the priestesses to see if we can up with a solution."

When no one else had any ideas, I said, "I don't know if this is anything, but the only book in the Claybourn's library that seemed to have any real knowledge about nether magic was with Baroness Silvadra by way of a Katie Nevilles, according to the catalogue."

"Baroness Silvadra?" Emma said. "I've wanted to meet her since I saw the pictures of her at her husband's funeral. She looked so stately in her grief. I always wanted to know how she bore it so well, especially as a newlywed." Emma's own grief flashed raw in her eyes then faded just as quickly. She put on a smile, realizing how her words had brought down the mood. "She's glamorous is all. I think she'd be interesting to talk to."

"Well, she made her feelings about my performance as the Dragon Fae quite clear at dinner."

"Really?" Sybil asked. Deacon and I had already told her about the dinner party, but we hadn't gotten into specifics of who said what.

"Yes, she was the most vocal about the failings of the Dragon Fae."

"And she has a book on nether magic?" Sybil asked rhetorically. She bit her bottom lip and sat back in her chair, her gaze off to the side in thought.

"What?" I asked.

She didn't respond.

"Sybil?" I said, a little louder.

She startled and straightened in her seat. "Oh, nothing. I was just trying to remember something Jaygar said." She shook her head. "So what do you want to do with that information? Are you thinking about approaching her?"

I didn't like it when Sybil hid things, especially since they tended to affect me. "I don't know. It's an option, but I'm not sure if it's a good one. I'm confident she has no affection for Malev or her presence at court, but I don't know how prone she is to gossip. She certainly didn't hold back about her feelings at dinner."

"Tarelle trusts her, so that's something," Alistair said. "I don't know how you're going to find a spiritstone, and if she has more than just a passing interest in nether magic, she might have information on how to get one."

"I'll ask her for the book back. It would help if we knew who Katie Nevilles is. We could ask the Claybourns, tell them we need the info for this silly game they think they're playing."

Deacon looked at me, as if waiting for me to say more. When I didn't, he said to the group, "We know from Tarelle that the Claybourns are believers in the Dragon Fae. We need to consider using them. As long as they're at Drake's compound, there's no risk of them leaking."

I wished he had spoken to me about this first. "As soon as we tell them the truth, it condemns them to stay there until Malev is dead. If we decide to change course and assume different glamours, they still won't be free to go."

Deacon tilted his head. "Their help may facilitate us killing Malev sooner."

I knew he was right, but I naturally resisted bringing outsiders in as much as possible. I faced Alistair. "I'll leave it to you to decide how much to tell them."

"We'll see how things progress with getting a spiritstone. How are you going to proceed?" Alistair left the decision to me, part of our new dynamic now that we didn't work for the Circle any longer. I'd hoped he'd give me more direction.

I hated to use the black market for the same reason I didn't want to ask Gordon. We didn't need rumors. I didn't even know how rare spiritstones were. Was it something a rich aristocrat might have as a collector's item? Or were they only of value to people who used them for shady purposes?

"We'll start with Silvadra. I'll talk to her tonight. If it feels right, I'll ask her about spiritstones. I'll keep it light and casual. She seems to have more serious things to concern herself with than gossiping that the Claybourns asked her about a spiritstone."

"Good." Alistair stood from the table, signaling the end of the meeting. "I trust your judgement. I'll let you know if we get anything from the Claybourns. Keep in contact as much as you can."

"Will do." I stood and Deacon followed, still holding my hand. It felt so natural, I'd forgotten. I took a good long look at him before applying my glamour.

We had our plan. All we needed to do was come up with some eccentric rich-person reason for wanting a spiritstone.

29

Per usual, it didn't take long for our plan to hit a snag. When we arrived at court, Silvadra was nowhere to be found. A little asking around revealed that we'd likely find her at the northeast corner of Fairtree Park where sorcerers played skizing, a magical chess-like game.

Walking through the crowded streets of Stardowns, I felt freer than in the vast halls of the palace. The noise and bustle was exhilarating because these people were just living their lives. There weren't machinations and plotting, political alliances being hammered out, spies around every corner. I hadn't realized how on edge I was until I allowed myself to smile at the beautiful chaos of everyday life.

"There's a rare sight these days," Deacon said from beside me as he turned to edge past a gaggle of children hounding their mother for sweets.

I shrugged. "I haven't had much to smile about."

"And now you do?"

I looked at him and smiled wider. "We're out of the palace, aren't we?" I spread my arms and accidentally hit a frazzled man muttering to himself as he hurried toward his destination. "Oops, sorry!" I said as I pulled my arms back in. The man shot me a dirty look and continued on his way.

Deacon laughed. "I didn't realize you hated it there so much."

"What's to like? This is nice, normal Elustrian activity. Normal people. Normal is a novelty to me. Why do you think I opted to walk instead of taking a cab?" Teleporting around Stardowns wasn't common. The city was too densely populated, and sorcerers ran the risk of appearing literally on top of someone else with nasty results.

While I enjoyed myself, Deacon bristled at all the people. A lifetime spent in near solitude would make Stardowns a shock to his system. He liked people more than I did, but I could understand experiencing a little claustrophobia on the city streets.

"We'll cut through the park. It shouldn't be nearly as crowded there," I told him as I crossed the street. If our information was correct, Silvadra would be at the far end of the park. I'd initially planned to take a path around the perimeter to gawk at the people and buildings, but cutting through would likely be faster anyway.

"Don't worry about me. We can go whichever way you like," Deacon said as he avoided a collision with a man levitating several wooden chests in front of himself.

The crowds thinned at the park entrance, and I could practically hear Deacon sigh in relief. We might as well have been entering a different world. The city around us melted away as we entered the tranquility of the park. Kids climbed trees, ran, and giggled as they played imaginary games hurling "fire" and "lightning" at each other that were nothing more than sparkly magic lights in different colors. Even the air smelled different, like grass and flowers instead of people and food. It'd be easy to forget we were on a mission and instead enjoy a leisurely stroll.

Fifteen minutes later, the whoops and hollers and claps of skizing observers filled the air. We went around a hedge and found about a dozen games in progress. In skizing, two sorcerers faced off across from each other, levitating their game pieces in the air as they tried to capture their opponent's dragon. There was no limit to the number of pieces a player could have in the game. It came down to the person's ability to keep all the pieces levitating in their proper positions while still moving their active piece. If any piece fell from its position, the player lost.

It took immense skill to control that many strands of magic. Holding a hundred pieces in a static position wasn't too difficult when they formed one whole, but as soon as most sorcerers tried to isolate one piece and move it on their turn, they all came tumbling down. Beginners worked up to control half a dozen pieces. Masters at the game could control more than a hundred. Silvadra appeared to have around a hundred and fifty.

At the far end of the clearing, the baroness played against a slight man with a long white beard. His back hunched over, but his eyes sliced the air with sharp alertness. Like most skizing players, his bony hands formed claws in front of his body, controlling his elaborate set of pieces. Silvadra, a consummate show-off, kept her hands in her pockets. With a shaking finger, the man made his move, taking Silvadra's grand sorceress, one of the most powerful pieces in the game. The crowd of onlookers gasped.

Silvadra didn't appear the least bothered. As soon as his piece settled, she countered, her water sprite taking a tree walker, leaving her opponent's dragon vulnerable. Hollers of disbelief rose from the crowd. She'd made the move without any outward expression of effort. If an observer missed the piece moving, they wouldn't be able to tell she'd done anything. It was the most skill I'd ever seen a sorcerer exhibit.

Her opponent's eyes frantically searched the playing area, trying to find a way out of the inevitable. When his face and shoulders fell, so did his pieces.

"That was the toughest game I've played in a while, Gayan. Thank you. You're a formidable player," Silvadra said as her pieces floated into an ornate box by her feet.

Gayan grunted in response and left with his skizing set. Silvadra looked around for another challenger, but the crowd had dissipated. The onlookers enjoyed watching her beat others, but none were eager to be beat themselves.

Accepting that she'd find no more opponents today, she levitated her box of pieces and turned to leave.

"That was quite the performance. I had no idea you played skizing," I said, coming up beside her.

"Oh, Jane, I didn't see you there." She gave me a polite smile of recognition then nodded to Deacon.

"I've never seen someone play like that before," Deacon said, genuine admiration in his voice.

"Do you two play?" For a brief moment, a spark lit her eyes, eager for another game.

I laughed and shook my head. "No, we don't even follow it that closely, but it doesn't take much knowledge to appreciate how good you are. When he took your grand sorceress, I thought you were done for."

Silvadra shrugged. "Sacrifice is always necessary for the greatest victories." She said it as if it were nothing and started to walk away. I worried she'd teleport home. If she did, it might be another day before I'd get the chance to speak to her.

"Before you go, I have a question for you."

Silvadra stopped and turned back to face me, raising her eyebrows. "Yes?"

"I was looking for a book in my library, *Walking With the Nether*, and it appears you have it, oddly enough, via Katie Nevilles."

"Ah!" Silvadra's face animated with fake enthusiasm. "Yes, of course. I hadn't realized she'd gotten it from you. I can go fetch it." She gestured behind herself, indicating she could leave now.

I dismissively waved my hand. "Only if you're done with it. We don't need it right away. We were actually wondering, since you obviously have an interest in that sort of thing, if you could help us find a spiritstone."

Genuine surprise filled her face. "A spiritstone? What for?"

"One of our little hobbies is collecting rare or peculiar magical objects and artifacts. We've gotten a little obsessed with finding one." Deacon and I had decided that this was the best reason to give. Any uses for a spiritstone could potentially cast suspicion on us. Rich people collected all kinds of things for no reason.

Silvadra considered us for a moment. I couldn't tell what she was thinking, and I didn't like it. Not many people were hard for me to read. Finally, she nodded and squinted. I could see her mentally going through a list of where she might find a spiritstone. "I'll ask around and let you know. I think I may be able to come up with something."

"Thanks. And we'd appreciate your discretion," I said conspiratorially.

"Of course, of course. Don't worry. I would never deal with someone who can't respect privacy. I'll try to have a lead for you tomorrow."

"Wonderful!" I said, clapping my hands in an imitation of Jane. "Thank you so much."

Silvadra smiled and nodded then went on her way.

"Do you hear that?" Deacon asked and turned toward the park exit.

It took me a second to filter through the normal sounds to understand what he meant. Shouting and angry cheers floated in from the street. We went toward the sound and emerged from the park into a mob.

30

The raucous crowd gathered around two sorcerers standing on levitating boxes a couple of feet into the air shouting out heated arguments.

"You are faithless and feckless, Jebidiah Pooflam. I wouldn't follow you into a bar, much less on this path of heresy you are leading the people down."

I looked at Deacon to see what he made of this. He had the same surprised look on his face that I assumed I had. Since when did religious zealots preach in the streets of Stardowns? Sure, religion had its place in Elustria, but adherents usually migrated to a temple or village full of like-minded people.

"And you, Instabul Caccina, are a simple-minded fanatic choosing to believe a fairy tale rather than facts. I preach no heresy, only facts." A few boos erupted from the crowd and Jebidiah raised his hands to silence them. "You're welcome to believe what you like. Enjoy your fairy tales, but don't lead others to sit around hoping for a savior instead of taking action against the fae queen."

Ah, that explained the anger. I'd wondered how the citizens of Stardowns were taking Malev's interference in the court. I still

171

didn't understand how Kelar let Malev close enough to enchant him. He really had been weak all along, relying entirely on Meilin. After this was over, we needed to demand that he choose an heir so when his idiocy finally got him killed, the kingdom wouldn't sink into chaos.

"It isn't hope. And it isn't a fairy tale. She has returned. The Dragon Fae appeared at the Feast of the Dragon, as has been foretold." Instabul looked out across the crowd with hopeful eyes. I glanced at my hands to make sure my glamour still held strong. Little hairs stood up along my arms as he spoke about me. Irrationally I felt like Instabul looked right through me and soon every eye would turn and see me.

"And what good has it done us? She appears, supposedly, and the next thing you know the fucking fae queen is making a fool of our king." Jebidiah raised a hand to the people, as if leaving it up to them. Claps and cheers answered him. I tried to gather whether the people hated Malev or the Dragon Fae or both.

"We must have faith in her," Instabul pleaded. "She will lead us out from under the fae queen's dark shadow."

A woman levitated a couple of feet off the ground to get attention. "If you ask me, this whole Dragon Fae business is just a ruse. It's to get us comfortable with the idea of fae rulin' over us." Grunts of agreement came from the crowd as she lowered back to the street.

I glanced at the people surrounding us. The woman's words appeared to have taken hold. It was the most disturbing idea I'd heard yet. It made my stomach churn for sorcerers to think that I was Malev's tool of oppression.

"We have to fight back against this fae queen before she gets her claws any deeper into our king," Jebidiah said.

Instabul shook his head. "No, we must wait for the Dragon Fae. She will lead us in our resistance."

"At best, she's a myth. At worst, she's an agent of the fae, directly opposed to our interests." Jebidiah pointed angrily at Instabul. "You would have us sit and wait for her until we find ourselves sitting in an entirely fae kingdom. The fae queen must be stopped. The high fae can't be allowed anywhere near Stardowns. They have an entire realm of their own. Let them stay there and leave us to our peace."

"Hear, hear!" The crowd cheered.

The people grew more agitated. Embers of discontent would take only a gentle wind to turn into fires of rage. That fire needed to burn the right people. Fae lived in Stardowns and had for centuries. The problem wasn't the fae; it was the high fae. Jebidiah made the distinction, but I doubted it would be honored by the masses. Something needed to be done to keep the situation under control.

"Let's kill the fae queen!" one of the sorcerers shouted above the cheers.

"Yeah, we can storm the palace. She can't protect herself from all of us."

"Let's do it tonight."

More and more suggestions came from the people on how to handle the fae queen's demise. Instabul shook his head at the crowd's foolishness while Jebidiah worked to bring a semblance of control back to the proceedings.

"Stop! We must not stoop to a different kind of foolishness. We will see the fae queen gone from our land, but we won't kill her the way she killed the Chancellor. We will get the king and the court to bend to our demands. Sorcerers have always been free to speak their minds. It is our birthright. I simply ask that you stand and claim that birthright, and if it turns out that our king denies it to us—"

Jebidiah's lips folded inward, and black smoky tentacles overtook his face, covering his eyes and entering his ears. When his hands flew to his face to ward off the smoke, they were likewise bound with the smoke, as were his ankles. I looked around for the source of the magic and saw a group of high-fae guards approaching, cool and collected. The leader unfurled his wings and flew to Jebidiah.

"We can't have any treasonous talk here in the king's own city." The fae looked out at the crowd, his accent thick with disdain. "Speaking out against your queen is indeed treason. Though you all will learn that soon enough." He gestured with a finger and the rest of the fae guards descended on the group, capturing those nearest them with the same black smoke and attacking any who ran or resisted.

Screams and shouts filled the air. Some of the sorcerers around me fought back with their own magic, but most tried to run. The fae used some type of magic that stopped the people within their circle from teleporting. There weren't enough fae to prevent some of the sorcerers from escaping, but I imagined that was intentional. They didn't want this to be secret. They wanted firsthand accounts of what happened to people who dared speak out against Malev.

I stretched my fingers, reaching for my magic, but Deacon's hand encircled my wrist before I could take action. "No, you can't. It would break our cover or at least make these identities useless. We need to get away."

Deacon pulled me through the crowd. The fae had come from the street, which left the park with less guards to maneuver past, though I didn't expect that to last long. Already the guards moved in to tighten up their perimeter. Most of the people who had escaped had done so into the park, and we aimed to follow them.

Deacon's grip around my wrist tightened as he pushed people out of the way. In the panic, most people tried to leave the way they came instead of taking the easier route to the park. This meant that we moved against the tide. It reminded me once again of Deacon's clarity of purpose. It was his job to save *me*, not anyone else. It was my job to take care of the people.

A big pot-bellied man stormed down the street, aiming to escape the fae with his size. Deacon took the opportunity to duck behind him and slip out toward the park unnoticed. I looked back as we walked swiftly away. The sorcerer now struggled against bonds as a fae guard laughed.

Deacon slowed his walk and linked arms with me the way a stately married couple might while out for an evening stroll. Once inside the park gates, he led us to a thickly wooded area where we wouldn't be seen.

"At least you had the good sense not to run this time," I said, remembering our first mission together. When Xavier, our mark, had spotted him, Deacon took off, giving Xavier no option but to chase.

Deacon grinned. "I've learned some things."

"Learned or always knew?" I asked. We both knew he had botched that mission on purpose to make the Dragon Fae prophecy come true.

"Let's just say I always do what's needed."

Yes, he really did. One of the many things I admired about him. "Good, because there's something we need to do now."

Deacon lifted his brow in question.

"It's been too long." I removed my glamour.

Deacon took a step toward me and kept his voice low. "We can't free those people. Not with that many high fae and without a plan."

"I know. But maybe we can let everyone else know they weren't taken in vain."

I could feel Deacon's understanding through our bond before I saw it on his face. He stepped back and removed his glamour.

"There's not enough room here for me to shift. I'm assuming you want to do a flyby?"

"With some style, yes."

Deacon nodded and stepped into the clearing. A few people milled about, talking about the scene on the street. No one knew what the Dragon Companion looked like. They wouldn't recognize him for who he was until he shifted. He looked around, gauging the amount of space he had. Then with a deep breath, his dragon emerged.

The few people around gasped and one screamed. Before word could spread, I sprinted from the trees and jumped on his back. His massive legs launched us into the air as soon as my hand touched his scales.

settled on his back, my thighs gripping his body, his massive chest breathing in and out, rumbling through my legs all the way up to my heart. It was like breathing air for the first time after being submerged in water so long that I'd forgotten the feeling. If I had any doubts about my identity as the Dragon Fae, I knew one thing for certain: I was meant to fly through the air on Deacon's back, the wind whipping through my hair, the cool air crisp in my lungs. I wondered how I'd ever settled for simply walking earthbound.

High in the air, with people on the ground pointing in disbelief, I removed my cuff. I could feel the sigh of relief from Deacon at our new freedom. If flight was air, being free of the cuff was sunlight. It lit me from inside.

I let my magic stretch out around us, then I gathered it up in a ball and released a torrent of sparkling yellow and red light in the dusk air at the exact moment Deacon released a breath of fire. The people below pointed up at the display, and I concentrated all of my magic on forming a shield around us. Gripping harder with my thighs, I leaned forward, and Deacon took my meaning. He dove toward the fae guards and their captives, releasing another stream of fire. The fae, scared that we'd somehow defeat them, teleported away with their prisoners.

Deacon took to the air again and circled around the park. People gathered below us whispering, shouting, cheering, pointing. I remembered a trick I'd learned as a kid to project my voice using magic. It wouldn't be long before the fae returned with a plan to capture me. This had to be quick.

"I am the Dragon Fae. I've heard you wondering if I really exist. If I've really come back. I'm here to tell you that my existence is not dependent on your belief. I'm here, even when you don't see me. I haven't abandoned you. We will defeat the fae queen. She will die by my hand. I swear it. Until then, have hope, resist, and keep the peace among yourselves. The fae are not your enemy. The high fae who would trample you are."

As if I had choreographed it, Malev's guards appeared. They'd had enough time to come up with a plan, so our only hope was escape. When the first guard appeared, I created a portal directly in front of Deacon and he flew us through it.

One of the fae managed to follow.

3 2

The portal hadn't closed all the way. When I looked behind us, the hand of one of the fae flailed on this side of the portal, shooting magic at us. I didn't doubt he had the power to widen the portal and come through.

I nudged Deacon's side and he swung around, easily dodging the fae's magic that shot blindly from the portal. I pulled the void blade from my waist. Deacon probably thought that I only meant to nick the fae, to void him. But I couldn't have his physical hand keeping the portal open. I'd only get one chance at this before more fae followed. As Deacon approached, I stood on his back, knees bent, waiting for the perfect moment.

Closer, closer. I had to get it right. Just a few feet away, I jumped and sliced the fae's hand off. The portal closed, and I was in a free fall with the hand. I could feel Deacon's surprise as soon as my weight left his body. He circled around and nosedived to my location, swooping beneath me only a couple of seconds before I would have made contact with the ground.

Deacon landed and shifted. "Are you all right?"

"Yeah, I knew you'd catch me." I hadn't doubted it for an instant. We were in northern Canada, a random, remote location where I

179

knew we couldn't be seen. "We need to get a move on." I put my cuff back on. It probably wouldn't hurt to keep it off while I made the next portal, but I didn't want to risk Malev knowing some magic to track portals with my imprint.

Before I took us to our final destination, I ripped off the bottom of my shirt and wrapped the fae hand in it. I didn't want him getting it back. Then I made a portal, and we stepped through into my room at Drake's compound. It was a safe place where we wouldn't be tracked. I didn't want to go directly back to the townhouse and risk Malev somehow finding out our identities. Besides, I was sure Alistair and Sybil would want to know about this latest development.

"You're back!" Pint flew up from the bed where he'd been napping. "Is the witch dead?"

"No, not yet." I scratched him behind his horns. Then I unplugged my phone from the charger and powered it on. "She keeps herself pretty well surrounded by fae. I mean, I might be able to kill her, but I would end up dead at the end of it."

Pint exhaled smoke. "Yeah, we don't want that."

I wasn't quite so sure, but I caught Deacon's eye and remembered my promise to him. I wouldn't turn this into a suicide mission. My phone turned on, and I searched my notifications. Still no reply from Trevor. Something wasn't right. I needed to check on him before I went back to Elustria. Since no one else knew his identity, I couldn't pass it off to anyone. "Pint, is Harry still being watched?"

"Yeah, Drake's still got people on him, and I go around and check every once in a while. He looks lonely, but he's safe."

After my recent stunt, Malev may send people to my apartment. I'd alert Drake to the possible increased threat. I put my phone in my pocket and really looked at Pint for the first time. "What's this?"

I put my hand under Pint's talons and lifted them up. They were painted a bright shade of pink.

Pint snatched his talons away and lifted his chin into the air. "Flora likes to play dress up."

Flora was one of Deacon's many nieces. In her human form, she was a chubby little angel just a few years old. She didn't seem to like the rough and tumble games many of the shifter children played. The one time I'd seen her, she was having a pretend party with imaginary friends. The thought of Pint playing with her warmed even my cynical heart.

"Aww, are you her pet now?"

Pint snorted. "No, I'm her fierce friend who goes shopping with her and gossips over brunch, thank you very much."

"Well then, no wonder you're tired. Where is everyone?"

"Alistair and Sybil are both here. They told the Claybourns who you are. If possible, they're even more excited about that than they were about their Enchanted Scrolls adventure. Everyone just had dinner. I think they're all downstairs talking."

Deacon asked, "When you say everyone, do you mean the Claybourns too?"

Pint glared at Deacon then addressed his answer to me. "Yep. Since they know the truth, no one saw much danger in letting them roam around the compound. They're giddy with excitement over you. They won't try to escape or betray our secret."

"Thanks." I gave him a little kiss on the nose and headed downstairs, Pint following. I wondered if he would ever get over his jealousy of Deacon. To be fair to Pint, Deacon had upended our lives. It must seem like he was the cause of all our troubles. Any truces Pint made with him were short-lived.

Laughter came from the large dining room. I hated to dampen the mood. Around the table sat not only Drake, Sybil, Alistair, and the Claybourns but also Farawyn, a fae who had helped us free Alistair from Malev's prison, and Korine, one of Deacon's sisters. All of the talking ceased as soon as we entered.

The Claybourns stumbled as they quickly rose to their feet and bowed their heads. "Please, sit." I said, acknowledging them with a nod. I didn't like the attention from people who didn't know me well enough to know that "prophesied hero" was very much just a title and not at all indicative of who I was. It was weird accepting deference from people when just a few weeks ago I'd regularly stumble into bed after having a whiskey to unwind after assassinating someone.

"We're just so honored to meet you. The Dragon Fae! And out of all the people of Elustria, you chose to kidnap us!" Jane Claybourn was beside herself with glee.

"It's really an honor," her husband said, with a little shrug of apology at his wife's exuberance.

"I just hope you can forgive us for disrupting your lives like this. I promise, I'm working hard to get you home as soon as possible." I really did hate involving innocents.

"Oh, no rush." Jane waved her hand in front of her. "This is the most fun we've had in a long time."

I wanted to like her cheery enthusiasm, but I really needed her to not be so excited about being kidnapped and held prisoner in a different world. It screwed with my sense of right and wrong.

"You just missed out on a wonderful dinner," Alistair said, gesturing for us to come take two of the empty seats next to him. The food had all been cleared away, but it appeared they'd had a couple dozen people at the enormous table.

"It's you all who missed out on the show," Deacon said, his hand on my waist as we made our way to our seats.

"Is that so?" Drake asked.

When I passed behind Alistair's chair, I dropped the wrapped fae hand on the table in front of him. "A hand for a hand."

Alistair looked up at me with soft appreciation in his eyes that was backed by hard steel. He leaned forward and unwrapped it as I sat next to him. "Whose is it?"

"One of Malev's guards who got cheeky and thought he'd follow us through a portal."

Pint laughed as he curled up in my lap.

"Why was he following you?" Sybil asked.

Deacon leaned forward on the table so he could see Sybil and everyone else. "Oh, that would be because she made an appearance as the Dragon Fae."

"Really?" Alistair looked at me, delighted surprise on his face.

"Yes. The opportunity presented itself, so I took it."

Deacon decided to flesh out my bare-bones version. "There was a crowd of people in Stardowns debating the existence of the Dragon Fae and how to get rid of Malev. Fae guards showed up and started taking people away. We escaped, but Nadiya thought it was the right time to appear. We did a little flyby, Nadiya reassured the people, and as soon as the guards returned, she made us a portal out of there."

"Fae were making arrests in the streets of Stardowns?" Michael Claybourn asked, his voice soft with disbelief.

It broke my heart to tell him the truth. "Yes, they took away not just the speakers, but the people listening to them too."

That subdued the Claybourns. For the first time, the joyous light left their eyes. As much as it annoyed me before, I'd give anything now for them to get it back. I was built to be cynical of the world, as was Alistair. But not everybody needed to know the truths of the world as we did.

"It's good you appeared. The people need hope," Sybil said.

"They need more than hope. I'm tired of just making appearances. No wonder the people doubt me. I want to do something. I want to kill Malev and get it over with. But I'm no closer than I was before. If anything, I'm further away because now I have to save our idiot king, too."

"On the subject of saving our idiot king," Jane said. "Michael and I are happy to help you get a spiritstone any way we can."

"Do you know where we could get one?" Deacon asked.

"Oh, no," Michael said. "She means money. We have a lot of it. It's just sitting there. You're welcome to take as much of it as you need to buy a spiritstone on the black market. The bank book is in my desk or you can go to Wolfman's in person."

"And they can do that new instant transfer thing we had setup last time we were in Stardowns, remember? As long as they have our imprints," Jane said to her husband.

"Oh, yes, quite right. I'd forgotten about that." Michael looked from his wife to Deacon. "There's a secure ring on my desk for doing transfers, if that's easier than going in person."

Deacon nodded his understanding, but I saw the disappointment in his eyes that they didn't have a lead for us.

"Thank you. That's incredibly generous," I said. "We asked Silvadra tonight about helping us locate one for our 'collection.' I don't know if anything will come of it."

"Ooh, Baroness Silvadra?" Jane put her elbows on the table and rested her chin in her hands. "What was she like?"

I didn't know what she was looking for. I imagined, like Emma, she thought Silvadra was glamorous. I only ever described people in relation to operational needs. "Interesting. She's the most skilled skizing player I've ever seen."

"I'll see what I can find out about getting a spiritstone," Farawyn volunteered.

"We appreciate it," Alistair said, "but don't compromise yourself. It won't do us any good if Malev comes after you or if she figures out our plan."

"What do the high fae make of recent events?" I asked. The only other fae I had contact with was Cassalina, and even if I trusted her completely, her view of things would be different from the average fae's.

"The queen's obsession with you is weakening her position. The high fae don't understand it."

"What's not to understand?" Korine asked.

"It would be like the Dragon Prince suddenly becoming obsessed with making sure the ants on this compound knew that he ruled over them. The fae are wondering why she doesn't just kill all the sorcerers or leave them alone. War they would understand. This obsession, they do not."

Korine nodded. As the Dragon Prince's sister, she understood better than most. Kings, princes, chiefs, they concerned themselves with war, with the many, not the individual. Drake had his own petty differences with Deacon, but no one for a second doubted that his people took precedence. Part of the reason Deacon had lived to see Drake inherit the dragon throne was because Drake saw it as beneath himself to kill a bastard who posed no real threat. Or at least that's what the clan believed. I knew that had Drake challenged Deacon, it would likely have ended with Deacon on the throne.

My phone vibrated in my pocket. I hoped it was a text from Trevor, but it was just a text from my carrier informing me of my next bill. "Drake, Pint tells me you still have people on Harry Harmon. I want to thank you for continuing to protect him. With recent developments, the threat may be greater now."

"Don't worry, I'll keep my word. He has protection from the clan as long as he needs it."

"I never doubted your word. I only want to apologize that I'm once again bringing danger to your people."

Drake started to speak, but Korine cut in. "We love helping out. It gives us something to do, a nice change of pace. Truth is, we all fight over that assignment."

I hadn't thought of it from their point of view. The dragon shifters at the compound were there for one reason: to safely procreate. They needed to increase their numbers. Their only other purpose on Earth was to play a part, so they thought, in fulfilling the Dragon Fae prophecy. Drake had thought he would have Deacon's place at my side. Protecting Harry was, at the moment, their role in the prophecy, and it was a change of pace from staying cooped up on the compound raising children and getting in each other's way.

"I'm glad it's not a burden. Now, if you'll excuse me, I need to go check on my tech guy before we head back to Elustria. It's late enough that he should be up." I stood, and Pint flew up from my lap and settled back on my chair.

"Is something wrong?" Alistair asked.

"He hasn't responded to any of my texts. It's not like him. He's a worrier. After this long without seeing me, I'd expect him to be hounding me, but he's gone silent."

I saw Drake perk up. If something had happened to one of my people on Earth, it could be a precursor to more trouble Earthside.

"Do you want some company?" Deacon asked.

Yes, I did, but I had to think about Trevor. His identity wasn't my secret to reveal. No matter how much I wanted Deacon with me, this was an errand I had to do alone.

"No, thank you. I won't be long." It felt strange keeping any part of my life from Deacon. We shared so much. We inhabited a unique place in history together, but I still had my secrets. Perhaps I'd see if Trevor felt comfortable with me revealing his identity to Deacon. I'd like for them to meet one day. "Stay here and eat."

"You need to eat too."

"I'll grab something on the drive." I couldn't believe it, but I actually missed Earth junk food. A drive-through sounded great.

Munching on some greasy french fries with the top of my Corvette down, I tried to enjoy the drive to Trevor's, but I couldn't shake the feeling that this was the calm before the storm.

33

*P*arking outside of Trevor's place, I appreciated how normal it felt to visit him. So much had changed in the last few weeks, but the house where Trevor rented a converted garage stood exactly the same as when I'd last seen it.

That was my hope talking. Of course something had to be different, otherwise I would have heard from him. The absolute best-case scenario was his phone was lost or broken. Experience told me never to pin my hopes on the best-case scenario.

I knocked on the door and got no answer. Unease solidified in my gut. I tried the door, but it was locked. Unusual. Trevor never locked his door. What had him scared? I forced myself to slow down and think it through. I closed my eyes and took a deep breath. With my enhanced senses, Trevor's scent reached me through the door. I could hear movement inside, faint, but it was there.

He might have his headphones on playing video games. That wouldn't be unusual. I knocked again, louder. "Trevor? It's Nadiya."

I still didn't get a response. I banged on the door. "I'm worried about you. If you're in there, let me know you're all right."

Still nothing.

"I know you're in there. If you don't open the door or give me some sign that you're all right, I'm going to break in. Fair warning."

This time there was a slight change. Fear tainted Trevor's scent. That didn't make sense. Was he scared of me?

"Trevor? What's wrong? I'm not mad. You don't need to be scared. Just let me in so I can see you're all right."

"Go away!"

It wasn't what I hoped for, but it was Trevor. "As soon as you tell me what has you scared."

"You. Leave."

My mind raced to catch up. I ran through my most recent contacts with him. What could I have possibly done to make him scared?

I gasped. Had I done something while I was strung out on the nether and didn't remember? "What did I do? Please, tell me. Trevor, I would never hurt you."

Silence.

"Please, Trevor." The pleading in my voice was completely foreign to me. I was losing one of the only friends I had, and I needed to know why. "If you give me your word that you're all right, I'll leave. But I'd really like to see that you're fine."

"I'm not fine." I could hear tears in his voice.

"What's wrong? Let me in, and maybe I can help fix it."

The lock turned, but the door didn't open. "You can't fix it. You're the one who broke it."

His voice was further away. I took the turning of the lock as an invitation and opened the door. In the far corner of the room stood Trevor, tears streaming down his cheeks. He lifted a hand to wipe them away but had to use his wrist owing to the knife he held. Whatever was wrong, he clearly wasn't in his right mind. Pointing a knife at me was useless at best and stupid at worst. Trevor knew that. He may kill people in video games, but he couldn't fight in real life.

The only conclusion I could make was that he genuinely felt

threatened by me. I held my hands up and relaxed my body in a small, non-threatening pose. He was more likely to accidentally hurt himself with that knife than me, but I didn't want to suggest he drop it. If it gave him comfort, fine. I wouldn't give him any more reason to suspect I had sinister motives.

"I'm not here to hurt you, Trevor. I don't know what's going on or why you're suddenly afraid of me. I got worried when I didn't hear from you."

"Why would I ever talk to you again? You're nothing but a liar." He dropped his hand to his side, still gripping the knife but not pointing it at me.

I didn't know how to take his accusation. Yes, I lied. All the time. He knew what my work entailed. "You're going to need to help me out here, Trevor. You know about the work I do. I keep things from you, sure, but it's for your safety more than mine. When it comes to us, though, the real stuff, I've always tried to be honest. I'm not going to pretend I've been perfect, but I wouldn't intentionally deceive you."

"Really? So when I talked to you about my family, about the harm a fae did to my clan, you didn't lie about being a fae yourself? You didn't take my family's pain and use it against us to get me to trust you?"

Shit. How did he find out? That was a question for a later time. "I didn't know until recently, and honestly, I'm still processing it myself. It's not like either of my parents or grandparents are fae. It's somewhere deep back in my ancestry. I still think of myself as a sorceress."

"Why should I believe you? Even if you did just find out, you should have told me. I know you knew during those last missions we worked."

I didn't know how to make him understand. All I could do was tell him the difficult truth. "I'll admit I hoped you wouldn't find out because I knew how much the fae hurt your family. I didn't want you to see me that way. I didn't want it to change your opinion of me."

"So you thought it'd be better for me to find out from someone else? If you didn't trust me enough to tell me the truth, then we didn't have the kind of relationship I thought we did." Trevor's tears had stopped, and he spoke with assertive confidence. He was in the right, and we both knew it.

"I should have told you. Maybe I would have eventually, once I came to terms with it. Everything in my life has changed since I found out. Everything. I wanted this one thing, my friendship with you, to stay the same." I didn't hold anything back. I needed him to believe me. I couldn't stand losing him. "I've thought of you like a little brother. My time with you has been the most normal part of my life. I would never, ever do anything to endanger that. And perhaps in trying to keep our friendship, I've lost it. But none of the time I spent with you was a lie. In some ways, it was the most honest part of my life."

Trevor shook his head and closed his eyes. "No. Don't do that. Don't use my brotherly feelings toward you against me."

"That's not my intention." I didn't know how to make him understand. "How much do you know?"

Betrayal cut across his face. "How much is there to know? How much have you hidden from me? How much of a fool have you played me for?"

He didn't know about the prophecy then. All he knew was that I had fae blood in me. "A few weeks ago, I was told that I'm the Dragon Fae, a mythical sort of hero to my people. My first argument was that I couldn't be because I'm not fae. I refused to believe it until it was proved that somewhere in my genealogy there had to be a fae to give me a drop of fae blood that can interact with fae objects. That's it. It's not who I am. I'm trying to defeat some really evil fae right now. I didn't tell you because I didn't even believe it until recently. You know me. We play video games together, and I need you to save my ass regularly with your fancy tech knowledge. How could I be the Dragon Fae?"

I could see him thinking it through, remembering all the times we'd hung out together. But then the suspicion returned. "So you're saying you're not fae, that you can't change your appearance? Is this even what you really look like?"

I knew this was one of the things that Trevor's clan particularly hated about the fae. The harm that was done to one of his ancestors was the result of being deceived by a fae's glamour. If I wanted any chance of salvaging our friendship, I had to trust Trevor with the truth.

"I can glamour. Again, it's something I just learned how to do. In fact, the only reason I even have that ability is because of this prophecy. If I had never been anointed as the Dragon Fae, I would have never been able to glamour because I don't have enough fae blood in me. This is what I look like. You met me long before I could glamour. I would never disguise myself in front of you."

I could see he wanted to believe me, but his family's justified hatred of fae ran so deep that he couldn't cast it aside. The whole reason he had agreed to start working with me was because his clan felt indebted to sorcerers for saving them from a fae. Befriending me wasn't just getting close to a fae, it was actively helping the enemy.

Trevor's breaths came in quick bursts as he struggled internally. I worried he'd hyperventilate. He shook his knife-wielding fist at me. "Fae lie. They trick and they deceive without any thought to whom it might hurt. You are a fae, Nadiya. Get out. And don't come back here. I don't ever want to see you again."

The hatred that settled in his eyes incinerated my heart. Trevor was one of the kindest people I'd ever known and the closest thing to a little brother I had. I couldn't bear being the cause of his anger, of turning him into the bitter young man before me. I knew if I wanted him to be Trevor again, I had to remove myself from his life.

"I understand. I just want you to know that I love you. And you know me well enough to know I don't say that lightly. If you ever need me, you have my number. I hope you don't let this experience change who you are. You're not a fool. You never have been. Your generosity and openness are your strengths. Take care of yourself, Trevor."

Tears pooled in his eyes but refused to fall down his flushed cheeks. His lips formed a hard line. It was time for me to leave.

In the car, I had no problem letting my tears fall freely.

34

On the drive back to Drake's compound, warm sunshine spread throughout my chest as I cried. It took me a second to realize it was Deacon. I'd forgotten about our bond. My emotions must have had him worried. I dried my tears as best I could and returned the warm feeling, or a least an imitation of it, so he'd know I was fine. Not fine, safe. He wouldn't buy fine.

I let Deacon's warmth soothe me. I couldn't indulge in tears right now. By the time I got back to the compound, I needed to be ready to work. But one question kept nagging me: how did Trevor know? Only one answer made sense: Malev. She had to have gotten into the Circle's records deep enough to find his identity. If she had his identity, then she must have everything. Alistair didn't even have Trevor's identity.

I put more weight on the gas and weaved through traffic on the freeway. Malev had somehow gotten word to Trevor that I was a fae. She meant to undermine me by attacking my foundation. I couldn't let her succeed. If she thought this would weaken me, she was sorely mistaken. Unbeknownst to Malev, she'd lit a fire that burned beyond her abilities to control.

When I pulled up to the compound, Deacon waited for me

outside. He watched as I parked then came to me as soon I opened my door.

"How are you? What happened?"

I closed the door behind me and sighed. I wouldn't lie and say I was fine. "I'm all right physically, but Malev just struck a blow to my heart."

Deacon waited patiently while I gathered my thoughts.

"She got word to my tech guy that I'm part fae."

His eyes showed a hint of confusion.

"He was helping me, a sorceress, because a sorcerer saved his clan from a fae. I tried to explain that I only just found out myself, but he took it as a betrayal. He was my only friend on Earth who knew what I did, and now I've lost him. He doesn't want to see me again."

Deacon wrapped his arms around me, and it took all of my self control not to cry as he whispered, "I'm so sorry," in my ear.

I indulged in the comfort of his embrace for only a moment. As I had just been starkly reminded, the job came first over my personal life. "I need to let Alistair know. The only way Malev could have found him was through infiltrating the Circle."

"How bad is the breach?" Deacon asked as we went inside.

"Alistair doesn't even know the identity of my tech guy. There are maybe two or three people at most, especially now that Meilin is dead, who knew that information. The identities of innocents who help us are our most closely guarded secrets. Not only is it a matter of safety, but these people aren't trained to handle themselves should they ever be found." My mind flashed to the picture of Trevor gripping that knife, fear and betrayal in his eyes. I shook it away.

"Alistair and Sybil are still here. As soon as I felt you getting upset, I told them to stick around. Farawyn went to Elustria shortly after you left, and the Claybourns are in their room." Deacon led me to the sitting room where Alistair and Sybil were.

I didn't bother saying hello. "We need to get word to Gordon that the Circle has been breached. Malev got to my tech guy."

The color drained from Alistair's face. In all the time I'd known him, I'd never seen that response. It unsettled me in a new way. No matter what went wrong, he always had a certain degree of composure that leant me confidence.

"I'll get word to him right away." Alistair stood, but just before he left, he asked, "How's your contact?"

"Physically, he's fine. He just feels betrayed and wants nothing to do with me now that he knows I'm part fae."

"I'm sorry." I could see he meant it, but he couldn't do anything about it. He made a portal and went to Elustria. Every second that Gordon didn't know the extent of Malev's infiltration put people in harm's way.

"That bitch," Sybil said, her voice lower than its usual chipper register. "She's trying to undermine your confidence. You can't let her." She stood and gave me a hug. Between her and Deacon, I was getting quite used to hugging.

When she stepped back, she said, "You can do this. We have several people discreetly asking about a spiritstone. As soon as we have a lead, we'll contact you."

Deacon put a hand on the small of my back. I enjoyed how he casually did that now. "Silvadra may come through with something. We only just asked her."

"I must really look like shit if you both are trying so hard to comfort me."

"We just don't want to see you doubting yourself," Sybil said. "We're here for you."

"I know." I forced myself to smile just to get the worried look off of Sybil's face. It didn't work. "We need to get back to Elustria. I'm going to tell Drake about the breach, and then we can go."

Deacon followed me back to my room to put my phone away. I wouldn't need it in Elustria. Fortunately, Pint wasn't there. I didn't want to have to convince him that I was all right.

"You ready to go?" Deacon asked.

"Just a minute." I went to the bathroom and splashed some cold water on my face. I couldn't do anything about Trevor right now, so I shoved all thoughts of him to the back of my mind to be retrieved after I killed Malev. After patting my face dry with a hand towel, I emerged from the bathroom focused.

"Now I'm ready."

Deacon nodded and led the way to the lounge. Soft music played in the background as a dozen or so shifters talked, drank, and made out with each other. Drake had a woman on his lap, and he kissed a trail down her chest. It reminded me a little of the first time I'd met him.

"Yes?" Drake said when I entered, not pausing or otherwise acknowledging me. My scent would have alerted him to my presence.

"May I have a word?" I didn't hint at any urgency. Drake would know that any request I made on his time would be important, and I didn't want to alert the others to a problem.

Drake kissed the woman's mouth then stood. He walked right past me and Deacon, and we followed him into his office. When he turned to face me after closing the door, he was all business.

"I just found out that Malev has breached the Circle. We have to assume that she has access to everything. I don't know how much information the Circle has on you and your people, but she has it now. I don't think you're in any immediate danger. She doesn't have a reason to mess with you, but you needed to know."

"Thank you. I appreciate it." Drake hid his stress well among his dragons, but away from his people I could see the strain on his face. I'd just added one more worry to his already burdened shoulders. "Are you going back to Elustria tonight?"

"Yes, right away."

"Julien has requested to speak with you before you leave."

Deacon grunted. I could feel the disgust rolling off him. It made me admire the fact that he'd done what he could to protect Julien while I was unconscious.

There'd been a time when I thought I owed Julien, but it had passed. My confrontation with Trevor had taken all my emotional energy. I didn't have any left, and even if I did, Julien didn't deserve it. I had more important things to deal with.

"He'll have to wait. If he doesn't like it, he's welcome to leave." Malev couldn't use him against me, and he didn't know anything that would be valuable to her. The only risk he took by leaving was to himself.

A hint of admiration entered Drake's eyes. "I'll let him know."

Drake left the room, closing the door behind him. Deacon and I donned our glamours, and I made us a portal. The pain from performing magic with the cuff barely registered. If anything, it was a welcome change from the emotional pain I'd been through tonight.

I put all thoughts of what had happened on Earth behind me as I stepped through to the townhouse. Instead of the quiet of our upperclass neighborhood, a low roar came from outside. Once the portal closed behind Deacon, we went to the window overlooking the street.

In the few hours we'd been away, Stardowns had changed.

35

People filled the streets in every direction. I opened the window, and angry shouts filled the air. The chaos near the park had found its way to the Claybourn's neighborhood.

Two distinct issues battled for supremacy in the commotion. The first was the arrests the fae made, and the second was the appearance of the Dragon Fae. The people called for action. It was the same debate as earlier, except now it seemed all of Stardowns took part.

I dashed down the stairs and onto the street. A powder keg had been lit at both ends tonight. Malev misjudged the mood of Stardowns. Normally, the people who lived in this area couldn't care less about the lower class denizens of the city. The class divide stood strong, but Malev gave the classes a common enemy to unite against. Upper class sorcerers didn't need any help trampling on the lower class sorcerers. The fae had overstepped their bounds, and the class structure of Stardowns succumbed to the need to keep fae out of sorcerer business.

And then there was the Dragon Fae. Another uniter of the classes. She held the hopes and imaginations of high and low born alike. How miraculous then that right when an adversary had reared her ugly head tonight, the Dragon Fae had appeared as a counterpoint. This couldn't have gone any better if I had planned it.

"This is good." I surveyed the chaos around me. "With all of this going on, no one's going to think twice about two old rich people looking for a spiritstone for their collection."

Deacon chuckled. "That's what you're taking from this?" He shook his head. "Look around you. This is all because of you." He stood behind me and wrapped his arms around my waist. His warm breath tickled my neck as he leaned his head down next to mine and surveyed the crowd. He nodded to a cluster of people who all had the same exhilarated expression. These people clearly weren't activists. They had a thrill about them that said this was a novel experience. "Do you really think anyone other than the Dragon Fae could have gotten those people into the streets?"

I focused my attention on that one cluster. With focus, I could make out some of what they were saying.

"We have to be ready. She's coming back. I know it. The fae bitch's days are numbered."

"We have to resist. What can we do? Protest?"

"March to the palace and demand the sorcerers who were arrested today be released!"

The group nodded in agreement.

A passing sorceress stopped and handed one of the group a flyer. "A bunch of us are gathering in the spice quarter. The vendors have all taken carts into the streets. There's food and drink. Come and join us!"

This excited the cluster of people, and they followed the sorceress on her way to the spice quarter. Other groups followed as well while some stayed behind to have their own discussions about the day's developments.

A large number of people in one area invited trouble. Malev could send her guards to make more arrests or to attack. It would be a foolish move, but Malev had already allowed her anger to cloud her judgement. Ultimately, it wouldn't affect her if things went badly in Stardowns. Within the safety of the fae realm, she could afford missteps in handling the sorcerers.

"We should go keep an eye on things." I moved toward the spice quarter, but Deacon's arms around my waist stopped me.

"No." Once he had me back against his body he continued. "We should go join in the celebration. That's what it is. We're not working tonight. It's just the two of us enjoying the return of the Dragon Fae."

The wiseass in me wanted to point out that according to him I was always the Dragon Fae, but I liked the idea of having tonight just be us. I'd had a hard enough day, and the days ahead would be nearly as difficult.

I nodded my agreement, and we walked hand in hand to the spice quarter. The entire way there, people were talking in the streets. Electric energy ran through all of Stardowns. The warmth of unity filled the air. No matter class or race, everyone stood together against the high fae. Nowhere was this more apparent than the spice quarter.

When we arrived, a sorcerer was speaking at the far end of the main street on an impromptu stage. He preached about standing up against tyranny, about keeping our eyes on the greater good and not letting petty differences stand in our way. Lawyers were already drafting a petition for the release of the sorcerers arrested today. Tomorrow, citizens of Stardowns would march on the palace with the lawyers to present the petition and demand their release. The era of standing by and doing nothing was over.

Then he stood aside and yielded the stage to a minotaur. I squeezed Deacon's hand until my fingers turned white and cold. It wasn't just any minotaur; it was Jaygar.

As far as I knew, he didn't know the identities we'd assumed. I didn't know why I felt so exposed seeing him here. It was a strange clash of worlds. I was here as Jane Claybourn and Jaygar knew me only as the Dragon Fae. Furthermore, he knew the reality of my self-doubts about my role. I'd told him as much when we first met.

Out of everyone here, his words were based most in reality. He'd actually met me, knew me as a person and not just a myth.

Out of the corner of my eye, I saw Deacon smile. He nodded toward Jaygar, and I focused back on the minotaur. He spoke about how the Dragon Fae was a uniting figure, that all the other magical races of Elustria stood in solidarity with the sorcerers.

The people seemed receptive to his message. Jaygar knew exactly what to say. He'd spent a good part of his life waiting for this moment. I'd worried since the arrests happened earlier that the sorcerers would take this opportunity to close ranks and point their frustrations toward any outsiders. I didn't see any hint of that. Jaygar had done his job well.

After Jaygar, a singer took to the stage, belting out nostalgic folk songs. The crowd joined in, including Deacon, who had quite a good ear. I couldn't judge his voice since it was still Michael's, but he matched the pitch perfectly. When the song finished, I clapped and cheered with the rest.

"You should sing," Deacon said from beside me.

I snorted. "You're only saying that because you've never heard me." I had a decent enough ear that I could hear when music was in tune, which made my lack of singing ability more offensive. If I couldn't hear pitch, then I could join in the singing freely. As it was, I knew just enough about music to know how bad I was.

"It's not about how you sound, it's about how you feel."

"If I sing, I'll feel awkward."

The next song started. After a few bars by the performer, the people joined in once again. This time, Deacon warbled horribly out of tune. I couldn't contain my laughter. He sounded ridiculous. The people around us turned to stare and then just laughed and sang louder. Deacon didn't take any notice of them. His volume only grew, and he stretched his arms out in front of him, gesturing dramatically with the song.

I laughed harder and reached for his arms, but he didn't yield to my pressure to put them down. I had only one option if I wanted the spectacle to stop: I sang.

My lips moved, but hardly any sound came out. In recognition of my effort, Deacon stopped gesturing and cupped his ear with his hand and leaned toward me. Wanting this silliness to stop, I took a breath and started to really sing. I flinched at my off-key efforts, but the longer I sang, the more I let myself sink into the festive atmosphere.

After a couple of songs, Deacon grabbed my hand. "Do you smell that?"

It was difficult to tell what he meant by "that." The street was full of interesting scents. He sniffed the air, and I looked in the direction of his nose. "You mean the food?"

Deacon pulled me over to a stall to wait in line. "This smells like something you'd like." He got a few kebabs and handed me one, waiting to eat his until I tried it.

I smiled at his eager look and took a bite. It tasted even better than it smelled, with a satisfying tang and heat from the spices. Deacon appeared to genuinely enjoy my appreciation of the food. It didn't take long for us to finish the kebab and move over to a beer cart to try some local brews. A band took to the stage and soon everyone around us was either dancing, eating, singing, or a mixture of all three.

Deacon threw back the last of his beer then stood behind me. He placed his hands on my hips. Only then did I realize that I'd been moving them to the beat of the song. Full of good food and drink, I didn't need much encouragement. I twirled and grabbed his hands, pulling him into the middle of the street. The delight in his eyes filled me with happiness.

We danced until sweat covered us both, and then we grabbed another beer and danced some more. The last time Deacon and I let loose like this was at our anointing. This time we were anonymous, just two more faces in the crowd. No weight of expectations or prophecy. Just us. If only we weren't glamoured. If only we could truly be ourselves.

The band took a break and both of us came down to reality at the same time. Our break was done. It was time to go home. Without saying anything, we held hands and walked back to the townhouse, leaving the noise and crowds behind. When we reached our street, it was back to normal except for some flyers that blew down the avenue like tumbleweeds in an old western.

In bed, we lay facing each other.

"Tonight was fun," Deacon said, his voice soft and warm.

"Yeah, thanks for that." Left to my own devices, I would have treated tonight like an assignment. Then I would have come back here and dwelled on my broken friendship with Trevor.

"You needed it." His hand reached out for my face then stopped, thinking twice of the personal touch. "Sleep well. We have a lot to do tomorrow." He rolled onto his back and closed his eyes.

I wanted this. I wanted him. Instead of resenting his presence as a partner, I enjoyed counting on him, trusting him. He made it easy to let go and be myself without fear or shame. I didn't ever want to be without him. Just the thought of going back to how it was before he came into my life physically hurt.

Our life wouldn't be this, though. It wouldn't be normal. Street parties, hosting dinners, going on vacations, those were never meant for us. When we bonded, we wouldn't retire to a little house in the country like Emma and Philip. Our life would be mission after mission, trusting each other as we spied and killed until eventually…

I died.

My heart clenched with pain. I didn't want to leave him. I didn't want to hurt him like that, but I knew I had to let him make that choice for himself. Perhaps he had already figured out what was just dawning on me: that the pain of losing him paled next to the pain of never truly having him.

Lying in silence, watching the steady rhythm of his breath, my vision did the same strange thing it did when he begged me not to turn this into a suicide mission. I somehow saw beyond his glamour.

My heart swelled seeing his peaceful face flickering in and out behind Michael's. I could watch him sleep all night, except, that's not what my body wanted. My hips shifted forward without my permission, and I groaned.

Casual sex wasn't an option for us. Our magics called out too strongly for each other. I didn't care at the moment that sex would partially bond us. Now that I'd made the decision, it didn't matter. But I couldn't have us wearing glamour our first time. I wanted Deacon. I wanted to look into his eyes, feel his skin beneath my hands, lick his chest. And I needed him to see me while he was inside me. Nothing short of that would satisfy me.

I whimpered. Exactly what I needed on a mission to kill the fae queen: sexual frustration. I couldn't have waited a few days to think all this through?

I'd just have to take care of myself until Deacon could.

36

I woke up to an empty bed and disappointment. Now that I'd decided I wanted to bond, I couldn't wait to tell Deacon. But wait I must, because once I'd woken, he sensed it and strode into the bedroom with a determined look on his face.

"Good. You're up. I didn't want to wake you, but we need to get going."

I went into work mode. "What's happened?"

In answer, he handed me a letter.

Gwindle Trekov, owner of Trekov's Treasures, may have that item you wanted for your collection. His shop is conveniently located on Starlight Avenue just before the turnoff for the palace. He's a delightful imp, and as he's used to dealing with your class of clientele, he's the very model of discretion.

-F

When Farawyn said he would help, I took it as a kind gesture, but I didn't think he'd actually know someone who operated on the black market. In my experience, these weren't savory creatures, much too harsh for Farawyn's delicate nature.

When we got to the shop, it all made sense. Trekov's Treasures was an upscale antique shop full of expensive paintings displayed to perfection on the tall upholstered walls. Uncrowded display cases stood throughout the shop with various antiques and precious items. This shop was exactly the kind of place Farawyn would love.

An imp, maybe two feet tall with little pixie wings, flew to us when we entered. "Welcome! I am Gwindle Trekov. It's a pleasure to have the Duke and Duchess of Claybourn grace my humble shop." He bowed.

Nothing about his shop was humble. Nearly everything on display likely cost a year's pay for most Elustrians.

"Have we met?" Deacon asked Gwindle.

The imp flew up to eye level to speak with us. "I'm afraid I've never had the pleasure. However, I make sure to acquaint myself with the appearance of all the nobility in the sorcerer court."

Smart business move since they were likely his main source of income. As an imp, Gwindle was a low fae. They were much more common in Elustria than other forms of fae and came in a greater variety than the high fae who stayed in the fae realm. Low fae didn't have their own court in Elustria, so they integrated into various magical societies.

"And what can I help you find today?" Gwindle asked. "A piece of art for your wall? Perhaps a first edition manuscript? Some antique jewelry?" He looked at me with his eyebrows raised.

"Actually, we're looking for something more rare than all that," I said. "We're collectors of magical items. For us, the rarity is important. When we have guests, we want to show them things they'd only expect to see in a Duchess's collection, things that anyone lower ranked wouldn't even think of having." I sounded like an ass, but if we could get the spiritstone without specifically asking for it, that would be best. Seeking out a spiritstone and buying one for our collection were two different things.

"I understand completely. If you'll come right this way to a private viewing room, I can show you items that I don't display to the public." Gwindle led us to one of several rooms separated from the main showroom by a thick curtain. Inside were four plush chairs and a table complete with several pairs of cloth gloves and a couple of jeweler's loupes.

Deacon and I sat while Gwindle went to collect the items. He returned and set a cloth-covered tray on the table. "I have a few things here that I think will interest you."

He folded back the cloth enough to reveal the first one: an ancient looking wand.

"This is a wand from the Mother Tree." The Mother Tree was the first tree that produced the magical wood needed for wands. "There aren't many of these floating around. This one is in such good shape because it was passed down through a sorcerer family."

Mages used wands, not sorcerers. A sorcerer family would have kept it strictly for display purposes.

"Interesting," I said politely.

Gwindle chuckled. "Now, now, Your Grace, I have more. This next one is quite the treasure, a real one-of-a-kind." He folded the cloth again and revealed a seashell. "Here we have a tide shell. Quite a rare item and heavily regulated, as you can imagine. It allows the owner to control the tides. I've only seen a few of these in my life-time. Most of the existing supply is in the hands of various govern-ments throughout Elustria. Use by a private individual, if caught, is a crime."

Ah, yes, it was only a crime if caught. The fact that rich people could willy-nilly buy this stuff confounded me. They really did play with a different set of rules than the rest of us.

"I haven't seen anything like that before, but I don't have much interest in sea magic, I'm afraid. You don't either, do you darling?" I turned to Deacon.

He shook his head. "Afraid not."

"Well then, moving on." Gwindle folded back the cloth to reveal a black stone about the size of a chicken egg. "This is a newer acquisition of mine within the last couple of days: a spiritstone."

I elbowed Deacon. "Remember that dinner party at the coast last month? This is what they were talking about." I wanted it to appear that our interest lay in one-upping our friends. I turned to Gwindle. "Is it true that spiritstones trap people's souls?"

"Quite true. In fact, this one here already holds a spirit."

I gasped wide-eyed. "That poor person! Who do you think it was?" I looked at the stone closer, as if I might see the person inside. This definitely put a crimp in our plans. If the stone already had a spirit inside it, then it couldn't hold another, as far as I knew.

"I don't know. The person who I acquired it from had gotten it for the express purpose of seeking revenge on someone. It sounded like quite a nasty affair. As soon as he used the stone, he sold it to me."

So this wasn't a person who died long ago. He was talking about someone who had, just a few days ago, been alive, walking and talking. How could he have a person's spirit trapped right here in his store and then try to sell it to someone?

"That sounds dreadful. It can't somehow get out, can it? It's like asking to be haunted." I put my hand to my chest in mortification.

Gwindle laughed. "There's no need to worry about that. The spirit can only be removed by a netherwalker."

While I had expected to get an empty spiritstone, this would have to do. We would need a netherwalker anyway, and we weren't likely to find another spiritstone.

"And what else do you have to show us?" I asked, eagerly eyeing the last bit of cloth.

"Ah, yes. Here we have one of the famed moonlight gems from the court of King Gustufson, the seventh dwarf king."

My eyes lit up at the sight of the sparkling gem, just as Gwindle intended. He'd saved the most impressive looking for last.

"Aren't moonlight gems used by elves?" Deacon asked Gwindle.

"Yes, indeed. That's why they're so rare here in sorcerer society. Your friends won't have seen many of these."

"It is quite beautiful. What magical properties does it have?" I asked.

"The elves use them because they can focus the power of the moons. That's necessary for some of their spells and rituals."

"Oh, so it doesn't have any innate magical properties of its own?" I sounded disappointed.

"The dwarves and elves would beg to differ."

"Well, we don't know any dwarves or elves."

"It does look a bit like that earring and necklace set you already have," Deacon said, appearing to subtly steer me away from it.

"That's true." I sighed and nodded. "It's beautiful, but not much of a conversation piece. Meanwhile, the spiritstone would give our friends a lot to talk about."

We weren't interested in the spiritstone for ourselves; we wanted it because other people found it desirable. If Gwindle did talk, I didn't want him to say that he'd sold a spiritstone to someone looking to use it.

"Do you know anything about the person whose spirit is in it?" I asked Gwindle. "It'll be a much better conversation piece if we can tell the story to our guests."

"I must maintain the privacy of the person who sold it to me, but I can tell you that the spirit inside the stone belonged to a sorcerer who insulted a sorceress's honor. One of her suitors, not willing to let the insult stand, captured the sorcerer's spirit and put it into the spiritstone to suffer through eternity."

That was a bunch of bullshit, though I gave him points for trying to turn it into a romantic tale.

"That is a good story. I don't know if I can get over having someone's spirit in my home. Can the spirit still do magic from in there? You said it was a sorcerer, so he doesn't need a talisman or anything. Could he curse us for keeping his spirit?" I put a little bit of fear in my voice.

"If it really bothers you, you could always pay a netherwalker to remove it. Or better yet, a deathwalker would probably pay you for the opportunity to feed off of it. There's a well-known deathwalker here in Stardowns named Althea. She lurks at the Black Talon tavern."

Deathwalker was a derogatory term for a netherwalker. Though, there was a distinction between the two. Deathwalkers got their name not just because they walked with death in the nether but because they looked like walking death from the effects of their addiction. They were nether junkies.

"See, darling, we can have the spirit removed if it bothers you." Deacon patted me on the leg then looked at Gwindle. "Though we'll stick to hiring a netherwalker. No need to mingle with the likes of a deathwalker."

"Quite right," Gwindle said.

I pursed my lips in thought, my eyes darting between the gem and the spiritstone. Then I smiled and focused on the spiritstone. "The people at the club will be so envious when we tell them we've got one."

Deacon smiled. "That's what I think." He turned to Gwindle. "We'll take the spiritstone."

I jumped in my seat and clapped my hands in excitement.

A few minutes later, and fifty thousand gold pieces poorer, we walked out of Trekov's Treasures with a spiritstone wrapped in a pretty gift box as if it were a fancy ring and not a person's spirit.

"Do you want to go to the Black Talon now or stop at the house first?" Deacon asked.

"The Black Talon. I want to see if there's any way to get this spirit back in its body." Somewhere this poor person's body sat decaying, and if there was any chance we could give him his life back, I wanted to try.

37

The Black Talon looked like the type of place one could find a deathwalker day drinking. Deacon took the lead when we entered and asked the bartender if he knew of an Althea who frequented the establishment. The bartender chuckled and gestured with his head to the end of the bar.

"What do you want with me?" a scratchy voice croaked from underneath a matted pile of gray and black hair. Althea turned her face toward Deacon, and I had to hold in a gasp. Her eyes were like two pits of black sucking in all the light around her. Her skin was an ashy gray like soot. It looked like if I scratched her cheek with my finger it would come away dusty. A skeletal hand lifted her drink to her thin lips.

And that's when the shaking became apparent. The bright green liquid in her glass splashed up the sides, never quite making it over the edge. My stomach churned as the memory of being strung out on the nether at Bubbles and Brews flashed in my mind. This was what I could have become, what I could still become if I ever let myself into the nether again.

Deacon knew the effect this could have on me. That was why he took the lead. He walked to her and tossed some gold coins on the bar. "I have a job for a deathwalker."

Althea cackled. "And you think your gold will buy me?" She looked at the bartender. "Ned, how much of a dent will this make in my tab?"

He looked at the gold coins and chuckled. "Not much."

"There you have it. I'm not moving from this bar for 'not much.'"

"No, but I bet you'll move for a hit. I have a spiritstone with a spirit in it. I need it out, but first I need to find the body it belongs to. You track the body then take the spirit out for me and I'll give you enough to pay off your tab and then some."

As soon as Deacon mentioned that he wanted her to take a spirit out of a spiritstone for him, he didn't need to say anything else. Her eyes widened and her jaw went slack. "Give me the stone."

"No, Althea," Ned said. "You take that shit outside."

She slid off the barstool and walked out of the bar without finishing her drink. When she passed by me, I was surprised by her height. Her back didn't hunch like I expected it would. It occurred to me that she wasn't nearly as old as she looked. Her appearance was simply the result of the nether. I shuddered.

When we got out on the street, she grabbed for the box I held, no doubt sensing the spiritstone in it. I snatched it away, out of her reach. "Not yet. We need to set some rules. If you want to get paid, you'll do as we say. The spirit in the stone was only put there a few days ago. We need to find the body. From what I understand, you should be able to use the stone to track the body. Is that correct?"

Althea nodded and licked her lips. "Yes. I'll need to hold the spiritstone to do it."

I opened the box and handed her the stone. "If you make one move to feed off that spirit, I won't hesitate to kill you."

Althea's lips twitched until she felt Deacon's hand close around her neck.

"I wouldn't doubt our intentions," he whispered in her ear.

Althea nodded. "I believe you."

"Good." Deacon released her neck. I had my void blade sheathed at my back, but there was no reason to let her know of it unless we needed to. It was too distinctive a weapon and would risk blowing our cover.

"Where are we heading?" I asked.

She held the spiritstone in her hand and closed her eyes. The relaxed look on her face as she delved into the nether magic resembled a child with a soother. I remembered that itch and the subsequent relief.

I shook my head. I couldn't let myself think about it. The allure was too great. Entertaining it for a second could be my ruin.

"He's a sorcerer. His body is that way." She opened her eyes and pointed to the east. "Outside of town. I can see it."

"If you can see it, can you port us there?" I asked.

She closed her eyes again then nodded. "Yes, it's clear enough for that."

We joined hands, and she took us to the spot. We stood on a green hill, far enough from Stardowns that the city was a speck in the distance. Althea held out the spiritstone in front of her, letting it guide her to the exact location of the body. We walked farther up the hill until she stopped. The ground cut away to a ravine about ten feet deep. A body lay sprawled at the bottom.

Deacon's hand flew to his nose, and I caught a whiff of it a second later. Decaying death. The smell didn't appear to affect Althea. She was too absorbed in the stone. I covered my nose with the back of my hand and peered at the body.

"I don't see any obvious injuries," I said. "Even if he fell down here, it wouldn't be fatal. The man wasn't killed; his spirit was just removed from his body. So, in theory, if his spirit goes back inside, he should be able to be healed." I looked at Deacon for his opinion.

He looked ready to puke, and I couldn't blame him. Healing this sorcerer would mean getting close to the body and licking or breathing on it. "I can try, but I can't give any guarantees."

That was the best we could do. "All right, Althea, release the spirit."

She closed her eyes and covered the stone with her hands. Her lips moved as she murmured whatever spell she needed. A white smoky wisp seeped from the stone and floated into the air. Althea maintained a strict concentration until the wisp was completely free.

Then she pursed her lips and inhaled, sucking the wisp into her.

"No!" I yelled.

Deacon tackled her to the ground as the wisp fought to free itself. I grabbed her jaw, keeping her mouth open so she couldn't swallow. With Deacon's help, I rolled her to her side and Deacon pounded her back, forcing her to cough up the wisp.

Once free of her mouth, the wisp flew to the body but recoiled before entering. I grabbed the spiritstone from the ground where Althea had dropped it then focused my attention back on the deathwalker. "You're lucky you're alive."

We'd threatened to kill her, but I was glad we hadn't. I couldn't stand in judgment of this woman. What she'd attempted was wrong, but I knew the force of addiction, the allure of the nether.

"Get out of here before we follow through with our promise to kill you," Deacon said, standing and releasing Althea.

She scrambled to her feet and scowled at both of us. "You think you're so much better than me, but you wanted to put that man's spirit back in a decaying body for your own purposes. When you've walked with death as much as I have, you know that death is not the worst thing in the world."

Before we could respond, she ported away.

Deacon shook his head. "Good riddance. At least we stopped her in time." Then he looked at me, saw the expression on my face, felt my emotions. "You could never be like her."

"I was her." Deacon didn't see it because he loved me. He knew who I was before my nether addiction, and he saw me now. At my worst, he had still loved me, and that made it easy for him to forget how bad I'd gotten. I hadn't been addicted long enough to wear out the patience of my loved ones.

Althea may have been an ass before she became a deathwalker. For all I knew, she was a genuinely bad person and the world would be better off if we killed her. But I didn't know, and that was the point. I only knew that she was a disturbing glimpse into my future should I ever succumb to the nether again.

Something ran into my leg and thumped my foot. I looked down to see a white rabbit.

Deacon saw it too. "Aww, that's cute."

I swear the rabbit glared at him. It hit my leg and dashed off to the edge of the ravine. Then it came back and repeated the process. This time, Deacon and I followed.

We both peered over the edge and registered the sight of the still decaying body, not a twitch of movement. The wisp hadn't gone into the body.

The rabbit thumped my foot several times in quick succession, looked at the body, then looked at me.

I met Deacon's eyes to see if he understood, but I saw the same confusion there that I felt. The rabbit jumped furiously in place, and realization dawned on both of us at the same time. When I looked directly at the rabbit, he stopped jumping and stared right in my eyes.

I could think of only one thing to say. "Fuck."

38

"**Y**ou don't think he could actually be in a rabbit, do you?" Deacon asked.

The rabbit nodded his head vigorously. I couldn't tear my eyes away from it. A sorcerer's spirit was inside a rabbit. I didn't know how to react to that.

"It appears that's what happened." I had enough to do. I drew the line at taking on the plight of a sorcerer who chose to inhabit a rabbit instead of his own body. I wasn't the one who put him in that spiritstone, and I did my best to help him.

The rabbit stood on his hind legs and then launched himself on the ground, thumping his front feet on the grass. His intent was unmistakable. He was demanding we do something.

I knelt down to his level and spoke directly to him. "You could have gone into your body, but you didn't. Now, I don't blame you. But you made your choice, and now you have to live with it."

I stood up, and the rabbit thumped my foot with one of his back feet.

"Do you want to just port us back to the house?" Deacon asked.

"I think we should go to Emma's. We need to signal the others that we got the spiritstone and come up with a plan. I don't want to use Althea again. We can't trust her."

I had another reason for wanting to go to Emma's. After my revelation last night, I wanted to talk to Deacon without our glamours, and Emma's was the only place in Elustria we could do that. Her garden would give us privacy and a somewhat romantic backdrop.

"Sounds good. There's no real reason to go back to the house."

I grabbed Deacon's hand and checked to make sure the spiritstone was still in my pocket. But before I could teleport us, the rabbit jumped on my foot and wrapped himself around my leg.

"Go away." I shook my leg, but the rabbit refused to let go.

"Can't you just port without him?" Deacon asked.

Technically, I could, but it wasn't easy to choose to port Deacon but not another living creature touching me. I'd rather he leave on his own. "Sure." I leaned down slightly and raised my voice. "You hear that? I'm going to port away without you, but I'm not very good at it. If I were you, I'd let go. Otherwise, you may end up half here and half where we're going."

The rabbit drew his head back, and I thought for a moment I'd gotten through to him. Then he opened his mouth wide and clamped down on my calf, his blunt teeth piercing my skin.

"Oww! You little shit." It was the best way to ensure that when I ported, all of him would come too. He was literally attached to me. "Let go!"

I shook my leg, and he lost his hold on me, which just caused him to sink his teeth in deeper as I flung his body to and fro. Deacon's laughter stopped me long enough to glare at him. "You think this is funny?"

"It may be the funniest thing I've ever seen." Deacon kept laughing, and I knew I wouldn't be able to resume trying to shake off the rabbit without succumbing to laughter.

I looked down at the little guy and couldn't bring myself to use magic to forcefully remove him. "All right. Fine. You can come. But

I'm calling you Fluffy." I bent down to scoop him up, and he finally let go of my calf. "I can see now why someone put you in a spiritstone."

Fluffy flattened his ears and looked up at me with wide, pathetic eyes. I could practically see his chin wobble and giant cartoon teardrops forming. I sighed. "That was mean. I'm sorry. I'm sure you were an absolute delight before you turned into a carnivorous rabbit."

Fluffy snuggled against my chest and Deacon took my free hand. I ported the three of us to right outside Emma's house. When we arrived, I put Fluffy down, and Deacon bent to look at my leg. He stuck out his tongue and licked the wound, using his power to heal it. His touch sent a thrill through me and reminded me of the real reason I'd wanted to come here.

I removed my glamour and stretched.

"Wait, do you really think it's a good idea to let him see us?" Deacon asked, gesturing to Fluffy.

"He's a rabbit. Who's he going to tell?"

"Can't he be enchanted to speak?"

Deacon was thinking of Pint. "No, not in this instance. Or at least I don't think so. If he can be, it won't be until all of this is long over."

Satisfied, Deacon removed his glamour, and I smiled. I'd missed him.

"Why are you looking at me like that?" Deacon eyed me curiously.

I could barely contain myself. Butterflies erupted in my stomach when I realized that Deacon could really be mine. Ever since I came to my conclusion last night, I'd been bursting to tell him.

"Nadiya! Deacon! How long have you been standing there?" Emma asked from the doorway to her cottage.

"Not long," Deacon said. "We need to signal the others. There have been some developments."

"Oh?" Emma looked between the two of us. I saw in her eyes that she sensed she interrupted something.

To avoid any further questions, I picked up Fluffy and presented him to her. "Here, do you want a rabbit? His name's Fluffy."

"Oh, look at him!" Emma brushed her nose against Fluffy's. "He's so cute."

"Yeah, but he's also a bit of an ass, fair warning." The warning was pointless. It was impossible for anyone to be mean to Emma. "Would you mind sending the signal for us? Deacon and I need to debrief."

Deacon looked at me, confused, but I ignored him.

"Sure." She looked between us again and then went inside, carrying Fluffy.

"Do you want to walk around the garden?" I asked Deacon.

"Sure," he said, puzzled.

I'd never felt so nervous in my life, and he had to feel it. I knew what I wanted. It was so clear to me that I couldn't believe I'd ever convinced myself that I didn't want to bond to Deacon.

Walking with him, I couldn't come up with the words to articulate what I wanted to say. What did I want to say? That I loved him? That I couldn't stand the thought of not being bonded to him for one more second?

Yes to it all. But my mouth couldn't say the words. Once I did, they'd be out there. I couldn't take them back. If he turned me down, I couldn't laugh and say I was just kidding. It hit me that I was about to say the most honest words I'd ever spoken, and I didn't know what would happen next. I'd be exposing myself in a way I never had before. No other relationship in my life had ever felt this way.

After a few turns around the garden, Deacon stopped me with his hand on my arm. "What's going on? I'm worried." His worry mixed with my nerves and made something anxiety-inducing. It made it even more difficult to speak. "Was Fluffy rabid?"

The exasperation in his voice as he searched for an explanation made me burst out laughing, and the tension broke. "No, of course not. Or at least, I don't think so. Even if he was, I don't think you can tell this soon."

"Then what is it?" He turned me to face him, and I looked up into his eyes. Those gorgeous green eyes. I wanted him to look at me forever. I wanted those eyes to move south, to savor every inch of my body.

My knees went weak.

"Do you want to sit down?" I asked, moving to the lone bench in the garden.

Deacon followed me and put a hand on my knee when we sat. "Whatever it is, Nadiya, you can tell me."

I knew that. Of course I did. But I couldn't look him in the eye at the same time. I didn't want to see his immediate reaction. I'd already be able to feel it through our bond. I didn't want to see him look at me like I was foolish or too late. I didn't want to see him look at me with pity if I'd somehow misjudged him or if his feelings had changed and he only wanted to bond because of the prophecy. I should trust him, and I did. I knew he wouldn't intentionally hurt me, but asking him to mask his immediate reaction to spare my feelings was too much.

I looked away, focusing on a flower bush. It was the only way I could get through this.

"Last night, I realized something, and now I feel like an idiot." To Deacon's credit, he didn't say anything, and that made me love him even more. He could tell how difficult this was for me, and he gave me space to say what I needed to. "It was a wonderful night. I don't know that I've ever had that much fun before. We had a good time at our anointing celebration, but that had the weight of prophecy around it. Last night was just us, or at least as much of us as possible when glamoured. It was wonderful and sad at the same time because I knew that could never be our life."

I felt recognition and understanding through our bond. Out of the corner of my eye, I snuck a look at him, and he appeared patient even though I was rambling. "Sometimes I wonder what life would be like if I hadn't gone into this line of work. Would we have met? Would you have given me a second glance?"

"Yes." Deacon's answer startled me into facing him. I'd meant it as a rhetorical question. "There is no alternate universe in which I would have simply let you walk by me and not done everything in my power to get to know you."

It was a sweet thought, one that I knew he believed, which made it even sweeter. "The point is, we can never know. This is the life we have. Our future is missions, spying, killing. If everything works out the way the prophecy says it will, I'm going to die sooner rather than later. I don't want to leave you. I don't want to hurt you like that. But I've realized that I'm too damn selfish. I can't stand the pain of not being with you any longer, of not being yours, of not walking in the world knowing that I'm tied to you as completely as a person can be. So I don't want to bond to you because of the prophecy, I want to bond in spite of it. But I—"

I was going to say that I understood if he didn't want to, if he had changed his mind, if it was all about the prophecy for him now, but I didn't get a chance. Deacon stood and lifted me into his arms, twirling me around and silencing me with a kiss. And through that kiss he transformed the nerves in the pit of my stomach into beams of joy.

After he set me down, he asked, "When do you want to do it?"

I could see the nervous hesitancy in his eyes as he asked the question. If I couldn't feel his emotions, it would be easy to misinterpret. He wasn't nervous about bonding, he was nervous about scaring me away with his eagerness. "As soon as possible. I don't want to go another minute without being bonded if I don't have to. We just need to wait for Sybil and Alistair to get here."

Alistair was the closest thing to family I had. I needed him to be my witness. Then I realized Deacon may not want to do it right away. He'd been thinking of this a lot longer than I had, and he might have his own ideas of how it should happen. I couldn't believe I'd been so selfish. "I'm sorry, you probably have people you want at the ceremony too. Your sisters?"

A soft smile lifted Deacon's lips. "No, I don't need anyone here. I just need you. This is our story. I don't even need Sybil to be the one to do it."

"Well, I think Sybil would kill me if I let anyone else bond us. Seriously. She'd make that whole part of the prophecy come true all on her own." I regretted it as soon as I said it. I didn't want to think about the prophecy or my death. This was a happy occasion. The happiest.

Deacon took it in stride and laughed. "You're probably right. I guess we should go inside and share our news while we wait for her and Alistair."

"Or we could kiss again," I said, my eyebrows raised in question.

Deacon obliged, and I sank into the kiss, relishing this stolen moment until we both felt the magic of a portal opening in Emma's living room.

39

When we walked into Emma's house, Sybil couldn't contain herself. She threw her arms around me in a hug and squealed. "You finally did it. You finally agreed to be bonded."

I looked over her shoulder at Deacon in confusion. "How did you know?"

She pulled back and looked at me with a little bashful blush. "I know I should have waited for you to share, that's the polite thing, but I couldn't help it. I told you that as the Oracle I'm in tune with your emotions. That strong mix of nerves and excitement and a signal to meet you here, what else could it be?"

"So it's true?" Alistair asked from behind her.

I walked around Sybil so I could face my handler, the man who'd been at times like an older brother and at times a father figure to me. "Yes."

Alistair nodded. "And you're doing this because you want to? Not because of the prophecy?"

"I'm doing it because I don't want to live in a world where I'm not bonded to him."

"Good girl," he said and kissed me on my forehead.

Emma and Philip congratulated us, and then Emma asked, "When are you planning to have the ceremony?"

"I know the timing isn't great with everything going on, but we'd like to be bonded as soon as possible." I looked at Sybil and Alistair, expecting them to tell me to wait until Malev was dead, that this was too much of a distraction.

"The timing is perfect," Sybil said. "It's important that you're bonded. It's essential to the prophecy and your mission."

Well, wasn't that romantic. However, Sybil knew how important my work was to me, and she likely thought it would help me not feel too self-indulgent for this break.

"We're happy to do it here, today," I said. I had to contain my smile at the thought of going to bed tonight bonded to Deacon. I may have felt like a lovesick fool, but I didn't want to look like one.

"The cuff needs to be off for the ceremony," Sybil said. "Nothing can restrain your magics."

Good, I didn't want to wear it. But that presented a problem. "Then we need to find somewhere else to do it. I can't leave my imprint here and endanger you." I looked at Emma and Philip. They had already been so gracious and taken risks for us. Leaving my imprint here would put a target on their house.

"Nonsense," Emma said. "This is your bonding ceremony. It should happen where you're comfortable and surrounded by loved ones. If you'd rather be bonded somewhere else, fine, but don't let something as silly as leaving your imprint behind be the reason you don't do it here. We're family. We'd be proud to have your imprint here. Besides, it's all going to be moot soon when you kill the fae queen."

It was decided, and everyone went into a flurry of action preparing for the ceremony. Sybil went back to Earth to collect Pint. Emma started preparing a celebratory dinner. Philip booked a room for him and Emma at an inn in the nearest village and prepared the guest bedroom. As a present, they were letting us use their home for the night. It was the only way we'd be able to consummate our bond without glamour or the cuff.

And that was how I ended up barefoot in Emma's garden, facing Deacon, knowing that prophecy or no, everything in my life had led up to this moment. Tradition dictated that the bride and groom stand barefoot on Elustrian soil. It connected us to the magic of our world. The entire bonding ceremony was about uniting our magics.

Sybil grabbed a dress for me when she went to get Pint. At first, I didn't think I had anything that I wanted to wear. The dresses at my apartment weren't me. They were the mission. I'd worn them largely to seduce other men into telling me what I wanted. Then I remembered a sleeveless lavender dress I'd gotten to wear with Harry to brunch. It fell just below my knees and was light and flowy. It was the only piece of clothing I'd bought because I liked it and not because it served some utilitarian purpose.

Deacon wore linen pants and shirt, with the sleeves rolled up to the elbow, revealing muscular arms that I couldn't stop picturing doing delicious things to me. The sly grin on his face showed he knew exactly the effect his appearance had on me. But with the way his eyes lit when he saw me, I knew I was having the same effect on him.

I had worried that I wouldn't be able to focus in the moment, that thoughts of our mission, Malev, Trevor, or even my previous engagement to Julien would interfere. But it proved a foolish fear. In that moment, I could think of nothing other than Deacon. The rest of the world melted away. There was no time before that moment. There was no future that wasn't wrapped up in him. We were a team, and we were stronger for it. Whatever came our way, I knew it would be easier to bear with him by my side.

We stood facing each other, holding hands, in front of Sybil and our small gathering of friends. I could feel their love and support in the air, but I couldn't tear my eyes away from Deacon's face. His green eyes were so full of love and desire. His face was the most familiar and comforting sight in the world. I wanted more than anything to kiss him, but Sybil was speaking, welcoming everyone to the ceremony, and it would be rude.

My attention shifted to Sybil when she said my name.

"Nataliana Kyrell, do you come here today of your own free will to be bonded to Deacon Wyvern?"

"Aye, of my own free will." When I answered, I could feel Deacon's joy, and I matched it with my own. More than anything, I needed him to know that I was here today for no reason other than to bond myself to him.

"Deacon Wyvern, do you come here today of your own free will to be bonded to Nataliana Kyrell?"

"Aye, of my own free will." He squeezed my hands as he answered.

Sybil handed me a bonding knife. Technically, any knife could serve as a bonding knife, but this one was clearly made for the purpose. The traditional gold handle was ornately carved with the seven moons of Elustria and vines of flowers connecting them together. A gold handle that wouldn't tarnish over time was considered lucky. The small diamond blade was impractical for regular use, but it made the sharp cuts necessary for the ceremony. It wouldn't be used for anything else. I wondered where Sybil had gotten one on such short notice.

Behind Sybil, Alistair looked at me with so much love in his eyes that I knew blood couldn't make a tighter family relation. Emma and Philip held hands, and Emma rested her head on Philip's shoulder. She glanced up at him with nostalgia. It was then that I knew the bonding knife came from them. It was their family's, used to bond Emma and Philip. I hadn't expected such a meaningful gesture.

"Thank you," I said to Sybil, then I made eye contact with Emma. "Thank you." She nodded and smiled, encouraging me to the next step.

I held up my hand and drew the diamond blade down my palm. I squeezed a drop of blood out onto the ground and then presented my hand palm up while blood beaded along the cut. I handed the knife to Deacon, and he did the same.

As a shifter, Deacon had to actively prevent his magic from healing the simple cut. He handed the knife to Sybil, and we stood facing her, our sliced palms up and hands touching so our cuts formed one line. Sybil took a cord braided from Elustrian fiber with magical filaments in it and placed it across the cuts on our palms.

Deacon and I closed our hands, squeezing the cord until it soaked up our blood like a wick. Then we kept clenching our hands, forcing more blood out of our wounds until the magic in my blood mingled with the magic in Deacon's.

When Deacon's magic touched mine, it was the most intimate feeling I'd ever experienced. His magic knew me, saw me, explored me in ways I didn't know possible. As the bonding happened, not only did his magic mix with mine, but that strange third magic—the one that came from the anointing and allowed us to feel some magical bond without being bonded—mixed and mingled with our magics too. As his magic flowed through the filament and filled my body, it felt like rays of sunshine originating deep inside me and bursting out in all directions.

"Your magics have bonded, strengthening each other, forming a magic mightier than the two parts," Sybil said. When a couple bonded, their magics did indeed get stronger, more potent. They fed off each other as long as the relationship was healthy. If an imbalance occurred, one magic could just as easily act as a parasite as we saw with Malev and Kelar, ruining the symbiotic relationship. But together, the magics of two bonded people could help move them toward their goals.

Sybil removed the cord, and Deacon and I held hands, our smarting palms a sign of what we'd done. Deacon leaned down and kissed me. Up until that moment, I had never experienced true joy.

"I wish you could know how much I love you." Deacon's voice filled my head. It so startled me that I pulled back.

"What?" I said in my mind.

"You can hear me?" Deacon's brow furrowed in confusion.

We both turned to Sybil, who grinned fanatically at us. "I told you you needed to bond."

40

DEACON

"You knew this would happen?" Nadiya said to Sybil.

Sybil shrugged. "I had a suspicion."

She must have known from our expressions what was happening. It made sense, a kind of extension of the bond we already shared from the anointing. Nadiya's eyes were furious. She hated it anytime someone kept something from her that directly affected her.

"It's all right. All that matters is that we're bonded now," I told her.

The sound of my voice in her mind seemed to calm her. *"This would have been useful to have earlier."*

"Yes, but you wouldn't have wanted it that way." I was glad Sybil had kept this information from us. If we had known, we might have bonded out of duty, to help us succeed in our mission, and I wouldn't have liked that. I wouldn't trade the knowledge that Nadiya wanted me, Deacon Wyvern, the bastard who had spent his life in exile, for anything in the world. Her love was the most precious thing in my possession. I couldn't imagine trading the security of it for an advantage on a mission.

What's more, I knew she felt the same way. I didn't need her to articulate it. I saw through this performance she put on. Her indignation was real, but it came from a lifetime of being tossed to and fro by the people above her. So much of her life had been dictated by others that she was desperate for every bit of control.

I took her chin and turned her face to me. Her face. I didn't think I'd ever get used to seeing it, certainly not seeing the way she softened for me. *"We're one now. Our destiny is our choosing. We can't live in the past, especially when we have so much future to live for."*

Her lips parted as I spoke to her mind, and I couldn't help it. I kissed her. Our friends cheered for us, and Nadiya melted into my love in a way that made me feel so damn lucky.

Emma ushered us all into the house and to a celebratory meal. On our way inside, Pint landed on my shoulder, and Alistair took Nadiya away for a few words.

"I guess I have to welcome you to the family for her sake," Pint said.

I didn't take his dislike of me personally. I understood. He only wanted what was best for Nadiya. In that, our interests were aligned. But he was loath to trust anyone else with her happiness. "Thank you, Pint."

"But just so we're clear, I only like you as long as you make her happy. The minute that changes, you'll find yourself on the wrong side of me. I know I look small, but I am pure dragon. You'd be amazed how much fire I can breathe at a time. You may think you're the only one who can take care of her, but I took care of her through four partners and giving her heart to the wrong man once already. I'm more than capable."

"I know you are," I said, and I meant it. Pint and I saw eye to eye more than he thought. I wished I had been able to do as I wanted with Julien, but I was playing the long game. I wanted Nadiya's heart, and I knew I could never get that by betraying her trust. As much as I thought it was my place to take that asshole down a peg or two, Nadiya didn't agree. Loving her meant respecting her, and it had paid off in the end.

When Nadiya returned to my side, she had tears in her eyes. A quick check of our bond assured me they were happy tears with just a dash of melancholy. She took my hand as we sat at the table and Emma passed the food around.

"Are you all right?" I asked.

"Yes, better than I ever thought I'd be." She gave me a stunning smile that took my breath away.

As long as she was fine, I didn't mind that she had secrets with Alistair. They had nearly a lifetime together. He would always have secrets with her, parts of her life that would never be mine. He had her past, but I had her future.

"Emma, this is wonderful. I can't believe you put this together so quickly for us. Thank you," Nadiya said once all the food was served.

Emma brushed off the compliment. "It's my pleasure. We've needed good news to celebrate."

The strength of women amazed me. Deep in her eyes lurked the shadow of grief from her daughter's passing, yet she was still capable of doing so much for others, of celebrating another's happiness.

Philip raised his glass. "And thank you two for bonding. According to Sybil here, if you didn't, the world would end in some disaster."

Everyone around the table laughed except for Sybil. "Well, not the end of the world exactly. It would have still existed in some dystopian form."

"Ah, well thank you for saving us from a dystopian hellscape." Philip raised his glass to me.

"I believe that thanks goes to Nadiya." I raised my glass to her. "I'm not the one who needed convincing."

"Bit of revisionist history there," she said. To the table she raised her glass. "As they say on Earth, better late than never."

"Hear, hear," Alistair said and downed his drink.

Throughout dinner, I couldn't stop looking at her. She threw her head back and laughed at something Alistair said, or was it

Pint? I didn't know. All I wanted to do was take Nadiya to the bed I knew waited for us and finally pleasure her the way I'd wanted to since I met her.

When Sybil had first come to me, I had expected to do my duty to the prophecy. I'd never expected to have a life that was my own. And then I saw Nadiya. I could still remember the sight of her when those elevator doors opened in Las Vegas. Her shock at my magic gave me a chance to compose myself without drawing attention. It was then that I knew I was in danger of falling in love.

But this was the family she needed. I couldn't take her away from them to satisfy my lust, especially when I didn't know when or even if she would get this chance again. I could give her myself over and over every night of our lives, but evenings with family around a dinner table were always going to be a rarity for us.

When the food was finished, we all retired to the living room with drinks in hand. The suns had set, and the atmosphere was cozy until a banging on the door startled us.

My mood immediately shifted as I scanned my awareness for any foreign magics. Nothing smelled or felt out of the ordinary. My eyes went to Nadiya's wrist, and I thought about her cuff sitting in the guest room.

"You all need to calm down," Sybil said to the room as she skipped to the door and flung it open. "Aww! It's a bunny rabbit!" She scooped Fluffy up and cuddled him as I relaxed back into my seat.

"Excuse me?" Pint said, his jealousy coming out. He was so obviously smitten with Sybil that I actually pitied him, though I'd be careful never to let him know.

Emma, noticing Pint's jealousy, spoke up. "Yes, he's ours. His name's Fluffy."

Philip turned to Emma in surprise. "He is?"

"Yes, Nadiya gave him to us."

"That's actually a long story that I really should let you know about," Nadiya said, looking at Alistair and Sybil.

I didn't want work to mar this night, but it wasn't my place to say anything. We'd all made commitments to something bigger than ourselves. Part of being with Nadiya was respecting that. She may be my bonded mate now, but she was still the Dragon Fae.

Alistair held up his hand to stop Nadiya. "Nope. Everyone, that's our cue. Time to leave."

"What?" Nadiya said, confused.

Alistair walked over to her and gave her a kiss on the forehead. "It is your bonding night. We aren't bringing work into it. Besides, I think we've all tortured you and Deacon long enough."

"I'm surprised he didn't kick us all out already," Philip said as he grabbed an overnight bag he had packed for himself and Emma. "There's a reason we traditionally eat before the bonding ceremony and then have a celebratory luncheon the next day."

"You all need to stop teasing him just because he has better manners than all of you. Of course he wouldn't kick us out of our own home," Emma admonished them. "I thought it was a lovely improvised celebration."

I didn't mind their teasing. Yes, I was eager to consummate our bond, but I wouldn't trade this night and Nadiya's obvious joy for anything.

Emma came over to me and Nadiya, and we stood to meet her. She placed one hand on my arm and the other on Nadiya's. "May you both have joy. Cherish it. Every moment."

"Thank you, Emma, for all of this. For making sure Nadiya got the celebration she deserves."

"You're welcome. None of us knows what tomorrow brings."

She was right. I looked forward to tonight, but I held no romantic notions that we'd have a leisurely morning in bed. We were lucky enough to be getting tonight.

Emma joined Philip at the door and left, followed by Alistair. Sybil carried Fluffy out and then called behind her for Pint.

The tiny dragon looked at us then flew to Nadiya. "Are you happy?"

Nadiya's smile radiated more warmth than Elustria's two suns. "Yes. It's different this time."

Pint nodded. "Then I'm happy for you."

Nadiya kissed him on the head. "You know this doesn't change the place you have in my heart."

Pint grunted. "Of course not." Then he flew in front of me. "I'm watching you, shifter. Take care of her."

I looked him straight in the eye. He may be small, and Nadiya could protect herself physically, but I knew Pint had watched over her heart and taken care of her as only a close friend could. "You have my word."

Satisfied, Pint flew to the door, and Sybil gave us a little wave as she shut it behind them.

And just like that, I was alone with my bonded mate for the first time.

41

NADIYA

erves and excitement warred in my stomach. It didn't make any sense. I'd been alone with Deacon plenty, especially on this mission. However, once the door shut behind Sybil, I was distinctly aware that things had changed. I wasn't alone with Deacon. I was with my mate, bonded to me forever.

And we still had one last step of the bonding ritual to perform. Only during the open vulnerability of physical intimacy would our magics complete the bonding.

I'd had sex with more men than I could count and a few women as well. Some might even have called me a whore. Why then did I feel like a blushing virgin in front of Deacon?

I knew this experience was going to be different than all the others. It would complete our bonding. It didn't help my nerves that this was also our first time together. Most couples had sex before their bonding. Our situation had been different because of the anointing. It wouldn't have been possible for us to have sex without it bonding our magics.

Speaking of magic, mine roared through my veins, racing to find its new half. I may have been nervous, but my magic had no hesitation.

"Shh. It's all right. There's no need to be nervous."

Shit, I'd forgotten that he'd feel all this through our bond. I panicked.

"Nadiya," Deacon said aloud. "Look at me."

I did, for the first time since everyone had left. It did nothing for my nerves.

"We don't have to do this tonight if you don't want to."

Fuck, how had I screwed this up so badly that he didn't know I wanted him more than anything?

Deacon chuckled. "You need to take a breath and think about what you want."

I wanted him near me, closer. For some unfathomable reason he still stood several feet away.

Without me saying anything, Deacon did exactly what I wanted. If this was a preview of things to come, I was in for quite a treat tonight. He tucked a strand of hair behind my ear and cupped my face with his hand. When I looked up to meet his eyes, I saw something I'd never seen in a lover's face before.

Total acceptance.

And that's when I realized: my nerves came from not knowing how to act. In every sexual encounter I'd had, I'd always played a role. Even with Julien I was trying to be the woman he wanted. But with Deacon, I didn't need the artifice. I only needed to be myself. In that way, it was a first. This would be the first time I'd have sex as myself.

I lifted my chin and met his lips. His kiss started soft and gentle, almost shy, testing boundaries to see how fast and far I wanted to go. I wrapped my arms around him and plunged my tongue into his mouth, not because I wanted to speed things up—though I did—but because I couldn't control myself anymore. This was the first time we'd kissed knowing we wouldn't have to stop.

Deacon didn't need any more invitation than that. He pulled me to him with a desperate fierceness that would have scared me if I didn't feel the same. My magic churned in my veins, rushing to every point where skin touched skin, frustrated by our clothed state. It was as if our magics were magnets, seeking each other out. Still barefoot from the ceremony, I placed my feet on his just to have another point of contact.

Deacon ran his hands down my back to my ass, grabbing hold, pushing my pelvis against his erection. He pulled his mouth from mine and latched onto my neck, sucking right below my ear with an intensity that would leave a mark. Shivers ran all along that side of my body. When he finished, a little burst of healing magic danced across the skin he'd just kissed. Through the haze of my desire I realized: Deacon could heal us. His magic would remove any marks from our skin that we didn't want visible.

The heat of my magic and lust surged as I considered the possibilities. I couldn't keep my mouth off of him any longer. I licked down the curve of his neck and barely controlled myself as I bit down on that lovely bit of flesh where neck gave way to shoulder. Deacon growled and thrust his hips. His pleasure surged through our bond.

Deacon's hands slid a couple of inches down to my thighs and nudged me up. My legs obediently wrapped around him, and he took us to the bedroom, unzipping my dress as we went.

"This isn't quite the sweet romantic lovemaking I had in mind for our first time," Deacon said, a note of apology buried in his rough tone.

I wanted to tell him to shut up and fuck me, but I thought better of being quite so desperate. *"I don't want sweet and romantic. I want you. I want you in me. I want every inch of my skin touching every inch of yours. We can take it slow next time. I'll let you do every sweet romantic thing you want next time, but my magic's going to tear me to shreds if I don't feel you inside me."*

It wasn't an exaggeration. For the first time I doubted the well-known fact that a person's magic couldn't kill them, because my magic seemed intent on getting to Deacon even if it had to rip through me to get there.

Another surge of Deacon's pleasure filled our bond at my

words. He pulled off my dress as he sat me on the bed, revealing my black lace underwear. Normally I'd take a moment to enjoy the hungry look in his eyes, but I wanted him to consume me.

When he crawled on top of me, I pulled off his shirt and gasped at the sight. I'd seen his bare chest before, marveled at the perfection that was only amplified by a pale patch of scar where he'd sacrificed his skin to make my cuff. But this time I wasn't limited to just looking.

I grabbed his biceps, squeezing the firm muscle I found there. Lifting my head, I kissed his scar, licking and then sucking it. I released the skin and moved to a spot just an inch away. I wanted to litter his entire chest with kisses.

Deacon reached around me and unclasped my bra. I let go of his arms only long enough for him to pull it away and discard it on the floor. I tried to resume my kissing, but Deacon wasn't having it. He pushed me back on the bed and roughly grabbed my left breast, massaging it in his hand, driving me crazy. His fingertips brushed across my nipple and I arched my back, begging for more.

He obliged, licking a line up the center of my chest and then flicking my right nipple with his tongue. Supporting his weight on his forearms, he took my right breast in his hand and covered it with his mouth. His tongue swirled around my nipple and then flicked it. My hips bucked against him as if they had a will of their own, and Deacon answered with a throaty chuckle.

His lips closed around my nipple and pulled, my hips rising with his mouth. Deacon chuckled again and released my nipple. He looked at my breast as if it were the most perfect thing in the world, then licked it and sucked on my nipple again. All the while he continued playing with my left breast. I'd never realized that I could get so close to the edge just from this. My panties were already soaked, and he still had his pants on.

I found myself in the horrible dilemma of not wanting him to stop but also needing him inside me. Deacon smiled, "Is there something you want?"

I couldn't take his teasing. I arched my back into him, distracting him so I could roll him onto his back in one quick motion. I straddled his hips, and fire leapt in his eyes when he looked up at me. Keeping my eyes on his, I reached down and lowered his pants, taking his cock in my hand. I squeezed the silky hardness and licked my lips. I wanted him everywhere, to taste him, to breathe him in. Deacon's eyes dilated as he watched my lips.

"Unlike some people, I'm not a tease," I said, then I went down on him, taking him in my mouth. It was his turn to buck his hips.

My magic swirled, approving of this new direction. Deacon's hand rested on my head, then his fingers combed into my hair for a second before he formed a fist. *"Stop."* His voice sounded strained in my mind.

I crawled up his body, and he flipped us around, kicking off his pants and sliding my panties down until they fell to the floor. He ran his hands down my body then buried his face between my legs. The first swipe of his tongue had me opening my legs wider. The rush of the room's cool air on my sex, the delicious probing rhythm of his tongue, the pent up desire, and my swirling magic all coalesced at my clit and exploded into a thousands lights.

My back arched violently, wrenched with the spasms of my climax. My knees snapped shut, trapping Deacon's head. This was it, my magic really would kill me.

Deacon laughed. *"You're not dead. I'll prove it to you."*

My orgasm receded and my legs relaxed, freeing Deacon who licked his lips as he climbed up to kiss my mouth. His hand reached down and steered his cock to my entrance. Waves of pleasure still washed over me. He waited until they'd subsided just enough, then he pushed inside me.

Hungry for him, my body clamped down, never wanting him to leave.

He pulled away from my lips and gasped above me. *"I won't be able to last if you do that."*

"I think you've waited long enough."

He answered in a growl. Then he thrust twice and pulled out. I felt bereft at the emptiness and couldn't control the little pout that escaped my mouth.

The head of his cock returned to my entrance. Deacon leaned over me again. His mouth descended onto mine, his eyes so wide and hungry that I thought he'd devour me.

Deacon's hips moved. He slid his cock up my slit and over my clit then back down again. By the third stroke, he'd mastered the amount of pressure, friction, and time that produced the most blinding pleasure. Then he slipped inside me again. A few thrusts and he pulled out. Then he repeated the process over and over until I once again danced on the edge of oblivion.

He entered me, and his hand reached down and massaged right around my clit, never touching the ball of nerves directly. His pace got faster, more desperate as he lost control. My hips met his frenzied rhythm. My breath came in short gasps. Everything inside—blood, magic, lust, love—crescendoed.

Deacon's fingers moved down, and his thumb pressed directly on my clit. This orgasm ripped through me more violently than the last. My entire body shuddered as my magic grabbed hold of Deacon and refused to let go. He moaned above me as he thrust frantically a few times then came, his magic washing over me, crashing into my magic, weaving and dancing together. The waves of my orgasm stimulated the waves of his.

Deacon rolled beside me and held me to him. He tried to pull out, but I clenched my muscles, not wanting him to leave me empty. He surrendered, and we lay in the afterglow of our lovemaking, breathing heavily, the occasional aftershocks of our orgasms running through us. Our magics had settled into a warm, heavy peace, like a deep, tranquil body of water.

"That was the bonding, right?" I finally asked.

"If you're asking if I've ever had sex that was in the same realm as that experience, the answer is no," Deacon said as his breathing slowed.

"Good. I was getting worried that I hadn't known what I was doing before."

Deacon laughed. "I doubt you've ever had any complaints."

"That's true." Though, most of the men I bedded ended up dead. I propped myself up on my elbow and smirked at Deacon. He raised his eyebrows, intrigued. "So, how long until you're ready to show me sweet and romantic?"

Deacon growled, and I spent the rest of the night learning the meaning of stamina.

42

DEACON

Magic woke me in the morning. I guessed someone had sent us a message, likely Emma or Alistair. Nadiya still slept beside me. She was rolled onto her side with her back to me, giving me a lovely view of the naked curve of her hip. The knowledge that I could put my hand on her waist if I wanted, that I could bury my nose in her hair and nuzzle at her ear until she woke up, that I could get her to roll over onto her back and let me touch her breasts, nestle myself between her legs, it was an intoxicating feeling unlike anything else I'd experienced. That knowledge gave me comfort, security, and the strength to resist.

We'd had our stolen night. I'd had Nadiya in my bed, and now it was time to give her back to the world as the Dragon Fae. I could do it knowing that when Malev was dead, the thrill of the mission would make our lovemaking that much better afterward. I could roll out of bed and check our message because I knew the world only got a part of Nadiya on loan. I had the whole woman.

When I stood from the bed, Nadiya didn't stir. She felt safe, otherwise she'd never sleep this deeply on a mission. I wanted to let her sleep as long as I could. She desperately needed it. Maybe the message would be nothing more than a congratulations and I could make her breakfast and let her wake up naturally. We'd make love and then eat.

I laughed at my own little fantasy. I'd already had more than I'd thought possible. Greed would only set me up for disappointment.

On the dining room table sat a basket with a note.

Enjoy your first breakfast together as a bonded couple then come to Drake's. We need to debrief, and there's news.

   -A

Inside the basket sat a traditional pastry breakfast, meant for the newly bonded couple to share in bed without the need for plates or utensils. Nadiya would love this. I added two glasses to the basket and got us a carafe of water from the kitchen. Nadiya didn't like juice in the morning unless it was spiked, and she wouldn't want to drink on a work day.

I took the one chair in the bedroom and sat watching her. A tree outside the window filtered the sunlight, throwing a pattern of light and shadow across her body. After a few minutes, she stirred. Wanting to see if I could get a laugh from her, I put my feet up on the bed and placed the basket right over my penis and then leaned back with my hands behind my head.

It took about a minute more for her to open her eyes, and I got better than a laugh. I got a giggle out of her, a light airy sound that made her seem so soft and happy. It was a glimpse of who she might have been had she not been trained to kill as a child, if she'd been allowed to simply grow up and be whatever she wanted.

"Is this your way of saying I tired you out last night and you're offering food in lieu of sex?" she said as she sat up and stretched.

I snorted. "Hardly." I removed the basket so she could see just how much I meant it, and that turned her giggle into a laugh.

"So why aren't you in bed?" she asked. In her eyes, I could tell she wanted me to lie, but I couldn't.

"We have been summoned." I got into bed next to her with the basket. "But before we go, we can enjoy the traditional breakfast in bed."

Nadiya eyed the pastries then eyed me. "I'd much rather we enjoy each other. We wouldn't even be late. I could go for a quickie."

I knew she could see how much I wanted that, but I couldn't give in. "You're not a pastry to be scarfed down. You're a meal to be savored. Besides, after last night, I know you won't be satisfied with a quickie. This is a trick to get me to help you skip work, and everyone will blame me. No, thank you."

Really, Nadiya would feel guilty if we indulged. I couldn't risk her resenting our time together. A little sacrifice now would pay off later. I had to believe that, because it took everything I had not to take her up on her offer.

"I'd make it worth it." She slid her hand down my chest, and I caught her wrist just before she reached her goal.

"I have no doubt of that. Really, though, we have work to do, an evil queen to kill, an incompetent king to save. Our schedule is crammed full. I promise, I'll make it up to you."

Nadiya sat back and pouted as she grabbed a pastry. "Fine. But don't think I'll forget this." She smiled as she took a bite of the savory pastry, and then her eyes closed as her entire body melted. "These are so good." She took another bite. "We could have avoided this entire argument if you'd just had me taste this first."

I almost fell for the challenge, but then I took a bite, and I was fine taking second place to these.

We finished off the pastries together then got dressed, each watching the other and mentally counting down the time until we could get naked again. Being desired by a woman like Nadiya, someone so sensuous, who could have any man she laid eyes on, gave me a high that I would ride all day.

&

At the compound, we were met with cheers and congratulations.

"It's done then," Drake said when he greeted us. I had my arm around Nadiya's waist, and my grip involuntarily tightened a little. "My sincerest congratulations to the happy couple. You did it on your own terms, and I admire that."

In his eyes I saw that it was finally over. He accepted that I had won and that it was the better outcome. If he had been the Dragon Companion as he'd always thought he'd be, their bond wouldn't have been done out of love. It would have been duty alone.

"Thank you. We treasure the blessing of the Dragon Prince." I didn't mind stroking his ego. We both knew I was the victor.

"The blessing of the Dragon Prince...and of your brother."

Nadiya felt the same surprise I did. It was the first time in my life that Drake had called me his brother. I hadn't realized how much it would mean to me to actually hear him say the word.

"Thank you, Brother." I didn't know what else to say, but it seemed we'd have time to repair our relationship later.

"Our sisters are dying to smother both of you in well wishes, but I convinced them to wait until after the business is done." Drake gestured to the table where everyone else had already taken their seats.

Nadiya felt a bit of nerves at the mention of my sisters. *"There's nothing to worry about. They love you,"* I said.

"Thanks, but I don't know how to be around them."

"Just be yourself."

"You are the only person who being myself works on."

She was wrong, but I liked that she knew it worked on me. I'd reassure her later. Now it was all business.

Around the table sat Drake, Sybil, Alistair, Jaygar, and Farawyn. I hadn't expected Jaygar, but it made sense given his recent activism in Stardowns. He was the one who started the meeting.

"Malev has changed course. She doesn't like that people rallied around the appearance of the Dragon Fae. This morning she executed the fae guards who arrested the activists outside the park.

Her public line is that they were acting without her approval and that she takes the freedoms of sorcerers, her subjects, seriously."

"And how is that working for her?" Nadiya asked, her eyebrow arching skeptically.

"About as you'd expect. Her attempt to placate the people has succeeded only in creating a rift along class lines. The higher classes have been mollified by her actions. It's the lower classes who haven't been swayed. They're one spark away from erupting into full rebellion."

The way Jaygar spoke, he didn't consider that a bad thing. But what we needed was an opening to kill Malev, not war.

Farawyn leaned forward. "More importantly, she's aware she's misstepped. Her aim is to take down the Dragon Fae, not alienate the sorcerers. In a strange way, I think she not only wants you dead, she wants the people to love her more. She wants to be right and for others to acknowledge that. She won't be foolish enough to give you an opening to garner support again. She's on a mission to win over the masses and show them that she is better than the Dragon Fae."

"It seems a weird obsession for the fae queen to have," Nadiya said. Everyone in the room looked at her as if she'd gone crazy. I could feel her discomfort through our bond.

"You're the only person who poses a real threat to her," Sybil said. "Before you, she walked in the knowledge of her absolute power. You've changed that. If you were simply a fae or a sorceress, she'd forget about you soon enough, but you're a myth, and myths live on forever, even longer than she will."

The discomfort grew. Nadiya regretted saying anything. I doubted she'd ever get used to being referred to in such a way. It was different for me because my role stemmed from hers. The sidekick wasn't a myth himself, just a supporting character. She bore the mantle of history alone.

Alistair picked up on Nadiya's discomfort and took over. "We need to strike now, while public sentiment is on our side. Gordon says the Circle has completely broken down. No one trusts anyone. He doesn't know how Malev got to your tech guy."

Sadness and anger flashed through the bond. Nadiya didn't let many people into her life. Those lucky enough to be welcomed into her inner circle had her complete loyalty. The range of emotions she'd had to deal with over the last few days was too much for anyone, and she hadn't had the opportunity to process or deal with any of it. I wished I could take her out into the desert, let her work through her emotions the way she liked. She needed an outlet.

Nadiya suppressed the sadness and anger to answer Alistair. "We have the spiritstone. All we need is a netherwalker to put Kelar's spirit into it and the opportunity to kill her. I'll need to do it as soon as his spirit is safe, before she notices. And on top of that, we need the damn talisman. Once Malev is out of the way, Cassalina is going to make her move for it, and I don't trust her."

"I can help with the talisman," Farawyn said. All eyes turned to him. "It's the Blue Crystal Talisman you need. As I said, the queen is making an effort to get the people to like her. So it's been suggested that she put on an exhibition for the people of Stardowns, and she's agreed. I'm good friends with the curator of the royal collection. I can make sure the Blue Crystal Talisman is included without drawing specific attention to it. I'll play it off as an appropriately rare item that is also visually stunning."

"Brilliant," Alistair said, nodding. "That's good work, Farawyn. Will Malev be at this exhibition herself?"

"Yes, as far as I know."

"Maybe as a welcoming show she'll stop cowering behind her fae guards," Jaygar said, his voice low and disgusted.

Farawyn smiled. "I think she might, especially after this recent episode with the protestors."

"So that will be our opportunity." Nadiya nodded, absorbing the possibility that the end was in sight. Killing Malev would lift a weight from her shoulders, and destroying the Blue Crystal Talisman would neutralize the threat Cassalina posed. With her plans on Earth foiled and Malev dead, she'd likely move to take the fae throne and be content with it. "All we need is a netherwalker."

"Use Silvadra," Jaygar said.

Sybil looked at the minotaur. "Are you sure? Even if we can trust her, she might let it slip to someone. I thought it would be best to use an outsider."

A tension passed between Jaygar and Sybil as they maintained eye contact, some subtext the rest of us were unfamiliar with.

"No, Silvadra is the best choice. She's available and loyal to the cause."

Sybil stared him down. "But…it doesn't have to be her."

Jaygar nodded solemnly. "Yes, it does. Besides, we don't have anyone else."

Sybil seemed crestfallen as she slumped back in her chair. This exchange confused Nadiya as much as it did me.

Jaygar looked at Nadiya. "I'll speak to Silvadra. She won't have any problem doing what we need."

If Jaygar trusted her, I had to as well, but that didn't make it easy. Our plan was only as strong as the weakest link, and if our chain broke, it was Nadiya who'd pay the price. It was difficult trusting anyone with her life.

"When will this exhibition take place?" Nadiya asked Farawyn.

"She wants it to start tomorrow. She needs a distraction from the recent troubles. I think it'll run for a while, but the opening is the best chance that she'll be there. I wouldn't expect her there every day."

Good. We needed this to be over. The sooner Malev was dead, the sooner I could take Nadiya away for a proper celebration of our bonding. I wanted to see the world with her, but I'd settle for a few days of just the two of us. I could hardly expect the world to stay together much longer than that before she'd be needed again.

"Then tomorrow it is," Alistair said. "Jaygar can talk to Silvadra today. You already have the spiritstone to give to her. You'll just have to find a way to get her close to the king."

"Tarelle," I said. "He likes us, he's a supporter of the Dragon Fae, and he's the only one who gets close to Kelar these days."

"Good," Alistair nodded. "So you can go with Tarelle and Silvadra to the king and send a message through your bond when his spirit is safe."

"No, I'll be with Nadiya at the exhibition," I said.

Alistair's face registered surprise at my defiance. "But we need a way to get a signal to Nadiya that she can strike."

"I agree, but it'll have to be a different signal. My job is to make sure Nadiya gets out alive. I can't do that if I'm not with her."

"I'll be fine," Nadiya said.

"This isn't negotiable." I'd already made her promise not to turn this into a suicide mission, and I trusted her to keep her word, but I didn't trust her to adequately assess the risk. She had a blind spot when it came to her own safety. *"Besides, it'll be easier with two sets of eyes in the room. With our new bond, I can be more help to you."*

Throughout our little exchange, I kept my gaze on Alistair until he relented. "Fine, we'll think of another signal. While Silvadra is taking Kelar's spirit, you two will get in place at the exhibition. As soon as you get the signal, attack. Once she's dead, get the talisman and get out of there."

"Actually," Farawyn said, "there's no need to worry about the talisman. I'll be there and ready to grab it in the aftermath."

"Even better." Alistair nodded. "Any additions from the Oracle?"

Sybil had stayed quiet after her tense exchange with Jaygar. She focused her attention on Nadiya. "This will work. It's part of the prophecy. Just remember, no matter what happens, your allegiance is always to the innocent."

Nadiya never needed reminding of that. It was her code, stamped into the fibers of who she was.

Alistair, knowing this, didn't wait for her to answer. "You're not going to have any support from the Circle. I can't even let Gordon know in case he's interrogated between now and then. This is all on you."

That didn't phase Nadiya at all. "It always is."

For her, that was true. It was on her to complete the mission, keep her partner alive, and continue on to the next objective. She didn't put the responsibility anywhere else, even when she should.

Everyone looked around the room and nodded. We had our plan in place, all we had to do was execute it.

Drake slapped his hands on the table. "We all know what we have to do. I'll expect you all back here tomorrow night for one hell of a celebration."

43

NADIYA

Everyone dispersed, and Drake came to me and Deacon. "Our sisters will have my hide if I keep you any longer. Go let them smother you in congratulations." He patted Deacon on the back.

I could feel Deacon's pleasure at the reference to their familial bonds. Once this was over, I vowed to foster those relationships. Deacon needed them, and he deserved them.

Drake turned his attention to me. "I've also been told that Julien is requesting you speak with him."

I didn't relish the thought of seeing him, but I'd already brushed him off the last time I was here.

Drake left us, and Deacon turned me to face him. *"You don't owe him your time. You deserve to be around people who celebrate you."*

He referred to his sisters, but I didn't think he realized how intimidating a room full of dragon shifters was, especially when they couldn't possibly think I deserved their brother. They couldn't be happy he'd bonded to me, a sorceress and fae mix who pulled him into a dangerous world of prophecy and assassination. What family wanted that? They'd prefer him settled in a proper home producing chubby little dragon babies.

"You go be with your sisters. I've got to take care of this."

Deacon saw the determination in my eyes and nodded.

I went down to the basement by myself. The guard at Julien's door recognized me and moved to the end of the hall to give me some privacy. I took a deep breath and entered.

Julien looked up from his book. Not wanting a repeat of the awkward silence from last time, I forged ahead. "I was told you wanted to speak with me."

"Yes, it's about time. I've no idea what's going on or what measures are being taken to protect me."

I hadn't expected that. "What do you mean?"

"The fae queen. I heard that she's married our king. That's more than just an alliance. Doesn't this put me at risk because of my connection to you? How do I know that I'm still safe here?"

"Here? You mean the compound full of dragon shifters? You want to know if this is a safe place?" What a spineless little man he was.

"It's not as ridiculous as you seem to think."

"Well don't worry, if everything goes to plan, the fae queen will be dead soon enough."

Julien's eyes narrowed. "You mean you're going to kill her."

"Yes," I said, as if it were the most obvious thing in the world.

I think it was my tone that bothered him most. His face twisted in disgust. "You really are a killer."

"Yes, a killer who is keeping you safe. Isn't that what you want? Malev dead so you don't have to fear her?"

"I just…" his voice trailed off, but I knew what he meant.

"You just don't want to think about the particulars. You want to go to the steakhouse but not see the animals slaughtered out back. Well, that's what I do, Julien. The world is a nasty place, and someone has to kill the bad guys so people like you can lie safe in your beds reading your books."

Hurt pricked his eyes, but I realized for the first time it wasn't his feelings I'd hurt. It was his pride, his sense of self. When I looked at him in front of me, I saw nothing, just a sorcerer. I didn't feel any connection to him at all.

I'd recently lost Trevor's friendship, someone whom I cared about, who knew me and accepted me in ways Julien never had. I realized then that the pain from Julien's betrayal was the grief of losing a dream, an idea, a hope for the future that was never meant to be.

When Julien discarded me, I'd never thought to fight for him to take me back. What I lost with Trevor had been real, and already I knew that as soon as Malev was dead, I'd do what I could to win back Trevor's trust. That relationship was too important to me to not defend it. Once Trevor knew the truth, I had faith that we'd mend our friendship.

Deacon was right. Why was I here? The happiness in our bond told me Deacon was having a wonderful time with his sisters. My bonded mate was up there enjoying himself while I tortured myself over a sorcerer who didn't deserve me. Julien didn't love me and never had. I'd never loved him. I hadn't even known myself well enough to love another person when we were together.

The thought that I might have bonded to Julien, that I could have made such a horrible mistake that would have prevented my current joy with Deacon, made my heart clench. The thought was so suffocating that I couldn't breath.

"Are you all right?" Deacon's voice came through and calmed me. The mistake hadn't been made. I'd narrowly avoided that path thanks to Julien.

"Yes, I'm almost done here."

I could tell from Julien's expression that he expected me to apologize for my harsh words. Nataliana, the girl he had been with, would have. "I do have something to thank you for, Julien."

He quirked an eyebrow in an annoyingly smug way.

"Thank you for saving me from bonding to you and making

what would have been the biggest mistake of my life." I didn't stick around for his response. It was none of my business. I merely turned and left the room, eager to join my family upstairs.

44

───

DEACON

he Starlight Palace bustled with activity. Tensions ran high from recent events, and all the fae running around preparing for tomorrow's exhibition didn't help. Speaking with Tarelle inside the palace was out of the question. Instead, we invited him to the Claybourn's townhouse for drinks. Even with his promise that he would come, I worried that he wouldn't show. Any number of things could keep him from attending, including the weather. A storm raged outside, the rain pelting the windows in a quick staccato rhythm.

While I sat watching the time, Nadiya paced around the sitting room. She didn't move with nervous energy. Instead, her steps were calm and measured. She kept her eyes closed most of the time, her hands gesturing lightly in front of her, working through tomorrow's mission in her head.

She was different after her talk with Julien, more confident and sure of herself. I'd hated her being alone with him, knowing he had the power to hurt her, but it appeared to have done Nadiya good. I hoped the ghost of that relationship would no longer haunt her.

A knock sounded at the door, and Nadiya stopped. I rose from my seat to welcome Tarelle inside.

"Thank you for coming. I imagine you're quite busy," I said as I closed the door behind him.

"I am, and I don't have much time, but I know you wouldn't have asked right now if it wasn't important." He used magic to dry his umbrella and then placed it by the door.

The last couple of days had taken their toll on him. Puffy bags dragged down his eyes, making them appear even more sunken than they were. It looked like he hadn't eaten or slept since the last time we'd seen him.

"Would you like something to drink?" Nadiya asked, playing the part of hostess. Since the duke was closer with Tarelle, I'd be taking the lead in the conversation.

"No, thank you. As lovely as that sounds, I'm afraid if I sit and drink, I'll never leave. The only thing keeping me going right now is staying in motion, so I'll stand."

"Have recent events really changed things so much?" I asked.

Tarelle closed his eyes and shook his head. "If only you knew." He opened his eyes, and they looked more weary than before. "Between trying to persuade people not to revolt and keeping the fae queen adequately happy, I'm stretched in too many directions."

"We heard about the exhibition tomorrow."

"Ah, yes. The queen's desperate attempt to calm the people and get them on her side. The Dragon Fae has her spooked. She's determined to distract people from her appearance. I hate to say that it might just work. People are excited at the prospect of being allowed inside the palace and seeing such rare treasures." Tarelle shook his head, saddened by the fickle nature of people.

"Will the king be there with her to open it?" I asked.

"Yes, why do you ask?" Tarelle's curiosity was piqued.

"We need you to get him to not come. Convince the queen that she should open the exhibition on her own, show that it's her idea, her gesture of goodwill to the people, not the king's. She wouldn't want it to appear that she's doing this because he told her to. Do you think you can do that?"

"I think so. But why don't you want him there?" A hint of suspicion entered his eyes.

"Because we need him to talk with Baroness Silvadra while the queen is at the exhibition," I said.

The mention of another friend seemed to help. "All right. I'll arrange it. Silvadra can meet with him for a late breakfast. It shouldn't be hard to convince Malev to do the exhibition without him. It's not as if she actually enjoys being in his company."

Real sadness filled Tarelle's face. It hurt him to see one of his dearest friends be used so horribly by someone. I didn't know what kind of man Kelar really was, but Tarelle did, and I could tell that he missed him.

"Is that everything you wanted?" he asked me, as if the only time he spoke to anyone anymore was to find out what was needed.

"Yes, thank you, friend."

Tarelle nodded. "Before I go, did you two see the Dragon Fae?"

The question took me off guard, and I looked to Nadiya for an answer. She stepped forward, and Tarelle seemed surprised, like he'd forgotten she was here.

"Yes, we did," she answered. "Did you?"

"No," Tarelle shook his head. "I had to hear about it. What was it like?"

Nadiya looked at me, and I nodded for her to continue. "It was wonderful. That night, there was a giant street party. We danced and ate and sang. The whole world felt young again."

Tarelle smiled. "Good. I'm glad you got to be there. Every morning I hope that if I can just keep Kelar safe for one more day, keep the fae queen from destroying us for one more day, the Dragon Fae will come take over and let me rest."

Nadiya stepped closer, locking eyes with Tarelle. "She will. I promise, she will."

A spark of hope lit Tarelle's face, and he nodded. "Then I should get going. I'll arrange everything for tomorrow morning." He went to the door, but before he turned the handle, he looked back at me.

"Oh, one other thing. Kelar and I were talking yesterday about that summer we spent at the coast, the one where you taught us how to fish. We were remembering that night you got us drunk and convinced Kelar to sing for everyone. What song was it again that you had him do?"

Tarelle looked right at me with rapt attention that drove away some of the weariness.

"I don't know," I said, shaking my head.

Tarelle nodded. "That's all right. It was a long time ago." He turned back to Nadiya. "Until the Dragon Fae comes." He nodded and walked out the door with his umbrella.

Nadiya stood beside me as we watched him walk down the street, out of sight.

"Do you think he knows?" she asked me.

I thought it over. We couldn't tell him the truth. Even if we trusted him, it was too great a liability. "No, I think he has hope."

"When it comes down to it, is there really a difference?"

I turned away from the window and looked at her. "Yes, hope will drive a man a lot further than knowledge will."

45

NADIYA

I looked in the mirror at Jane's reflection. Only a few more hours and I could discard this glamour for good. Malev would be dead, Alistair avenged, and the sorcerer king would be free of fae interference. Farawyn would get the Blue Crystal Talisman, and we would destroy it to keep it out of Cassalina's hands.

Jaygar had sent word last night. He'd passed the spiritstone to Silvadra, and Tarelle would get her in with the king. The signal we'd worked out was a simple one. Silvadra and Deacon each had a mood stone. They were simple objects, toys really for children. Mood stones came in pairs. When a person held one, they could make the other change color with their mood. When Silvadra had completed the spell, she would turn the stone green and that would be our signal to proceed.

With my void blade securely fastened to the small of my back and covered by my top, I joined Deacon downstairs where he was eating. He gestured to a plate he'd made for me. "Eat something, then we'll go."

I picked up a sausage but stayed standing. It tasted good, but I'd rather eat when the mission was done. Before I could say as much, a letter appeared in the middle of the table. Deacon grabbed it before I could, depriving me of an excuse not to eat.

I watched his face fall when he unfolded it. *"Shit,"* he said.

I popped the rest of the sausage in my mouth and grabbed the letter.

Tarelle's been arrested.

   -J

"Fuck." There were no other details, no explanation. It could be coincidence.

"Should we postpone?" Deacon asked. "Malev may know everything."

I shook my head. "No. I don't care. This ends today. Tarelle didn't have enough information to give away our plan. We did that intentionally in case this happened." We'd have to think of some way to make this work without him.

"Our cover may be compromised. We could be arrested as soon as we show our faces at the palace."

"If Malev knows, she wouldn't leave anything to chance. We would have been arrested at the same time as Tarelle to prevent us getting away." That would be the smart move, at least. I couldn't let this development change anything. I needed to finish this. I was tired. "We have to do it today. Who knows what Malev will do tomorrow?"

I could tell Deacon didn't want to give in. He knew me too well. He knew that even if it wasn't smart, even if it was dangerous, I would still run in to kill Malev. Our definitions of failure and success weren't aligned. For me, the worst outcome was Malev getting away. For him, it was me dying. Maybe he was right. Maybe I was foolish. Perhaps that time in the nether had made me too comfortable with death. I didn't know. I only knew that I wanted to kill Malev.

Deacon shook his head, and I could feel his sadness through our bond. "I can't risk losing you."

"Every day that we wake up, you risk losing me. That's our life."

I could feel his conflict. He didn't want to deny me. I could play on that, but I didn't want to. I didn't want to manipulate him. That wasn't the kind of relationship we had.

"Do you remember your promise to me?" Deacon asked.

It took me a second to realize what he referred to. "Yes. I won't turn this into a suicide mission. I don't break my promises."

"I know. You would never intentionally break a promise to me, but I worry you might accidentally."

He had a valid point. I didn't know how to assuage his fear. I couldn't honestly dispute what he said.

Deacon nodded, a decision made. He came to me and placed a soft, gentle kiss on my lips that made me feel treasured. Then he rested his forehead on mine. "Thank you."

"For what?"

He chuckled at my confusion. "For not manipulating me into doing what you want. For not arguing that you really won't, no matter what, get yourself killed today. For not lying to me."

Our bond intensified as love for this man filled every part of me. Deacon's love responded, and I felt like I would burst into light. I gasped. I couldn't endanger this bond. I'd protect it as much as I was able.

Deacon stepped back, his face fixed in grim determination. "Let's go. We don't want to be late."

🔥

As it turned out, we didn't need to worry about these identities after all. On our way to the Starlight Palace, sorcerers handed out flyers on almost every street corner. They announced that the opening day of the exhibition had been reserved for the commoners of Stardowns.

"Could one thing go according to plan today?" I said after reading the flyer. We had to trust that Tarelle had arranged for the king to not be with Malev today before he was arrested. At the palace, we could find Silvadra, and Deacon would take her through the secret passages to the king without Tarelle. But with this new development, Silvadra might not even be at the palace.

"We'll just have to assess the situation when we get there. We can always glamour ourselves as commoners," Deacon said.

"Yes, but Silvadra can't." Her distinctive appearance with silver snake tattoos curling up her face meant everyone would recognize her.

"We'll figure out a way." Deacon kept walking as if nothing were wrong.

I had to admire this latest move of Malev's. The chatter that filled the streets was all about how Malev seemed to value the ordinary people. Savvy of her considering that commoners believed in the Dragon Fae more than the nobility did. People truly were fickle.

We walked the entire way to the palace. It gave us a better sense of the atmosphere, and I wanted my magic rested and antsy to be unleashed when I needed it later. At the gate to the palace, guards watched as the crowd entered. It didn't appear that they checked identification, but they did scan people's faces, looking for anyone recognizable. Most nobility wouldn't try to sneak in as a commoner just to see Malev's trinkets. They would view it as beneath themselves.

"Look at the nobles' gate," Deacon said.

There stood Silvadra waiting for someone. The original plan only called for her to meet Tarelle and go to the king. She didn't need to know the Duke and Duchess of Claybourn were involved at all. I trusted that Jaygar hadn't told her any more than she needed to know to complete her part of the mission.

"I guess it doesn't matter now if she knows who we are. In the next hour, this is all going to be over one way or another," I said.

"I agree. Let's do what we have to. We've come this far."

That's what I loved about Deacon. Once he committed to something, he was all in, no wavering. He'd voiced his concerns earlier, but we'd decided against postponement. He would do whatever it took to finish this mission.

We approached the noble's gate, and when Silvadra turned our way and saw us, Deacon reached into his pocket and pulled out the mood stone. He tossed it in the air and caught it, making it change to red. Silvadra checked her mood stone and saw it was an identical shade of red.

The baroness shook her head and laughed. "Of course." She looked over her shoulder at the guard and raised her voice. "Can you believe it? They're not letting any of the nobility in. I guess we'll have to have breakfast somewhere else. Fancy coming to my place? I'll port us."

She reached out her hands, and as soon as we formed a circle, we appeared in the middle of a forest, not a house in sight.

46

DEACON

Nadiya appeared as confused as I was about our location. From the scent, I was quite certain I'd never been here before.

"Sorry for the locale, but given the circumstances, I don't trust that we won't be overheard even in my home," Silvadra said. "I assume you heard about Tarelle's arrest?"

"Yes, do you know why?" Nadiya asked.

I noticed Silvadra didn't mention Jaygar was her contact. I appreciated the precautions she took. If we were going to get through today, we needed to trust each other's judgement, and she'd just proved hers.

"No idea, but I didn't get any message saying I was no longer needed, so I figured I'd wait at the palace. I didn't expect to be refused entry."

"It's the day for the unexpected," Nadiya said.

"I'd say so." Silvadra pulled the spiritstone out. "Nice to see you managed to find one of these without me. All of my sources came up empty. I can't believe I didn't suspect something when you asked for one. You really had me fooled. I don't suppose you have a plan for how to get me to the king."

"We have our ways," I said. Then I spoke to Nadiya. *"I'm thinking we glamour as commoners, disguise Silvadra as best we can, and take her to the king through the secret passages. Then we'll go to Malev, and Silvadra will signal as she always planned to. Does that sound all right?"*

"If you're confident you can get us to the king, that sounds like the best option."

With us both on the same page, I relayed the plan to Silvadra. "We just need some way to hide your appearance so we can get past the guards at the gate. Once we're in the passages, it won't matter."

"I can wear a mask and a cloak. That's the best I can do, but if I hunch between the two of you, I doubt I'll attract attention. There are so many people at the gate they can't possibly get a good look at everyone."

"Will that be enough?" I asked Nadiya.

"I think so. We can glamour ourselves to be taller than her, make her disappear a little more between us." Then she spoke to Silvadra. "Where are you going to get the mask and cloak?"

"From my house. I can use my satchel to fetch them." She placed her hand on her satchel, and it glowed. "If there's anything else we'll need, let me know now. I can't summon anything on palace grounds because of the wards against portals." She pulled a mask and cloak out of the bag and put them on.

At first, I didn't think the mask would work. It was clearly fake, something to use at a party, but once she put on the cloak and arranged the hood, the shadows obscured enough of it to make it look real.

"That'll work as long as no one looks too closely," Nadiya said. "And even if they do notice something is off, they won't suspect it's you, which is the most important thing." Then she looked at me. "Your turn."

I changed my glamour, taking the opportunity to widen my shoulders and add an inch of height. I gave myself a bit of a baby face so as not to appear too intimidating with my size. I stood next to Silvadra, and when she hunched over, I had a good five inches on her.

Nadiya nodded her approval then changed her own appearance. I recognized it immediately as one of the characters from her favorite TV show, only a little taller and slightly less attractive. I grinned.

"Stop. I'm in too much of a hurry to come up with anything else. I didn't want to accidentally imitate someone at court."

"It's good. I like it."

We were interrupted by Silvadra. She straightened and looked at the two of us. "That's incredible. It's really you, isn't it? You're them?"

At first I thought she meant that these were our real identities, but before I could say anything, she shook her head and continued.

"There I was, sitting at your table, deriding the Dragon Fae for not doing enough, and you were right there."

"I don't know what you're talking about," Nadiya said. If that was how she wanted to play it, I'd respect her wishes.

"You can deny it all you want, but my contact told me I was doing this today for the Dragon Fae. I didn't realize you were her. I feel like a fool."

"Why do you think she's the Dragon Fae?" I asked.

"The only people who can glamour are fae, and the only fae who'd be willing to do whatever it is we're doing today is the Dragon Fae."

"You don't know what the mission is today?" Nadiya asked.

"I only know my part in it, and believe me, I will do it well." She hunched over again, pulled the cloak around her and lowered the hood. Then she took my hand and Nadiya's, and we found ourselves outside the palace gate.

Getting through the gate proved easy. Nadiya and I towered over Silvadra and no one even noticed she was there. Once in the courtyard, I led us to the entrance to the passage. We didn't have much time. I'd need to get Silvadra to the king, hope he didn't have anyone with him, then take Nadiya to the great hall where Malev would be.

All this in less than fifteen minutes.

"It's incredibly dark in the passages. I'm going to move quickly, so stay close and keep hold of our hands. If we get separated, we'll never get this done in time," I said as I took Silvadra's hand. She nodded in response and took Nadiya's hand. "We won't talk again until we're there."

I entered the passage when I was satisfied no one would see us. As soon as the door closed behind Nadiya, I took off, walking as fast as I could without tripping up Silvadra. I had no idea where Kelar would be, but I knew the general layout of the palace and headed toward his sitting room.

Without slowing, I talked to Nadiya. *Do you want to go to the great hall on your own, and I'll join you?* That had been the original plan.

"No, without Tarelle to get us in, we don't know what to expect. You may need me to fight whoever is minding the king."

"And if it's fae?"

"We'll have to hope that the three of us together can take them."

After a couple of minutes, I got my first whiff of Kelar's scent. It was in the general direction of his sitting room but slightly farther away. The closer I got, the more I realized he did have a fae with him. From the scent there was only one, but it still presented a challenge.

I stopped at a peephole and looked through. There sat Kelar in his bedroom, a single fae keeping him company. We needed to figure out a plan, so I took us one room farther then stopped and whispered to Silvadra, "Cast a shield around us so we can speak."

She obliged.

"The king has a single fae with him. We're going to have to get rid of him somehow."

"And Malev can see everything Kelar can, so we need to do it in a way that won't tip her off," Nadiya said. "Is there a way we can lure him out of the room?"

"Wait, Malev can see through Kelar's eyes?" Silvadra asked. I had assumed she knew that was why we needed her to trap Kelar's spirit. This surprised Nadiya as well.

Rather than give anything away, Nadiya answered simply, "Yes."

I could barely make out Silvadra's eyes in the darkness, but I saw the moment all the pieces slid into place. "You're going to kill Malev."

Neither one of us answered her.

"That's why I'm here. If she can see through his eyes, then she's got a hold on him. You can't risk him dying when she does, and that's why you need me to trap his spirit." Silvadra nodded. "I had wondered why. It's a strange request, being asked to trap your king's spirit in a spiritstone."

And yet she had agreed to do it without any more information. I don't know if that made her loyal to a cause or foolish. Then again, it was no more foolish than the things I'd done for this prophecy.

"We're running short on time here," Nadiya said. "Unless someone comes up with something, we're going to have to kill the fae and hope Malev doesn't notice."

"No, you don't need to do anything." Silvadra pulled the spiritstone from her bag. "I don't have to be close to him as long as I can see him. The fae in the room won't know what's happening. It'll be like the king just drifts off to sleep. As soon as it's done, I'll send you the signal as planned."

"Are you sure you can do that without tipping off the fae?" Nadiya asked.

"Yes, the only way he'd know is if he could smell my magic behind the wall, but I doubt he's that sensitive."

"I agree," I said. "The chances that he'll be able to smell your magic are slim. I'll take you back to the peephole. It should take us about three minutes to get to the great hall. Try to time it so you're done after we get there."

"Understood." Silvadra took my hand and removed the shield. It would be that much less magic for her to maintain and for the fae to potentially smell.

I lead her back to the peephole. When she let go of my hand, I took Nadiya's, and we ran to the great hall.

47

NADIYA

We made it to the great hall just as Malev entered to open the exhibition. Deacon had the mood stone in hand, and it still glowed red.

"You focus on Malev. Let me worry about the stone. I'll tell you the second it turns green."

My hand gripped my void blade, ready to strike. The great hall was filled to capacity, and I pushed my way forward, Deacon at my back.

That was when I smelled it: fae, and not just Malev. I looked around but didn't see any guards.

"She has a dozen of her guards with her. They're not in uniform. She has them blending in," Deacon said.

I spotted a few of them, but not all twelve. The crowd made it difficult to home in on who precisely the magic came from. *"Shit, I don't know what to do."* I'd made a promise to Deacon, and I'd do my best not to break it, but how could I kill Malev and make it out alive with twelve fae guards and no ability to teleport?

"The stone's green."

I could feel Deacon behind me, but I still didn't know what to do. Malev's demeanor changed. Fury swept across her face, and the twelve guards I'd struggled to identify materialized as one in front of us, pushing the crowd back then standing in front of their queen.

"She knows," I said, but there was nothing we could do. Kelar's spirit was outside of his body. The time to strike was now. We couldn't orchestrate this again.

"Think this through. How can we do this with the best chance of survival?" Deacon asked.

I wasn't fast enough to evade twelve fae, and that wasn't counting Malev. We didn't have the element of surprise since she knew Kelar's spirit was gone. I looked around the massive room, hoping for a strike of inspiration, perhaps an alcove that would give me a better position or something to lend me an advantage. Along the walls were display cases filled with items included in the exhibition. Perhaps there was something in them that could help. But how could I possibly look through them quickly enough to make a difference?

Then I caught sight of Farawyn standing against the wall behind a display case. He had a serious expression and kept looking down at the case in front of him, twitching with every surge of the crowd. He must be standing guard over the Blue Crystal Talisman, ready to snatch it as soon as Malev was dead. As a fae, Farawyn might be able to help, but he didn't know what I looked like. I'd have to figure this out without him, but knowing I had a supporter in the room did give me a little confidence.

Malev stepped up on the small dais prepared for her and raised her hands. Apparently she was going through with the opening, though I didn't doubt she'd be whisked away as soon as she was done.

The crowd stilled, and the woman next to me shifted her weight. A piece of paper she held scratched my arm, and I reflexively looked down. It was the flyer about the first day of the exhibition being only for commoners. It dawned on me then that Farawyn wasn't the only supporter I had in this room. Malev had targeted the commoners because they'd always had a stronger belief in the Dragon Fae than the nobles did. I was standing in a room filled with sorcerers who supported me.

They just didn't know who I was.

"I have an idea. We'll probably still die, but I think it's our best chance."

"I'm listening," Deacon said.

"I told you I could kill her with speed and surprise. The only problem with that is the dozen guards who'd kill me before I can kill them."

"So how do you plan to kill them without dying yourself?"

"I don't. You and the supporters of the Dragon Fae will do it for me. We drop our glamour, and you shift. The guards are all in a line in front of Malev. Take them down with your breath. The people in this room will support us once they realize who we are. In the chaos, I'll take out Malev. The two of us can't do it by ourselves, but if the sorcerers in this room join in like I think they will, we can pull it off."

Deacon's approval coursed through our bond before he could say anything. I couldn't guarantee I'd survive, but at least this way we had a fighting chance. We would win or lose together.

"Get on my back. I'll jump up and shift while you lose the glamour. If I time it right, I'll be midair when I change so I don't hurt the people around us."

I got behind him and wrapped my legs around his waist as Malev proclaimed the exhibition open. The crowd cheered, and Deacon seized the moment. He launched into the air and shifted as I shook off my glamour. Screams and gasps filled the air. Deacon blew a stream of fire at the fae guards.

"Long live the Dragon Fae!" Farawyn shouted, and the crowd erupted. The sorcerers around me attacked the guards. They weren't fighters, but they used whatever magic they had at their disposal.

The great hall was barely wide enough for Deacon's wings, but the room had plenty of height. I stood on his back and drew my void blade. I could end this with one strike.

I leapt from his back, my dagger above my head, ready to plunge into Malev. Her eyes looked ready to shoot fire at me, but it was her hands that hurled magic my way. I blocked her attacks with my dagger and landed on the ground in a roll. I swept my arm out, trying to get a cut on her legs, but she levitated out of the way.

As I stood, I snatched the cuff from my wrist and stuffed it in my pocket. I'd need every resource available to me, and even then I wasn't sure I could take her. My only cause for hope was that, just like me, she couldn't teleport away.

Malev surrounded herself with a shield. No amount of magic or fire from Deacon would be able to penetrate it. She didn't seem to know that my dagger could make short work of it.

Heat hit my back, and I turned to see a charred fae smoking from Deacon's breath. I caught sight of sorcerers lying dead on the ground along with some of the fae. I couldn't concern myself with the guards. Deacon and the others would take care of them. Some of the sorcerers even flung magic at Malev, but it glanced off her shield. I was the only one who could take her down. She had to remain my only focus.

Malev unleashed tendrils of black magic toward me. They latched onto my legs, burning my skin. Using magic, I cut through them. I wanted to avoid using my dagger and tipping her off to its power. I just needed to get close enough to slice through her shield and nick her.

As soon as I cut one tendril of magic, another latched on. They burned unlike anything I'd ever felt before, and once my mind got past the shock, I noticed they pulled me toward Malev. All I had to do was endure the pain long enough, and she'd bring me right to her.

Deacon roared, and I felt him push his healing magic through our bond. The pain lessened, but she kept wrapping me in the burning tendrils. Deacon roared louder.

"I'll be fine. Just a little longer." I hated that he could feel the pain

too, but he kept sending healing waves through our bond. It took the edge off just enough that I didn't go mad.

Malev pulled me right to the outside of her shield. "I finally have you. You're not so strong now that you face me directly, are you?" she taunted. "I had thought to kill you quickly, but you're not strong enough to fight me off. Perhaps I'll take your hands one at a time, like I did your little friend. Would you like that?"

The tendrils around my wrists tightened, burning through the skin until they hit bone. The pain had me almost delirious. If she cut off my hands, I would be dead. I gripped my void blade harder and used the last little bit of lucidity I had to send a message. *"Deacon, help. I need your strength."*

If I was delirious from the pain, then so was Deacon. I didn't even know if my message got through to him. My vision blacked out as I felt bone burn away. At least I tried. That was all I could tell myself.

A surge of light came through our bond, and with it one last burst of healing magic. My vision cleared just enough to see the glee in Malev's face. With all my strength, I willed my hand to grip the void blade and swing. It cut through the tendril of magic holding my wrist, and Malev noticed as soon as it broke free. Realizing the threat my dagger posed, she released her other tendrils on me and focused them all on my dagger hand. This time, I was prepared for the pain. My other hand could barely grip. I couldn't feel half of my fingers, but I wrapped them around the hilt of my void blade as best I could, fortifying my dagger hand that I felt sure would break any second.

With every bit of muscle and magic inside me, I pushed forward. The dagger sliced through the tendrils as if they were nothing. The sharp blade didn't need any force, just direction. When the last tendril snapped, the resistance against me gave way, and I lunged forward, falling to the ground. My void blade went through the shield but didn't make it to Malev.

The damage to my hands was too extensive. I had no fine motor control, and my grip on the dagger gave way. As I fell, all I could do was twist my body so I landed on my side and not my face.

I looked up and saw confusion in Malev's face. Trying to seize the moment, I searched for my void blade. I found it lying on the ground in front of me. A few inches in front of it stood Malev's ankle with a single drop of blood dripping from a tiny nick.

48

DEACON

I thought I knew what pain was.

I'd had the skin cut from my body to form Nadiya's cuff. I'd gasped on the edges of death from poison. I'd watched as the woman I loved lay unconscious, no guarantee that she'd fight her way back from nether sickness.

None of that compared to the white hot pain I'd just experienced. Malev's magic had a potency I'd never encountered. And now Nadiya lay broken on the ground. I sent her every bit of healing magic I could, but it hadn't been enough.

I focused on Malev. Nothing stood between her and Nadiya. The only thing I had left was my body, my massive bulk as a dragon. I could be Nadiya's shield. But as I moved toward them, Malev didn't attack. It was then I noticed her scent had changed. Her magic was gone.

Nadiya had voided her.

Triumph filled my chest. I roared, and with one swipe of my talon, I sliced Malev into four pieces. I shielded Nadiya with my wings, protecting her from the gore. Then I turned and licked her wounds. I was spent, but every bit of healing I could give her would help her gain strength, which in turn would give me strength to keep healing. It was a virtuous cycle that I needed to start before I collapsed.

"Is she really dead?" Nadiya asked as soon as she had the energy.

I looked over my shoulder at the four pieces of Malev splattered across the floor and then back at Nadiya. *"Yes. Sorry I deprived you of the satisfaction."*

"No, you did good. Thank you."

I was glad she wasn't upset, because I didn't feel bad. Killing Malev gave me a pleasure different from any other I'd experienced. She'd harmed my mate, and killing her set my world right again.

"How are your hands?" Our bonding enhanced her healing and accelerated the process of us both gaining back our strength.

She looked at her hands, and her fingers twitched. *"The pain's a lot better, but I still don't have strength."*

Someone approached, and I roared, instinctively hiding Nadiya with my wings. A frightened sorcerer stared back at me. Then I noticed the condition of the great hall. The fae guards were all dead, as were several sorcerers. If there was any noise before, my roar silenced it. Our world had shrunk to just the two of us, but around us time continued.

"My void blade. We need to get it."

"Don't worry. It's under my talon. No one's going to get it there." I continued licking her wounds, quicker now. Each lick imparted exponentially more healing which gave us both more strength.

"Is she all right?" one of the sorcerers asked. I couldn't speak in my dragon form, but I nodded.

During the fighting, some of the sorcerers had fled and spread word of what was happening. Chaos sounded outside as people approached.

"We need to get to Silvadra. She needs to put the king's spirit back," Nadiya said as she sat up.

"Take it easy," I said, but I moved back, giving her more space.

She clenched her fists, able to execute the movement, but without much strength. She looked around, and I lifted my talon, knowing what she searched for. With a loose grip she grabbed her void blade. It took her two tries to sheathe it.

"We have to go. Can you shift back?"

In answer I resumed my human form. *"How do you want to get out of here? If we use a passage now, everyone will see, but I don't know how feasible it'll be to move around the palace any other way."*

Nadiya surveyed the room, ignoring the calls of the people for a speech or some explanation. *"Get ready to go through the passage."* With a wave of her hand, she plunged the great hall into darkness. Before anyone had time to react with their own light, we slipped into the secret passage, and I led us to Kelar.

49

NADIYA

ithout my cuff, my magic swirled inside me, ready for action. It had recovered much quicker than my hands. The pain was largely gone, but I didn't have any strength in my grip and movement caused an electric shock through my nerves. We were almost done, though. All we had to do was make sure the king was all right and then leave him to clean up the mess he'd made.

When we got to the peephole outside Kelar's bedroom, Silvadra wasn't there. It took me a second to realize that she was inside the king's room. We entered, and she stood from the bed where she'd been sitting next to Kelar. Her mask and cloak lay discarded on the ground.

"It's done?" she asked, hope in her eyes.

"Yes," I said.

She closed her eyes and took a deep breath as she smiled. I let some of her obvious joy fill me too. We had done it.

When she opened her eyes, they had tears in them. "There was a commotion outside, and the fae left. I didn't know what was going on."

"We don't know what's going to happen now," Deacon said. "It's chaos outside. News is spreading and there's no telling what the remaining fae will do. If we're lucky, they'll just return to their realm. We need to get the king back."

"It's time, then," Silvadra said with a strange sadness. She retrieved the spiritstone from her pocket. The wisps of Kelar's spirit left the stone and made their way to his body. The first one entered, and then the next, but after that they shifted, moving toward Silvadra.

"Stop!" I yelled.

Deacon reacted, lunging for Silvadra, but she held out her free hand and threw him against the wall, holding him there.

"Silvadra, stop!" I hurled a bolt of magic at her, aiming to disrupt her. She easily brushed it off with her own shield. "Why are you doing this? Don't make me hurt you."

She stopped, and when she spoke, she thankfully exhaled some of his spirit. "Hurt me? You can't possibly hurt me. My magic is far more powerful than yours, and I didn't just tire myself out killing the fae queen."

A heavy sadness fell in my chest. "Why?"

Something, maybe shame, entered her eyes, and then she went back to inhaling the king's spirit. I gathered up another burst of magic, but it glanced off her shield just as the last. I needed to stop thinking about brute force. I could penetrate shields. I sent my magic out, probing for weaknesses. It would only take one.

"We don't have time. The king won't survive if she takes his spirit. It's either him or her."

Deacon was right, but I didn't want to face that. Sybil's words came back to me. My allegiance was always to the innocent. I didn't have a choice here.

"I'm so sorry," I whispered as I gripped my void blade. Pain shot through my hand, but I bore it. I wanted to give her a quick and clean death. With one swift movement I thrust my dagger into her heart. She slumped onto the bed, exhaling Kelar's spirit. It joined the rest of the wisps in the air and entered his body.

Deacon came behind me and placed his hands on my shoulders. I shook my head as I looked down at Silvadra. Her silver snake tattoos no longer slithered with magic. Tears wet her cheeks.

"She was crying as she did it. There was shame in her eyes. Why? Why did she do it?" My voice cracked, and my vision blurred with tears. I couldn't hold them back, and they streamed down my face. Why did she make me kill her?

"You know what they say about netherwalkers."

They were all a little mad, all addicted to the nether. But she hadn't wanted to take Kelar's spirit. I could tell. I knew what that addiction felt like. I'd fought it. Why couldn't she fight it too? Why couldn't she have let me help her?

My allegiance was to the innocent, but weren't we all innocents? Didn't we all move about tossed by the winds of fate and chance? Why did I get to go through nether addiction and end up a hero while Silvadra ended up dead? And why was it my hand that killed her?

"It's going to be all right. Just stay strong for a little longer, and then you can fall apart in my arms for as long as you need. I promise. But for now, the king's waking up, and we still need to check on Farawyn and the talisman."

I nodded and dried my eyes. Then I pulled my dagger from Silvadra and wiped the blade on the sheets before sheathing it. "Help me lay her out on the bed. She deserves some dignity."

Deacon obliged, moving her head to a pillow and covering her with a blanket. I closed her eyes and took the spiritstone from her hand. If one didn't look too closely, she and the king looked like a couple asleep.

"Do you think something's wrong?" I asked Deacon.

"What do you mean?"

"The king. Shouldn't he be up by now?" If I'd killed her and it didn't save the king, I'd never forgive myself. Not for the king's death, but for hers. My personal feelings on the matter were clear. If I had to choose between Kelar and Silvadra, I'd choose Silvadra.

But that hadn't been the choice. It had been between innocent and not.

The door to the king's room burst open, and in came Tarelle. He ran to the king's side, placing his hand on the king's forehead and grasping one of his hands in a concerned gesture. "Kelar? Can you hear me?"

Jaygar followed Tarelle. The sight of him stirred embers of anger inside my gut. If I stoked them, they could overtake this grief.

The minotaur came up behind Tarelle and nudged him out of the way. Jaygar produced a vial and lifted the king's head to drink its contents. He spoke to Tarelle. "The priestesses made this for him. They said the constant use of fae magic on his mind would take a little while to heal. This should help him along and get him to wake up."

Jaygar left the king to Tarelle and registered Silvadra's dead body. Sadness passed so quickly over his face that I might have imagined it. "How did she die?"

Deacon opened his mouth, but I silenced him with a touch to his arm. I didn't need him to explain my actions. "She started taking the king's spirit. I had to stop her to save his life. Her magic was too strong for me, so I voided her."

He nodded, seeming satisfied, and looked at me for the first time since entering the room. "Good work."

"Good work?" I said, my voice low, simmering with anger. If I let myself speak any louder, my screams would echo through the halls of the palace. "You told me to use her for this. If we had gone with someone else, my magic could have stopped them. Silvadra didn't have to die."

My anger seemed to have no effect on Jaygar. "By someone else you mean a deathwalker. That wouldn't have worked. They would have consumed Kelar's spirit before you even killed Malev. I knew we could trust Silvadra to withstand the temptation while you worked. This was always a possibility once she started returning his spirit and saw the wisps, but I knew you'd be here to stop her if you had to."

Just like that he had calculated the acceptable cost of the mission. Silvadra had been deemed expendable. The logical part of me knew it was the same formula that had controlled my life since I'd joined the Circle. Risk and reward, acceptable losses, they were all calculated for each mission. The difference was this time I had to kill the acceptable loss on our side.

"Jaygar's not our enemy. Fighting with him won't change anything." Deacon sent a cool, reassuring wave of calm through our bond.

He was right, but I wanted to fight because the alternative was unfathomable. If I fell into my pit of grief, I didn't know how long it would take me to climb out of it.

"I won't let you go through this alone. Trust me to carry you." Deacon's hand rested on my shoulder.

I did trust him, more than anyone, more than any sane person should trust another. I placed my hand on top of his in acceptance.

50

DEACON

I'd never seen Nadiya cry like she did over Silvadra. She had been pushed too hard for too long. I wanted to take her home, but I didn't know exactly where that was. Besides, we still had to destroy the Blue Crystal Talisman. Power-hungry psychotics wouldn't take a break so the love of my life could process having to kill a friend.

Fuckers.

"Do you know if Farawyn got the talisman?" I asked Jaygar.

"No idea. I spent all morning trying to free Tarelle. Once you killed Malev, the fae must have known somehow. They debated about what to do then left. I got him and headed straight here."

"Then we need to get back to the great hall. Farawyn was there earlier." I went to the secret entrance, Nadiya's hand never leaving mine. I knew she would prefer Jaygar not come with us, but we might need his help. The sooner we finished here, the sooner we could get away from everyone, so I didn't object when he followed us.

We emerged into a nearly empty great hall. Everyone had been cleared out, and Sybil stood with Alistair over the pieces of Malev.

Bodies of fae and sorcerers littered the floor. Glass from the broken display cases crunched underfoot.

Sybil turned at our entrance and came to Nadiya. I'd never seen her so somber. It wasn't like I'd imagined it would be. I'd pictured celebration at Malev's death, but I'd never expected so many others would die with her.

"You look horrible," Sybil said to me and Nadiya. "You don't need to be here. Go to Emma's."

"We need to get the talisman," Nadiya said, and walked right past Sybil to the spot where Farawyn had been. Alistair looked at her with concern, but she ignored him. "He was standing right here and it was in front of him, I'm sure." Nadiya used her magic to sift through the rubble. The items that had been on display were strewn about haphazardly among the glass.

I searched with her but couldn't find it. "It's likely Farawyn took it and left. He knew the importance of it."

"Or it could have been looted," Nadiya said.

"Trust Farawyn. The simplest, most logical explanation is that he has it and is waiting until he knows it's safe to return." I put my hands on her shoulders, trying to give her some comfort, to let her know that it was all right.

She shrugged me off. "We should go look for him."

Alistair intervened. "No, we'll look for him. You go rest." He took Nadiya's hand and looked into her eyes. What he saw there clearly worried him. "You're done."

She looked at me for support, but I shook my head. "He's right. Let the others look for him. Us being here isn't going to help."

"With Malev dead and the fae gone, the Circle has taken control until the king is ready," Alistair said. "I'll get Gordon and everyone on it. We'll find Farawyn and the talisman."

"Are there crowds in the courtyard?" I asked. We needed to get outside of the palace grounds before we could teleport to Emma's. I'd prefer not to subject Nadiya to a bunch of gawkers.

"It would be best to take the passages," Sybil said. "I'll go with you and make a portal once you're outside the gates."

"I can port us," Nadiya said. "You stay here and help with the search."

What she really meant was that she wanted us to be alone, but Sybil was undeterred. "There's not much I can do here. Alistair will take care of the search. I think the sorcerers of Stardowns are tired of taking directions from fae."

Nadiya wanted to say something else but decided it wasn't worth the fight. I gestured for Sybil to come with us.

As we made our way through the passages, Sybil spoke. "I'm sorry today was so difficult."

"You don't know anything about it," Nadiya said in a matter-of-fact tone. She was right, but that wasn't Sybil's fault.

"I assume you mean Silvadra. She's dead, isn't she?" Sybil asked.

"Yes," I answered before Nadiya could. The last thing she would want was to break down in tears in front of Sybil, but the only way she'd avoid that was by getting mad, and Sybil didn't deserve her anger.

"I thought that might happen. It's why I didn't want Jaygar to use her for this."

That explained their strange interaction when he'd suggested Silvadra. My gut told me that she knew the netherwalker would die because of prophecy. If that was the case, she was wise not to mention it. Nadiya was sick of the prophecy, and after today, so was I. Without it, I wouldn't have Nadiya in my life, but I wished there had been some other way for us.

When we exited the palace into the courtyard, it was a beautiful day. The clouds had dissipated after last night's rain, and all above us blue sky stretched out. Sybil used some type of fae magic to keep people from looking our way as we walked to the gate.

Outside the palace grounds, she made a portal. "I'll send word as soon as we know anything."

"Thanks," I said. Nadiya had already walked through the portal, and I joined her.

51

NADIYA

*D*eacon stayed true to his word, as I knew he would. Emma had food and drink waiting for us, and then she and Philip left us alone, giving us use of the guest bedroom in yet another gesture of extraordinary kindness. On the bed, Deacon let me fall apart. I cried, we made love, and I cried some more. Through it all, he held me.

I wouldn't have had the strength to get through it without him. He let me mourn for Silvadra, for my friendship with Trevor, and for the normal life I'd never have. He bore my grief with me, and no matter how thoroughly I searched our bond, I never found any disgust at my self-pity. The only emotion that answered mine was love. The only magic that touched mine was healing support.

So when I woke to an empty bed after falling asleep in his arms, I knew it had to be serious. Nothing else could have pulled him from me.

"Where are you?" I asked. I couldn't feel him in the house. Emma and Philip were gone too, but I thought I smelled their magic on a breeze coming through the window.

"I'll be there soon."

A portal opened in the living room, and I went to meet him.

Sybil must have made it for him, but she didn't step through. The portal closed behind him, and I could tell from his face that it was bad. Then I realized the grief I felt in our bond wasn't from me.

Deacon took my hands, and we sat on the sofa together. "Farawyn's dead. They found his body outside the palace but still on the grounds where he couldn't port. Alistair came and asked me to examine the scene with him. That's why I was gone when you woke up."

Gentle Farawyn. My eyes watered as I remembered his defiant shout, "Long live the Dragon Fae." He hadn't been a fighter, but he'd fought for me, for what he thought was right. In many ways, he was one of the bravest people I'd known.

"But why did Alistair want you there?" The Circle had plenty of agents he could have used.

"Because he wanted to be sure." Deacon took a deep breath. "The scent of Cassalina's magic was on him."

The talisman. Farawyn had done his part, and she'd killed him for it.

That bitch was going to need more than an army of dwarves to protect her.

ABOUT THE AUTHOR

Caethes's writing is influenced by her observations of this imperfect world and the flawed characters who inhabit it. She enjoys playing RPGs and making up complex backstories for her avatar and the characters she encounters. Caethes has lived in seven states and is always looking for the next place to call home with her husband and dogs. She currently resides in Florida where she's often found at theme parks when she's not writing.

Join her Facebook reader group:
CaethesFaron.com/fbgroup
Contact her:
CaethesFaron.com/contact
Visit her site:
CaethesFaron.com